THE SHOP ON COPPINS BRIDGE

THE SHOP ON COPPINS BRIDGE

Elizabeth Daish

CENTURY

LONDON

First published in Great Britain in 1985 by
Century Hutchinson Ltd.
Portland House, 12–13 Greek Street,
London W1V 5LE

ISBN 0 7126 9405 6

Printed and bound in Great Britain by
Anchor Brendon Ltd, Tiptree, Essex

For Derek, Simon and Sally
who love the Island

Chapter 1

From the back of the newspaper office of the *County Press*, shadows glanced off the windows, receded and took shape as the clerk walked slowly to the main window at the front and fixed the oil-lamp on the shelf by the bulletin board. The shadows paused, trembled and grew thin as the clerk turned up the wick of the lamp with maddening deliberation and trimmed it with scissors before replacing the large glass globe over the flame.

Satisfied at last, and making the most of his fleeting power, he fastened a sheet of paper to the board which hung in the window, covering the last bulletin, making it lie true to each corner and then he stood back as if awaiting applause.

The waiting crowd shifted and tried to get closer, craning their necks to read the latest news that had threatened for so long.

'What's it say?' A man at the back of the crowd pushed through, fighting to get a glimpse of the clear copperplate writing, and a way opened for him when some of the men heard his voice.

'It's war!' said a voice from the front.

'Another bloody war?' The thickset man in a well-cut light overcoat now pushed him aside. 'Let me see. Another false alarm, more like,' he said. 'We've had enough of them to know that they'll never fight when it comes to it. It's one thing to shout and another to fire the first shot when they know that the whole might of the Empire is against them.' He looked round at the faces of the men listening, then back at the board. 'When it comes to . . .' he started, and stopped, the words on the bulletin making a lie of all his hopes. It was short and even the least educated in the crowd could understand.

'What is it? Read it out! We can't see it!'

The man at the window who had moved away turned. 'I told you. It's WAR. It says that a state of war exists.' He gave a snort of derision. 'It says some fine words about us fighting for Queen and country, and everyone doing his duty, but all it means is that Kruger is fighting and our boys will be killed.' He shouldered his way through the crowd. 'Read it for yourselves. It's got it all there, even the date and time it all started. Ten past three on the afternoon of October the eleventh in the year of 1899.'

Someone cheered and tried to slap him on the back, but the speaker pushed him aside. One after another the men went up to read the news and sank back as if suddenly believing it. Bert Cooper stood and watched, the thin spiral of smoke from his cigar wasting in the damp air. 'Another bloody war,' he muttered and spat into the gutter.

'It's right, then?' Walter Darwen stared at the backs of heads and the now misted glass of the office windows where the hot breath of those determined to read and to extract the last vestige of drama from the bald words had to be wiped away before the words became clear once more. One or two of the local hotheads were shouting and trying to get an audience, but few listened.

'About time we taught the Boers a thing or two. They've asked for it long enough. Did you hear that they arrested one of our journalists? It's true – one of the men on the *County Press* knows him. That was before they declared war. They said he spread lies about them when they started moving troops.'

'What do you think?' asked Walter Darwen.

Bert took his cigar from his mouth. 'True enough, I reckon, and bad for trade. All trade in Johannesburg has stopped and hundreds of families are on the way to the Cape, driven out of their homes.' He threw down the stub of the cigar.

'That's right, Mr Cooper,' said Fred Cantor, eagerly, and Walter moved to one side, wondering if there was anything that Fred didn't hear. He was forever sidling up to listen to other men talking and some of his gossip was true. 'Nothing left. Driven out of their lawful homes with no food nor clothes nor money, and no hopes of getting any.'

'I never thought they'd fight. I knew they'd push as hard as they could, but not that,' said Bert.

'We couldn't let them get away with it, Mr Cooper,' said Fred Cantor as if he had signed the declaration of war himself. 'They stole the gold from the train to the Cape and I heard they mean to take over the mines.'

2

'They're nothing but a band of brigands,' said Bert. His face reddened.

'Do you have much tied up in gold?' Walter Darwen smiled. 'That really hurt, didn't it?'

'Gold has always been safe,' said Bert. 'I don't believe that it can last. As soon as our troops get out there, they can guard the mines.'

'I thought you were against war, Bert?' said Walter.

'When it comes to protecting property, any man would fight,' said Bert Cooper, with the same determined look he had when trying to convince the local council that he was right.

'Even you, Bert?' Walter turned up the collar of his overcoat and looked at the dark and starless sky. It was common knowledge that Bert had not been well enough to fight in the other clashes and had escaped the Irish Troubles and made a packet while other men left widows and orphans.

'I would, if it was on my doorstep,' said Bert. 'But for that kind of fighting they need professionals.'

A man in a black jacket and cloth cap waved unsteady arms and shouted, his eyes refusing to focus on the bulletin board, 'Think they can fight? I'll take 'em on, one at a time. I'll go out there on the first boat. Who'll come with me, to fight for our Queen? I'll go! I'll be first to volunteer.' He stared with bloodshot eyes and clenched his fists as if the Boers were among the crowd at the bulletin board.

Someone laughed. 'Go home! Go home before your missus catches you shouting and gives you a box on the ear.' Another man went up to him and told him he'd had one over the eight, but others stood silent, their eyes sliding away from his glassy stare when he accused them of being cowards, too frightened to go with him to the enlistment booth.

The rain started in earnest now, as it can do after a sultry day on the Isle of Wight. Men on the pavement pulled down hats and turned up the collars of their coats or jackets. Some moved to the shelter of the wide arches under the Town Hall on the other side of the road and some went away home. The street grew slimy with newly-laid dust and trodden horse manure and the air stirred hardly at all. Bert looked once more at the board and muttered that the least they could do was to quote share prices to put his mind at rest, but Walter just stood in the doorway and thought of his wife, Jane.

A woman, standing apart under the broad archway leading to

3

the main entrance of the Town Hall held a child wrapped in a shawl. The child coughed with dreary regularity but even her mother took no notice.

Bert turned away and rejoined his companion. 'So it really is war. I don't know what Annie will say. She didn't want me to put money out of the country.' He laughed, grimly. 'But you know Annie. Doesn't like anything out of her sight. What she'd say if I joined up, I hate to think.' He walked across with Walter to the more sheltered side of the arches where Maudie Dove stood with the child. 'I should never have touched them. Got a tidy bit in Transvaal Gold that even Annie didn't know of.'

Walter Darwen smiled. 'Too greedy, that's your trouble, Bert. Never could leave well alone, not even at school. Always wanted that bit more and devil take the loser.'

'You'll have something to worry *you* if it gets any worse,' said Bert, sharply.

Walter shrugged. His tone was still good-humoured, his smile without malice. 'That's one worry I don't have, too much money.'

'There'll be other matters,' said Bert. 'What of your business? Who'll look after that if you go? Who can you expect to look after the shop, your other business interests and that wife and family of yourn? Not to speak of the animals. Think about that and then try to tell me how to run my own affairs!' He buttoned up his overcoat and squinted up at the sky. 'There's a lot to think about, Walt, mark my words. I'm off home before it pours down.'

The woman with the child plucked at Walter Darwen's sleeve. 'What are they saying, Mr Darwen?' she said, timidly.

'War, Maudie!' he said brusquely, moving away. Something about Maudie Dove repelled him. It could be the whiff of dirty linen and the sour smell of the child in her arms, but whatever made him turn away now made him stop and look more closely at the pale but pretty face, as if he was unwillingly attracted to her poverty.

'Not war, Mr Darwen? What shall I do?'

'Wait a minute! Your Ben is in the army, isn't he? You poor little soul, he'll be one of the first to go.' Maudie sobbed and Walter shifted uneasily, pulling at his moustache and trying to look stern. 'Yes, you go home now, and try not to worry. Get that little one home in the dry. It shouldn't be out in this.' He half-smiled as she stopped sobbing. 'That's right. Home for you and I'll ask my wife to look in on you tomorrow. This business may come to nothing. There's no cause for you to worry. It came as a shock but they'll sort it out soon.'

'Thank you, Mr Darwen.' Maudie seemed to accept his clumsy reassurance as gospel truth and hitched her shawl closer before stepping out into the rain.

Walter stared after her, seeing the natural grace that the shabby clothes and slovenly shoes couldn't hide completely. Maudie had been a pretty child even if her mother was a one for hanging round the barges when the men came ashore with money in their pockets. Some said the man who fathered Maudie was Dutch and it could be true if the fair hair and good skin gave any hint of it.

Jane would listen to no gossip about the girl, but then, Jane didn't gossip like most of the women in the small town. Walter looked down the road, past the yellow lights reflected in the black wetness of the street, towards his shop, hidden beyond the bend and the rise up the hill. He stayed under the arch and tried to make up his mind to go home.

Would Jane weep for him if he went away? Would she want him back as Maudie wanted her Ben? A twinge of anger mixed with sadness made him envy Ben. Not for Maudie, dirty little slut as he thought her, but for having his woman waiting, ready and able to lie with him and give him comfort. It was near on four years, he thought with wonder. How long could a man stay away from the pleasures of bed? He glanced towards the Square and the lights of the Wheatsheaf spilling out on to the cobbles. Was that the only alternative?

The vision of Jane, his beautiful Jane, faded as he walked slowly to the bright lights. If he went home, what was the use? The Doctor had been very convincing. Eight babies in as many years and the last one dead, nearly taking Jane with her. Fred Cantor sidled along the wall and then away, seeing that Walt Darwen was in no mood for him, and recalling the time that Walt went wild and gave him a black eye just because he tried to sell him some of the new-fangled sheaths that were said to stop pregnancies. It was hurt pride as much as natural revulsion that had made Walter lash out. Did all Newport know that he no longer slept with his wife? But Fred had been scared enough to keep quiet about the snippet of gossip brought home by his young daughter who cleaned at the doctor's surgery.

'"No more babies," he said,' Dora had told him. 'It's true, Dad.

If she has any more, she'll die, and with seven living, they can't afford to lose her.'

Walter looked once more down the main road then hastened his steps. No need to get wet through. A wave of beery air, warm with promised comfort, escaped thankfully from the stuffy snug bar. Walter hung his hat and coat on the tall bentwood stand and sat in his usual corner.

'Still wet out?' said Olive Grace, the landlord's widowed sister. She wiped the table top with an ale-damp rag and smiled, wondering when one of the best-looking men in Newport would see her as she was, a woman without a man. 'Quite a bit of excitement up at the Press window, Mr Darwen.'

'I was there,' he grunted. 'The usual.'

Mrs Grace sensed his need to be alone and brought a carefully-filled tankard of her best ale. She put it before him and Walter relaxed, viewing the room quizzically and listening as more and more men came from the bulletin board. He made a place for Peter Fry who came to sit by him.

'Well then, Walt – what now?' Walter sipped his ale. 'Not worried, are you?' persisted Peter Fry. 'You haven't money tied up like Bert. That doesn't hit you, with your business doing well and your bits of local trade.'

'There's a lot to think about,' said Walter, frowning.

'They couldn't take you. You did your duty and more in Ireland. They wouldn't call you back.'

'It might not be a case of calling back,' said Walter, slowly.

'You wouldn't volunteer? You'd be mad. You've a wife and seven children, and what about the shop and your other bits of business? You couldn't be expected to leave Jane with that lot.'

'As everyone tells me,' said Walter dryly. 'But as I see it, there's been trouble with South Africa for years. They've had some skirmishes about a deal of injustice. Kruger has been trouble for thirty years and if he's not stopped, he'll be trouble for another thirty and by that time all our assets over there will have vanished. He needs a lesson and to be stopped before he does more harm and he needs to know we mean it. He must stop for good.'

'So you think we should rush off to defend a lot of foreigners and to put Bert's money back in his pocket?' He laughed. 'You won't catch me on that lark. Leave it to the regulars. Plenty of men who've taken the Queen's shilling without you and me leaving our families.'

6

Walter drained his tankard and signalled for more. 'They aren't all foreigners,' he said. 'Some are as British as you and me. They pay high taxes but have no say in running the country. How would you like to live like that? They have no vote and are harassed at every turn, not knowing what's to happen from one week's end to the next.'

'If they choose to live there, they must sort out their own salvation,' said Peter. 'They have money and gold and in any country that means power.'

'That Paul Kruger is as clever as a fox. Not educated but clever,' said Walter. 'He knows that if he gives the Outlanders the vote, they might vote him right out of power, so he stirs up trouble. The Dutch Church preaches independence and the Dutch farmers think the Outlanders want power. He's told them they can treat the Kaffirs as they like.'

'The Kaffirs are the natives there?'

'The blacks who have some rights, surely. It was their country once, but poor critters, they are still like slaves, even if they have permission to marry now.'

'We can't tell another country what to do. It's all thousands of miles away and it's different there.'

'Have you seen Kruger's pictures?' Walter stuck out his jaw as he did when he was obstinate. 'As awkward a cuss as ever I've seen. He'll never give equal rights to the Outlanders or anyone else, nor disarm his forts unless he's pushed. Some men have to be pushed before they yield an inch.' He leaned back and lit a small cheroot. He was warm and comfortable now and a kind of excitement grew as the evening wore on. Even Mrs Grace looked quite a tasty bit, with that purple flower pinned to her dress and her more than generous curves pushed up over her stays.

Peter ordered more ale for them both. 'Be honest, Walt. Would your heart be in it? You've a lot to lose and everyone doesn't think as you do. There are many in this country who think the declaration is wrong, and the Irish are for Kruger, and the Germans, or so I hear. The Americans keep quiet but I think they wouldn't be sorry to see us beaten out there.'

'Does that mean you as well, Pete? Are you for Kruger, too?'

'Of course not, but I think he has as much reason to hate us as we have to hate him. I agree that he needs to be kept in check, but he'll be fighting for his own, as we will. It's no use talking, the papers say one thing one day and change their tune the next. Half the time I don't know what to believe.'

7

Walter laughed. 'Let's hope they don't call on you then, Peter or you'd be hard-pressed to decide what side to fight for.'

Peter flushed. 'I'd fight if I had to. I'm as patriotic as the next man but pray God it doesn't come to that.'

The door swung open to admit the drunk in the black jacket. A bottle stuck out of his pocket and his eyes were rimmed with red. He leaned against the wall to gain his balance and blinked in the bright light. 'Who's coming? Come on, who has the courage to fight for our lovely Queen? Come and take the Queen's shilling.' He began to walk round the room, staring into faces and stumbling against chairs. He sang the National Anthem in a hoarse and quavering voice.

'Quieten down,' said Walter. 'Let peaceful folk sup their beer without that row and sit down before you fall down.'

The man's eyes focussed on the local businessman who every other person in the room respected as honest and hard-working and yet good for a drink and a song. 'It's Walt Darwen,' the man said, thickly. 'Walt Darwen who fought in the other war. He fought in all the other wars. 'He breathed heavily. 'Come on, Walt. You'll come. They need men like you. They want all the good horsemen they can get. They told me they want men like you.' He sank into the tub chair by the piano and tried to play a tune until someone shut the lid down hard on his fingers. As the laughter faded, Walter looked up to see what had caused the silence.

Three men stood in the doorway, non-commissioned officers from Albany Barracks. After a full minute of silence, a sudden rush of offers to buy drinks for the soldiers made Mrs Grace quite flustered. Walter smiled wryly. He recalled being fêted when in uniform, when the country had need of him, and he also recalled the indifference on the public face when hostilities were over and there was no longer a threat to life or liberty.

The sergeant held up a hand in greeting and grinned across the smoke-filled air. Walter knew him from the visits he made regularly to the Barracks to deliver fish and vegetables. The sergeant had been there when Walter had renewed the contract to supply fish and fruit to the officer's mess. Walter beckoned to him and Peter moved to make room. 'What's this, then?' Walter nodded towards the drunken man who sat sucking his knuckles. 'Not enlisting already?'

'We set up a booth by the Town Hall. Quite a few takers,' the sergeant said. 'We get more when the news is bad and tomorrow, it will be too late to back down. Some were too young so we sent them away, and some were half-drunk like him over there.'

Walter wiped the ale froth from his moustache.

'Interested?' said the sergeant.

'I've done my duty,' said Walter. 'I've far too much doing in this town to think of going overseas.'

The sergeant watched him over his drink. 'Pity. It's men like you we want.' Walter looked up. 'You were with the Horse, weren't you? The Royal Horse Artillery?' He nodded as if impressed. 'Did well, or so I heard. Better than most.'

'You heard that?'

'I may be mistaken, but you *are* Walt Darwen, non-commissioned officer who won the silver spurs for horseman-ship. Best in regiment?' Walter reddened and waved a deprecating hand, but the man continued, 'That's darned good. I pride myself I can sit anything on four legs but I'm not that standard. Do you still have horses? Get any practice? You look fit and sturdy.'

'I have a working horse who draws the cart,' said Walter, cautiously.

The sergeant laughed. 'I don't want your nag. I saw it when you came up to the Barracks. We do need mounts but that's none of my business. I want men. I want men like you who are experienced and can set the right example to the recruits. You know how they need licking into shape. They need discipline badly.'

Mrs Grace came with the sergeant's beer and he put a hand round her waist and gave her a squeeze. She laughed and Walter knew that if he was in uniform, women would almost expect such casual signs of appraisal. It was nothing, but it showed the glamour of uniform and the affect it had on women like Mrs Grace. 'Another?' she said to Walter Darwen, with the respect due to a man well-known in the community, but her smile lacked the coquetry she had shown the sergeant.

The sergeant nodded although Walter protested that he'd had enough and should be on his way home. Mrs Grace brought another full measure and the sergeant raised his own to Walter.

'There's too much at stake here,' said Walter. He looked at the soldier with a kind of desperation. 'I've a wife and seven children and so much to do that the days need to be twice as long. I'm tied.'

9

'You could be safe, just training recruits. You could still be proud to serve the Queen.' Walter shook his head. 'Not you, then,' said the sergeant, then leaned forward as if the matter was dismissed and they could talk freely. 'But it's bad luck for you. Don't you ever miss the company?' He loosened the top button of his tunic. 'Don't tell me you never think of the old days? What of the freedom, the companionship of other men, the horses. I tell you, I've never seen finer beasts than the ones they have now. Bred for the Artillery, in special stables from good stock. Not a wrong 'un among them.'

'But if I went, it wouldn't be with the Horse. I'd be just another volunteer. I might end up in the infantry!' he frowned as he imagined the ultimate indignity.

'So you would – if you wait to be called. I think there are many who hold back now who will be taken later and sent to anywhere they need an extra pair of hands. If you enlist of your own free will, now, you have a choice.'

'What do you mean?'

'You can enlist in your old company with your old rank and pay.' He shrugged as if regretting having to tell Walter something he couldn't do, and turned away to speak to his corporal.

Walter sat brooding and from time to time, the sergeant glanced at him but said nothing.

The atmosphere in the snug became charged with fumes and patriotic fervour. Three men came in, looking half-frightened and half-proud that they had enlisted and Mrs Grace sang songs for them as they clustered round the piano. She sang old songs, sentimental songs and the drunk wept openly. More ale was consumed, the sergeant waited and Walter wished with all his heart that he had gone home when Bert did.

A terrible force plucked at his loyalties, his stabilities and the whole fabric of his life. Memories evoked by the uniforms and the talk of regimental life filled his mind, coloured and softened by the ale.

'I'm on my way,' said the sergeant, and a group of men followed him to the door. Several stopped there and turned away to their homes up above the town, but more went with the sergeant to the booth by the Town Hall.

Peter Fry sat hunched over his beer, thinking that Walter Darwen was every kind of a fool, and wished he had the courage to join him.

Chapter 2

One yellow gaslight irradiated the bend in the High Street and misty rain swept over the low stone parapet of Coppins Bridge. Jane Darwen looked out of the second-floor window of the house above the shop and craned her neck to see what was going on up the road, but the worsening weather kept any who might want to be out, at home.

It was nearly ten o'clock after a leaden evening and it was unlikely that anyone would want fish or vegetables at this hour. 'Edward?' she called to her eldest son. 'Time to fix the shutters.'

Edward and his brother Jack lifted the heavy wooden shutters and placed them over the windows of the shop front, sliding in the heavy bolts that secured them each night, and the thin light from the street was blocked out.

Jane came down the twisting stairway and closed the door behind her. She put another lighted candle on the counter of the shop and two spare candles in holders by the first. What was the point of wasting gas? If someone came to buy, a knock on the door would bring one of the girls. All of Newport knew that the Darwens were there behind the closed shutters and willing to serve.

Hurrying feet and muffled voices from outside brought an air of disquiet and urgency into the quiet shop but Jane tried to ignore them, moving the candle to cast a better light over the fruit she was sorting. Rumours, she thought. There had been rumours for weeks and every tongue in the town told a different tale. The shop had its fair share of idle gossips, ready to fancy the very worst that could happen and Jane was sick at heart, even now the dark wet night was shut out and the boys were laughing in the back room. The golden light from the candle was dim and did nothing to relieve the gloom.

11

'Edward? Have the girls gone up yet?'

'Yes, Mother.' Her eldest son stood against the light that now escaped from the main living room of the old shop, and she wondered if she would feel less depressed if she lit the gas in the shop while she worked, but candle-light was cheap and usually, the fruit sorting had a tranquillizing effect after a busy day, with Jane alone in the shop in the soft light.

'Then it's time you all went up,' she said.

'Father not home?'

'Not yet.' She smiled, seeing the anxious look in the eyes so like his father's, blue and deep-set and with a manliness too old for his twelve years. 'I expect he's on his way back from the *Press* windows. They're all coming back now.'

'Can I wait to hear what they said?'

'Time enough in the morning. You've school to go to and your father may need you to fetch Bess from the arches, early. Tell Jack to go up and stop teasing Sidney.'

Edward grinned. His mother might be out of sight, but she knew to a T what Jack was up to. 'I'll get them up the stairs,' he said, and Jane felt calmer, knowing that with Edward, she had a son who would help her in anything she asked of him. 'Sidney's got chalk dust all over his face. Can I take some warm water into the scullery?'

'The tank is full, but make sure you fill it for the morning,' said Jane. 'And make sure you all wash well. It's clean underwear tomorrow and clean socks, so leave the dirty in the basket.'

She returned to the sorting, and the light faded behind her. Edward, her eldest, was born when there was time to play with a first child and to love him in a special way because he looked so like Walter; and there was still time and laughter in their loving, as husband and wife. He would not need anyone to check on his filling the tank at the side of the big kitchen range so that warm water would be ready in the morning for the family to wash, heated by the banked up fire that never went out, winter or summer except for twice a year when the chimney was swept.

She tossed a rotten orange into the box under the counter. Some people had time to waste, standing in the rain waiting for news. Bad news came fast enough without chasing it. As if there wasn't enough in the daily papers. Some said the war had started already, while others swore that Kruger would steal and run. South Africa was hundreds of miles away. It could be on the other side of the moon for all she knew, so how could a quarrel so far

12

away affect her or her family?

The three boys came in with their candles in wide-based brass candle holders. 'Father in the Wheatsheaf?' asked Jack.

'He is not.' Jane sounded slightly more Irish, a sign that she was upset. 'He is trying to make some sense of the bulletins and will want some peace when he comes in.'

Sidney, the youngest son, kissed his mother's cheek and she wanted to hug him fiercely, as the still damp skin reminded her of baby bathing and cuddles that would be rejected now by her growing family. How they grew. She sighed. Edward was quite grown-up in his manner, but Jack was still harum-scarum and if she knew the signs, would be so all his life. Sidney, no longer the youngest since Emily was born, and Caroline lived and died in one short month, was quiet and in a dream most of the time, drawing pictures and making models of cardboard and soft wood from the orange boxes.

'Good night, boys. Remember to say your prayers.' She touched Edward on the arm and smiled. 'Thank you, Edward. I don't know what I'd do without my big son when your father is out.' Edward's rather stolid face lit up with pleasure and he looked back at her as the others climbed the stairs, then followed and closed the stair door behind him.

Jane opened the door again, as she did every night. 'Quiet, you girls,' she called. 'Not another word or a giggle out of you or I'll come up with the hairbrush.'

'Goodnight,' said a voice trying not to laugh. Jane smiled and closed the door. Emily had the giggles again and it was Clare who had made her laugh and then kept very quiet herself. Clare and Janey, were far more grown-up than either Jack or Sidney, even though there was but a year on either side of them, and yet, Lizzie, Clare's twin, seemed young for her age, a thin and sometimes whining child who seemed to need attention all the time.

Jane listened. The children were asleep for sure, and horses and then human footsteps passed the door, the sounds magnified by the stillness of the wet street. Rain ran down the gutter into the deep drain that took it to the River Medina and threatened to overflow on to the road, leaving a blockage of sodden leaves. Footsteps came softly now, and the distant hooves were muffled on the slippery hill, but she recognised Walter's step as he crossed Sea Street. She looked up when he came in but still held a specky apple in her hand.

'Any news from the mainland?' she said.

13

Walter tapped the scarred wood of the front door. 'Everyone in?'

'At this hour, I should hope they were all in their beds,' she said, shortly. Walter bolted the door. 'Well, then? You look as if you lost sixpence and found a ha'penny.'

'It's war, Jane. It's really come and it's serious.'

'Holy Mother,' whispered Jane. 'I've heard all sorts today. I've heard enough different tales to make my head spin until I didn't know what to believe.'

'Well, we know the worst now and it's still a shock. Arthur says he'll sell his horses before the army take them, but as I told him, who will want to buy horses at a fair price when the Military can commandeer them as soon as they have men enlisted? The ones they don't take will have nobody left to work them or to care for them. I'm glad I have only Bess and Blackie.'

Walter stood watching his wife. The candle glow softened the hurt in her eyes but there were creases of strain that he had never noticed before, little lines round her eyes and mouth and a tight look to her chin. It was a long time since he had studied her so intently. There had been a time, but not now. There was always so much to be done ... he was out of the shop and house for hours at a time, fetching stock and ordering from the warehouse by the quay and buying fish from Aaron Sheath. The contract from the Barracks took time, not that he could afford to grumble at that as the concession to the officers' mess alone made it well worthwhile and the wives of 'other ranks' were glad to buy fresh fish at the gates of the married quarters.

Walter was tired and rather full of ale. He watched Jane's deft hands sorting the fruit, putting the unblemished in the window and the bad ones in the box under the counter. The slightly bruised, or specked, went for the horses and pigs and the children could cut out the rot and eat the rest of the better ones.

She was overworked already. What would she do if he had to go away? He pulled on the ends of his moustache and stood quietly. The children were good with the horses and the pigs and ducks in the pens under the archways of the railway, but now, there would be more to do. He shifted uneasily, remembering the brickyard. He dreaded her reaction on learning that he'd bought a share in Bert Cooper's brickyard. She looked gentle enough, but he knew just how violent the storm of her Irish temper could be, and how scathing she was when aroused.

14

Jane's face was pale and she felt cold. She knew about war, the Troubles in Ireland when Irish fought Irish and the British soldiers had come. Walter, in full uniform, had been a dashing figure and she had been helpless. She'd not needed asking twice but had come over the sea to Newport and the shop as his bride. She looked at the man she had married. He was still young and healthy. What if he had to go? She threw away a good orange and put a badly mildewed one on display. Walter reached across and removed it and suddenly she was very annoyed, as if he had reproached her. If he left, at least nobody could tell her what oranges went where. She knew it was childish. He wouldn't go, until the regulars had gone and they conscripted men into foot regiments. She glanced at him guiltily, as if she had wished him in the front lines. She sighed. Nothing she thought or wished would be of any account. Walter made his own decisions. It would be as he wanted it, as always.

He had shown her that as soon as they met, all those years ago. He'd wanted her and she had to make up her mind, quickly. 'Well?' he'd said. 'Are you coming to England with me? I've no time to argue the toss. I've a shop at home that needs a mistress, and enough for two.' He'd never said he loved her, even after eight children, he'd never said the words, but he was often loving, with moments of great tenderness and Jane respected his inability with words even when his need of her was intense. She pulled back her thoughts to more immediate matters, knowing that he would make up his own mind and the family must follow.

'What will I do if they take you away?' She looked at him directly, the dark brown eyes sad. 'What will I do if you go over the water? What will I do with the ducks and the horses and the pigs? And who will fetch the fish to the Barracks?' Her voice broke and she couldn't bring the anger she desired to her words. 'And *who* will manage the brickyard?'

So she knew about that. Walter had expected it for days. It only needed Bert Cooper to tell his wife that Walter Darwen had bought a share in the brickyard for it to be all over Newport and half the Island. Even knowing that Jane would hear, he had lacked the courage to tell her as he knew she'd be hurt, disliking Bert and his waspish wife Annie so much. He shuffled his feet and looked like Edward in trouble. 'I was going to tell you,' he said.

Walter fiddled with the door bolt until Jane wanted to scream. She sorted oranges as if each one was important and a personal treasure. The set of her head was proud and stiff and close to tears. Walter lifted the box of bad fruit on to the counter ready for putting outside. 'Any tea?' he said.

Jane pushed the thick dark hair from her face. 'Yes, it's ready. We'll have a cup.' She left him to snuff the candle and went into the living room, putting the hot flat iron on a trivet and a kettle in its place. Already a spiral of steam came from the spout of the kettle that had been on the hob all the evening. Half-finished ironing lay over the big table and the room was warm and filled with the scent of ironed linen. Jane riddled the fire in the range and made tea.

Walter watched the steam rise and cleared his throat. It was going to be more difficult than he'd imagined. How could he tell her? His heart ached with unaccustomed emotion as he saw the familiar room, with Jane standing there, her hair escaping in tendrils round her now hot face. Her whole being spoke of homely comfort, strength and great beauty. Inside, a cold nucleus of fear threatened to surface. – I must be mad, he decided, without hope.

'Well, what did it say?' she said, handing him the large moustache cup filled with strong sweet tea. Her wide eyes missed no expression that crossed his face.

'It was just the declaration and they didn't put out the usual bulletin,' he said. 'I saw Maudie Dove up by the Town Hall. She wanted to know about it and I couldn't tell her much. Her Ben is in it and she's upset, gal. Really upset. She doesn't know when she'll see her man again and the child looks rough. Take her some specks in the morning and a nice bit of skate.'

'Walter!' Jane could feel him sliding away again, avoiding the most important subject. 'What is it, Walter? There's something more, isn't there? It isn't even about the brickyard, though that's bad enough.'

'As I was saying, seeing Maudie in a state upset me.' He buried his face over the cup.

'What have you done?' Jane put her cup down and pushed aside the linen. She sat looking at him, their eyes level, and slowly, Walter put the cup aside. They were silent for a full minute, their individual fears becoming one. He could hardly hear her words but he saw her lips quiver. 'You volunteered,' she said. 'Walter Darwen, you have volunteered, and I don't think you know the half of what it means!'

16

In the Wheatsheaf, it had been something to make other men envious and proud that a friend could make sacrifices for the Country. They had cheered him on, seeing it a foregone conclusion that Walter Darwen who had such a good service record should be one of the first to go, whatever happened to those he left behind. The songs had done it, too. Those damned songs with Mrs Grace looking at him as if she admired him more than she did the sergeant, and was a part of the new life he could command.

The sergeant had stood there in his uniform and raised a glass to toast the 'little lady up the road at Osborne', and it had all been charged and patriotic. It had mattered! It was important for him to choose what unit he joined. Women didn't understand these things. Jane saw the flash of anger under the shame. If he had to go, it must be with the Horse. He must go proudly with his old regiment. His gaze left her set face. 'Yes, I volunteered,' he said.

Jane took the iron from the range and spat on the heel to test for heat. She folded a sheet so violently that a wave of warm clean scent went across the room, making the lamp flicker. Walter half-rose in his chair but Jane stayed him with a withering look. 'Sit where you are,' she said. 'We're quiet now. If you have to go away there are matters to settle.'

It was long after midnight before Jane packed up the fire and put the flat irons away in the cupboard under the window. She filled the iron kettles from the tap in the yard and put them on the stove, knowing from long experience the exact position for them to be singing in the morning. She saw that Edward had filled the water tank at the side of the range and took a little comfort in seeing it brimful.

Walter wearily emptied the boiler in the outhouse and raked out the ashes under it. He layed fresh kindling and sticks for the next crab-boiling and stacked wood ready to add when the fire caught. He ignored the warm water in the tank and washed his face under the yard tap before stumbling up the unlit stairway to the bedroom.

Jane lay in her shift, easing herself to the edge of the feather bed, heavy with misery. The full realisation of the situation came like news of a death in the family and she wanted to weep but had no tears.

Walter groped for her in the darkness, a small boy seeking comfort but she stiffened and turned away. Not that! Dear God,

17

not that. It would be unbearable. Another baby, or if the doctor was right, something worse while he was away. She remembered the times when she was full of joy with a baby kicking inside her and now, she might as well be barren. She wanted to turn to him, to take him into her arms to hold him close. – Dear Mother of God, she prayed silently. Let it pass. She wanted him and needed to tell him that everything would be all right and that nothing mattered but the two of them, loving again.

Jane clenched her hands and bit her knuckles to stop from crying out. She dared not ask for any comfort or it would be too late, and since Caroline, her last baby, she had lived in fear.

'No more children, Mrs Darwen,' Dr Barnes had said. 'No more if you value your life. You have too many responsibilities to the living to risk another baby.'

'You mean until I am well again?'

He shook his head. 'You will have to be strong and ... er ... resist any advances from your husband.' The doctor blew his nose vigorously on a silk handkerchief. 'Your husband must choose between total abstinence and losing you. It would be madness,' he added. 'And you have seven live children to feed and clothe and bring up in the way you would wish for them.'

Jack had looked round the door when the doctor bound up her legs after placing half-crowns padded with rag over the two varicose ulcers. 'Go down, Jack,' she said, hating a young child to see his mother so, and thinking he would be frightened.

'No, stay, Jack.' The doctor handed him the smelly dressings he had discarded, with the old half-crowns still in them. 'Put these under the tap and get the coins, my lad. Wash them in hot water and share them with your brothers and sisters.'

'But Doctor Barnes!' Jane was shocked.

'You don't know your own son, Mrs Darwen. He isn't moved by a bit of dirt. He'll be up here the next time I come, but you'd better tell him that half-crowns don't grow on trees.' Jane knew that it was his way of saying how much he respected her and wanted to help and what he'd said about Jack was true. Each time he came to dress the ulcers, he repeated the warning. 'No more children if you want to live.' He patted her hand when she was well enough to venture downstairs. 'I've told your husband and he's a good man. You'll have no more trouble,' he said.

Jane had stifled her natural warmth, knowing that the doctor was right. She must concentrate on caring for others and to be honest, seven live children were enough. She loved each one and even dreamed of Caroline, growing up into a beautiful girl. If she'd lived, she would have been nearly four.

Walter turned away and in a few minutes was sleeping. Until this night, he had never wavered and had been resigned to the situation even though abstinence was a bitter blow to him. Jane was glad to hear his deep breathing. She sighed tiredly but no sleep came. The clock in St Thomas' tower struck four and she was still hovering between sleep and waking.

At six, she crept out of bed and filled the heavy ewer with warm water and brought it up to the washstand in the bedroom. As she washed, Walter watched her. Jane twisted her dark hair into a shiny black bun in the nape of her neck and some fine hairs refused to be tamed. He stifled the lust that rose in him and wished she was less beautiful. In the queenly way of the dark-haired Irish, her breasts were high even after feeding her babies and she moved with grace and ease and a lack of self-consciousness that made her stand out among other women. She sensed him watching and smiled.

She buttoned her bodice. 'Don't worry,' she said softly. 'We'll manage somehow.'

The first kettle was hot and five mintues after Jane opened the damper and stirred the coke into flame, she was able to pour boiling water on the first pot of tea of the day. The house was quiet as they sat in the living room together, and Jane clasped a mug of hot tea between her hands and gazed into space. Walter gulped his and called the boys to go with him to the stable before breakfast and getting ready for school. The girls made the beds and Jane's tea grew a cold bronze skin on the surface of the mug. She shivered and put it from her.

'Is breakfast ready, Mother?' said Lizzie. 'We've done the beds.'

'Holy Mary! It's late. Go back and make sure you've all got clean pinafores then hurry down.'

Jane threw cutlery on the table and cut bread. She sliced bacon into the frying pan and made fresh tea.

'Where's Father?' asked Emily, pinching the stiffly-gophered frill on her pinafore.

'He's gone with the boys to get the cart.'

'Where's he going?'

'Eat up your bacon and don't ask so many questions,' said Jane.

Clare looked up from her plate. 'Is it true that we are going to fight the Boers, Mother?' The others stopped eating and Jane was aware of many eyes staring. She drew in her breath sharply and bent to cut more bread.

'I don't want Father to go away,' said Emily. 'Is he going away to leave us?'

'It's true that we are at war, but even if your father had to join the army, he would stay in Portsmouth and train new lads. They need men like him to do that training before they go as real soldiers,' said Jane.

Emily sat still, her breakfast forgotten and large tears welling up in her eyes. Clare tossed her head angrily, obviously disturbed and in a while would try to blame someone for her own anger. Lizzie sniffed. It wasn't going to be easy, but Janey smiled as if she knew what went on in her mother's head.

The shop door burst open and the boys rushed through the living room on their way to the scullery to wash. They brought with them a smell of horses and Sidney kicked a lump of dung from his boot, breaking the tension as he was bustled out to the yard to wipe his boots. Janey took out soap so that they could wash in the yard under the cold tap, with strict instructions not to venture in until they smelled sweet.

Walter gave Bess a nosebag of hay and hitched the reins over the cart. Jane raised her eyebrows and Walter nodded, all buoyancy gone. Jane saw lines on his face that she had never noticed before.

'More news?' she said, with a calm that surprised her.

'Another bulletin and it's bad. They posted a notice by the board telling all enlisted men to report at the Barracks this afternoon.' Walter sat down heavily and reached for his moustache cup, as always when he came in from the stables, full of strong dark tea. 'I'll go to the warehouse, but first, I'd better see Aaron.'

'Not until you've eaten,' Jane said, firmly. She handed him a plate piled high with food and re-filled his cup. Now it was certain that he was leaving, Jane was calm. Knowing made it easier to plan and she was clear-thinking, efficient and her mind buzzed with everything that must be done. She cleared dishes and chivvied the children off to school early, calling Sidney from the privy in the yard where he escaped as often as possible to read a book.

'I've lots of time, Mother,' he protested.

'Once your head's stuck in a book you'll never get to school,' said Jane. She lowered her voice. 'And your father needs a bit of quiet this morning.'

Sidney ran after the other children, banging the shop door behind him and racing over the bridge to catch up with the girls. To him, a bit of quiet for Father meant that Walter had drunk too much last night and was bad-tempered this morning. The threat to the family had not yet registered.

Jane put away the last dish and Walter searched the crowded mantelpiece for the pipe he so rarely smoked. Jane dusted off a scallop shell and set it by his elbow on the table. She could just recall the last time he had sat with a pipe. It was when Emily had scarlet fever and they had wrapped the tiny girl in red blankets before taking her in the hospital cart to the Isolation Hospital at Fairlee. Walter smoked in silence now but his eyes never left his wife as she bustled to and fro, washing the dishes in a bowl at the table, as it was cold in the scullery, wringing out the dishcloth and hanging it by the range and tipping the greasy water outside the back door, down the drain there.

Jane flicked dust from the curtain of red chenille that festooned the mantel, matching the bobble-edged table cover which now covered the table. She tidied the long dresser and returned the blue and white plates to their places beside the huge platter used only for Christmas dinner and on the rare occasions when Walter brought home a sucking pig, the runt of the litter.

Walter knocked the glowing ash from his pipe. 'I'm sorry, Jane,' he said, with difficulty.

Jane felt her hands trembling. This was terrible. She could bear it if he was brusque and demanding and she knew what he expected from her, but now, he was abject and unsure of himself and her heart ached. He saw her discomfiture and regained something of his normal manner, even managing a smile.

'I've thought it out,' he said. 'I'll go and see Sam Walmsley at the fruit warehouse and ask him to give you any help you need. He's a good friend and I've put many a bit of business his way in the past. Then there are the Sheaths. Aaron is too old to be called up, so he can bring the boat up under the bridge from his cellar door and give you fish straight into the cart. He might even do a run up to the Barracks now and then, but I wouldn't want you to expect it.'

'There's no call for him to do it. The boys must do that. They can go in the evenings.'

'It's time they did more,' said Walter. 'You can get a girl in to

21

help in the house and the girls must help in the shop.' He pulled at his moustache.

'What of the brickyard?'

'Bert Cooper will look after the pigs if he can have two of each litter. He'll see to the workmen, too.'

Jane went pink. 'Trust Bert Cooper to do nothing without a good return. You call him a friend but when it comes to money, he's a leech.'

'He'll do it right, that's the important fact.' Walter laughed. 'But you'll need to keep an eye on him, for all that. I'll tell him that you'll check the accounts at the yard every week. That should keep him on his toes. I think you frighten him, Jane.' He saw her doubt. 'If he's ever ill or has to go away, you'll need to be in the picture.' Jane nodded, reluctantly.

'Bert Cooper will never be called up. He'll keep very quiet and find some excuse. Bert is very good at looking after number one!'

'He's not as bad as he's painted, Jane. He's a bit livelier than most of the crowd over the bridge and he is a very good businessman.'

'He's a gambler and he drinks more than is good for him, Walter. He's a coward, too. He's scared sick of Annie in one of her moods and that is the only reason he isn't a womaniser. She'd ferret it out of him in half a minute.'

'Come now, Jane, I've had some good times with Bert,' said Walter, mildly, rather pleased that Jane showed some spirit and had discarded the serious, concerned expression that made him feel so guilty.

'The only times I've seen you the worse for drink were when you'd been with Bert. You know I've no time for him or for his family, except Dan, and Annie is the meanest woman in Newport. She is also the biggest trouble-maker.' Jane sniffed. 'Annie Cooper thinks a black satin afternoon apron and a gold pendant watch makes a lady of her.'

'I'm not over-fond of Annie, myself.' Walter smiled at Jane's bright colour and flashing eyes, loving it when she was on the verge of a paddy. 'I know they rile you,' he said, 'but they are important in this town and Bert has a finger in most things. If the war goes on, we'll need all the friends with influence we can get.'

'Well, Annie needn't think she'll get something for nothing when she comes to the shop! She feeds her family on stale cabbage and speck fruit. Says she wants it for the rabbits, but I know better.'

'Think what you like but be careful. If the shippers stop bringing fruit and the farmers have to grow less because the men are away, you'll have to build up the brickyard and the livestock.'

The shop-bell jangled. 'I'll go,' said Jane. 'And you'd better be over to the warehouse.'

Chapter 3

Walter looked over the bridge but Aaron Sheath and his boat were not there. He turned the horse towards Quay Street, across the swing bridge and stopped at the fruit warehouse. Bess stood still, knowing that this would be a long wait and Walter gave her some apple, cut from a pile of bruised fruit on the back of the cart, and went into the office.

Sam Walmsley looked up and waved Walter to a chair. He put down the newspaper he was reading. 'Bad,' he said. 'Don't know what we're coming to. Her Majesty has given her consent to a state of war, so I suppose we must take it that we fight in a just cause, but I'd have thought we'd had enough after all the ructions we've had everywhere the British flag flies. Still, I suppose all the silly young 'uns will wave the flag and flock to enlist.'

'Some of the married men, too,' said Walter and blew his nose, hard.

Sam dropped the paper and stared in disbelief. 'Not you, Walt? You haven't volunteered? Now stop chewing your moustache and tell me. God Almighty, it's true! I can see it in your face.'

'It's true, Sam. I must have been out of my mind.' He moved restlessly under the intent gaze of the older man. 'I want to fight for my country and I have the greatest respect for the throne, but now, there's Jane and the children.' He stopped and shrugged his helplessness. 'I didn't think they'd want me so soon, but I've to report this afternoon up at Albany.' His voice trailed away into a near-whisper. 'So soon, Sam. What will become of my family if I'm away for months or even years?' He put his head in his hands. 'What am I to do, Sam?'

Sam Walmsley spoke briskly. 'Come now, you make it sound as if it's the end of the world. You were a bit of a fool to volunteer

24

but you'd have been called up soon enough, I suppose. They can't afford to leave good horsemen like you. No, you'd have to go, so it might as well be now and cut down the anguish. As to the family, Jane has a good head on her and they ain't babies any more.'

'Will you keep an eye on them, Sam?'

'Bless you, Walt, I'll be a father to that pretty wife of yourn. You tell Jane that if she suffers any rudeness or abuse from anyone – and that means *anyone!* – to send one of the young'uns running for Sam Walmsley. Mind you tell her that. Jane is proud but she might need me before it's all over.' He gave Walter a penetrating look. 'News gets round when a pretty woman is alone and she might be glad of a man behind her. I wonder if you know just how much she is admired? And it isn't always by the ones who would treat her with respect.'

'If I thought that any man would...' Walter stood up.

'You should have thought of that afore, Walter. You know your Jane and I know men. Jane can look after herself as far as most things go, but I'm just telling you she must rely on someone.'

'Thanks, Sam,' said Walter, gruffly. 'You're a true friend.' He pulled out a list. 'Now to business. I'd best stock up for the week. I'll give you the order and one of the boys can bring the cart.'

They went to the inner passage that smelled of fruit in all stages of ripening. A curious gassy scent from the pungent stored apples mixed with the smell of bananas, ripening in semi-darkness. Sam pulled aside a muslin screen and looked at the huge stems of bananas. It was quiet and eerie in the banana shed and Walter was aware of faint claustrophobia. He selected two stems and Sam put labels on two more, as yet unripe. Small speckled Canary Island bananas were ready too and Walter took twelve hands of the deep yellow fruit. 'Jane will like a few of these,' he said.

Sam gave the next stem a sharp tap. 'This batch seems clear. Last batch we found a black'un.'

'A snake?'

'They come on the barges. We found one or two ourselves but none of my men have been bitten. There was one over in Portsmouth Harbour killed a man. All over in five minutes, so they say, and the doctor could do nothing.'

He checked the list and they loaded oranges, lemons and a huge crate of compressed dates. Walter added apples and dried peas and packets of herbs and Bess shook her head, asking for more apple before she started again, needing only a touch on the rein to go along to the arches under the railway bridge where the ducks and pigs were fenced in and the ducks could forage in the water on the river bank.

Walter went through his chores mechanically. The pigs squealed over the swill and the fruit, and the ducks gathered for the scattered grain. – Is this the last time I shall do this? he thought. He caught two ducks and wrung their necks, tossing them on to the cart as a surprise for Jane.

Jane. All the morning, Walter thought of his wife as he had seldom thought of her in the last year. For once, he wondered how she had felt during the time when they had to keep apart in bed. He had never asked her and yet he wondered if she could have any feeling left for him that wasn't rooted in habit or duty.

Sam Walmsley had hinted that other men could lust after his wife if he was away. It was small consolation to know that she dared not give her body to anyone if she wanted to live. He thought with an overwhelming guilt of the times he had left her alone with the children while he went to Ashey Races or down to the farm at Wootton. She was alone in the evenings after the children were in bed and he knew it was all wrong, but what was a man to do? If he'd stayed close to her, she'd have made him relax, smiling at him in that soft Irish way of hers, and he would have wanted her too much. The doctor was right. They dared not have another child and the only escape was with men in the Wheatsheaf.

He backed the cart and climbed on again. He couldn't erase the picture of Jane from his mind, this time with Caroline, the two faces waxen against the white counterpane, scarcely breathing, Jane exhausted from loss of blood, and the little one dead before many days passed. He needed Jane far too much to risk her life even in the emotions of leaving.

He eased Bess towards Sea Street and looked up at two of the windows. That was no answer, for the local whores who hung about the quay and went with foreign sailors would give him more than he wanted and he could never live down that disgrace. The thought of sharing a bed even with no physical contact with Jane, after sleeping with a slut made him grunt with disgust and give Bess a totally undeserved flick of the whip. The problem remained. Bert could go to Portsmouth and see his fancy-piece with Annie none the wiser, as a lot of business was done over the

Solent. Anyway, Annie, with her buttoned-up mouth and skinny arms, might well welcome the respite!

A liaison with a local widow like Mrs Grace? Walter shrugged. In the Wheatsheaf, after a few drinks, she looked fine, but he had seen her in daylight, as faded as the purple flower she had worn and which had looked almost alluring at night. He grinned to himself. Jane had a name for women who wore artificial flowers in the bosom of a dress. Besides, he thought, adultery was a word mentioned behind closed doors as one of the deadly moral and social sins. It was Jane he wanted, to hold her in his arms and hear the soft soothing words, receiving her warmth and pleasure.

Was it bad for her? Could a woman cut off all that, easily? Women like Annie and Amy the cousin at Wootton might, but Jane had been an active and loving partner, contrary to the accepted idea that women endured sex as a duty. The Wheatsheaf and the company helped but it was hard for them both.

At the bridge, Aaron put down his yard broom and wiped the sweat from his beard with a tattered fragment of butter muslin. A strong smell of fresh fish came from his clothes and the flagstones of the cellar glistened with scales. Huge rush baskets full of stiff blue and silver shapes sat on slate shelves and Walter nodded, appreciatively.

Aaron sluiced the last of the fish guts into the river and leaned on the broom. 'Heard you'd volunteered,' he said. 'What – I said – Walt Darwen? *Never*. Not Walt. He'd not do anything so daft. He's got more sense.' He looked sideways and grinned.

'You heard right, Aaron. I'd like to know who told you so fast. I went up to the booth with the rest of them. If you'd been in the Wheatsheaf, you'd have seen how it was.' He reddened. 'I had to do it, Aaron. If I held back now, they'd put me in a foot regiment later, and I have to go with my old unit. I couldn't be pushed into just anything,' he added, defensively. 'I need to be with animals.'

Aaron glanced at the flushed face of the man he'd known from childhood. 'You'll suit the uniform, Walt. Have all the girls after you again, like last time.' He gave a high-pitched giggle, guaranteed to annoy, with his usual genius for finding a raw spot. 'Might be a good thing for you, a bit more female company.'

Walter smiled, grimly. – He's wondered about me and Jane for a long time, he thought. No new baby for four years. People drew their own conclusions.

'Anything worth eating, today, Aaron?'

27

'All of it. All prime, of course. When did I ever sell fish that you wouldn't take?' Walter smiled. Aaron had his raw spots, too. During the last heatwave, he had forgotten to put fish in the cool cellar where the walls were thick and the cold river water lapped the floor at high tide. He had gone for another catch and the whole town stank of rotting fish which had had to be dumped in the Medina. Aaron still had boys shouting after him when he walked through Sea Street.

'Any oysters?' said Walter.

'Oysters?' said Aaron with great politeness. 'What do you need oysters for? A fine set-up man like you don't need oysters.'

Walter gritted his teeth. 'I need a barrel for the Mess and I want some special for Jane. She likes a fat oyster.' Aaron flicked open a shell with a thin blade and handed the opened fish to Walter, who sucked it down and nodded. 'Very good,' he conceded. 'Jane'll like them.'

'Are you so tired of England that you want to go off and fight a lot of foreigners? It's a long way, South Africa. Should have thought you had better things to do,' said Aaron. 'I lay it made Jane mad when she knew. She's a sensible woman with no time for the Boers or any other trouble-makers. Leave others to get on with their own business and minds her own.'

'She was at first, but we've talked and she's with me,' said Walter. 'You know how she hates people being put-on. I told her what the Reverend Moffat said about the way the Boers treated the blacks and she was very angry. Did you know, Aaron, that although they are free, they're still treated as slaves? They have to step off the pavement if white people pass and they have to carry a bit of paper saying where they live so that police can check that they stay in their own districts. The Outlanders who are as white as you and me are treated the same, or nearly as badly.'

'Carrying a bit of paper is nothing to go to war over.'

'It's not just that, it's Kruger's whole attitude. He's gathering arms and the Boer farmers are prepared for trouble. If we don't get fair deals for all parties under the law there, we'll lose the Cape. Kruger tried to convince people that we want the land and mines but he only says it to make the Boers rise against us.'

'The Cape? We can't lose the Cape. That's part of our Empire! Under the crown. It's as British as Portsmouth Harbour. It's ours, solid as a rock. He's got a nerve to try and take it away. He'd better watch out!'

28

'You see!' Walter laughed at the other man's anger and his red face. 'Even you get hot under the collar when you hear a bit of the truth. More people should read the papers and learn what's happening overseas. If we stay here, on our Island, and look no further than Southampton, we're blinkered and we could lose the lot.'

Aaron spread his sacking apron to dry on the wall. 'Is all that true or was it the ale talking in the snug? They talk a lot of rubbish up there.'

'It's true. I believe in the Empire, Aaron, and I'm a loyal subject.' He shrugged. 'Whatever my beliefs, I have to report to the Barracks this afternoon.'

Aaron covered the fish baskets with clean cheesecloth and filled a skip with freshly-boiled shrimps. He added a cage of crabs and one of lobsters and handed them up to Walter on the cart. He slapped Bess on the flank and called, 'Good luck,' and watched the cart until it reached the front door of the shop.

Jane was waiting with blocks of ice from the ice factory over the bridge and she took the baskets, arranging the fish on the scrubbed marble slab in the window. The basket of shrimps was set on the counter with a pint mug ready for scooping them out and Walter took the two ducks to the outhouse and plucked and drew them, scalding the insides and stuffing them with sage and onion and fresh breadcrumbs. It was nearly dinner-time and he knew that Jane usually ate bread and cheese with a cup of tea while she worked, after the children had gone back to school, but he called her and made her sit at the table with a dozen oysters open and ready for eating, and a crust of fresh bread. He poured a glass of stout to go with them and went to serve in the shop while she sat in peace, eating her favourite food and wondering if it would choke her.

Walter served fish and vegetables and tried to remain good-humoured even when every customer asked about his enlisting. It was difficult to parry the pointed questions and he knew that half of the people in the shop were there to find out what they could.

'Good morning, Pete,' he said, as Peter Fry came in for a piece of skate and some catfish. Two women standing by the door as if uncertain whether to enter and buy something, nudged each other and came closer.

'How is it, then?' asked Peter. 'You really did it, then?'

At any other time, Walter would have taken Peter into the

29

living room and given him cider while they talked, but today, in spite of the prying eyes, he was determined that Jane should enjoy her dinner quietly.

'I volunteered,' said Walter, 'as most men will have to do before long – whether they like it or not.' He saw Mrs Pointer stop laughing and knew that she had nagged her husband out of the idea of joining up. It wouldn't hurt her to be warned, he thought. 'If I go now, I have my old pay and conditions in my old regiment.'

'You'll have your old rank?' Mrs Pointer couldn't keep quiet. Pete winked. They all knew that Jeff Pointer had been a sergeant.

'Yes, Ma'am. Nothing lost, but if I'd waited, I would have lost my stripes most likely, and had to walk.'

Walter smiled, and looked at her with raised eyebrows, as if wanting her to order. She looked confused but couldn't very well leave the shop with nothing, so she asked for half a pint of shrimps.

'Good for trade,' said Peter when they were alone.

'Nine days' wonder but I feel like a freak at a fair. They all know me. They've seen me a million times but now they think I must have grown two heads. It's impossible to sneeze in this town without them all knowing that I used my sleeve.' For that reason, it would be good to get away, Walter decided. Maybe even if the war hadn't come, there would have had to be changes.

'I nearly went up there,' said Peter, 'but my mother is getting on and Mary would have her in the workhouse as soon as look at her if she was helpless.' He looked unhappy.

'You've had a weak chest all your life, Peter. No call for you to kill yourself or to get killed,' said Walter, mildly. 'You can't ride and you couldn't stand the strain of the life. They'll need some honest men left in the town after we go.'

'Anything I can do while you've gone, Walt? You know that. Anything at all.'

'I'll tell Jane,' said Walter, but he knew that Mary, Peter's wife, wouldn't let him come within ten yards of a pretty woman.

Peter took the thick pieces of skate and the coley for the cat and the shop was empty. Walter put the bell on the edge of the counter and went back to Jane. He waved aside the oysters she had kept for him, preferring his bread and cheese, so Jane took another oyster.

'You be sure to have some when I'm away,' Walter said. 'You've only to mention them to Aaron and he'll see you get some. They're very strengthening.'

'I'm strong enough, now,' she said.

Walter fumbled for words. 'You will take care? Look after yourself? You must let the others do more and not get too tired.' He took her hand and there was agony in his eyes. 'What would we do without you? What would any of us do?' He drew her towards him, about to take her in his arms.

'Walter,' she said, softly. There were tears in her eyes. The shop-bell jangled and the moment was gone. 'I'll go,' she said. She went into the shop with downcast eyes. – He does care, she thought. Poor Walter.

'Oh, it's you, Maudie. I was coming to see you later when I'm not so busy. What can I get you?' Jane forced a smile.

'Oh, Mrs Darwen, I'm frightened out of my wits.'

'I know, Maudie. My husband told me. I'm sorry that Ben is going away, but so are plenty more.'

'It isn't that, Mrs Darwen. It's the child. I don't know what to make of her. I left her in bed and came down. Could you look at her for me?'

'What about Dr Barnes? He must be back from his visits now. It's him you should be calling, not me.'

'I didn't want to bother him. If it's nothing, he'd only be cross with me, and besides, I can't – I haven't anything to pay him with.'

'Why is that?'

'The Army allowance hasn't come. I had to pay my rent or she said we'd have to leave, and there wasn't any money over.'

Jane looked at her, steadily. 'When did you last have something to eat, Maudie?' Maudie looked uncertain. 'Come into the back room,' said Jane. 'You'll be ill yourself if you go on like this. You have to eat to look after the child and your home.'

Walter took one look at the girl's heaving shoulders and runny nose and disappeared into the outhouse, muttering that he would boil the crabs. Jane stood over the girl while she ate oysters and drank strong tea. Her colour began to come back and Maudie sighed.

'Now, I'll tell my husband where I've gone and I'll catch you up. You've left her long enough as it is,' said Jane. She went into the yard but the door to the outhouse was shut. Jane hesitated, knowing that Walter would be lighting the kindling and the draught from the open door might not be just what he wanted now, so she scribbled a note and put it in the jar on the table where he would see it, locked the shop door after her and put up the Closed sign. She clutched her shawl about her and hurried round the corner to Sea Street.

It took at least an hour to heat the boiler and get the crabs done and she'd be back before he knew she had gone. There was plenty of time to say goodbye before he left for the Barracks, and Maudie really did need help.

Chapter 4

Jane hurried through Sea Street to the tall narrow house where Maudie had two rooms. The wailing of the child became louder as she went up the stairs, and gasping breaths between frightened cries made Jane run up the last few steps. She pushed open the door and peered into the dark little room. The curtains were drawn tightly across the window and there was no air.

Even Jane felt like gasping in the foetid atmosphere and she went to the window to open it. 'You'll stifle her,' she said. 'There's no air in here. No wonder she can't breathe.'

'The window doesn't open,' said Maudie.

'Then you must prop the door open on to the landing.'

'I can't do that. If I leave the door open, the landlady complains that the child makes too much noise.'

Jane set her lips and propped the door open wide. She pulled back the curtains so that she could see what was wrong and saw a small child picking fretfully at the sheet. Her eyes were dilated with fear and the effort of breathing. Each breath came in harsh labouring spasms and her chest heaved desperately in an attempt to drag more air into her lungs. Jane and Maudie stood over the bed and the child held out her arms, but didn't seem to know which of the women was her mother.

Jane listened carefully and said, 'Leave the door as it is. She must have more air. I think it's serious enough to fetch Dr Barnes. I'll go.'

She held up a restraining hand as Maudie tried to stop her. 'Maudie, now listen to me. She must have the doctor to see her. Don't worry. He'll get his money. Keep her face cool with a damp rag but don't give her anything to drink. She can't breathe properly or swallow, so you'd only make her choke if you gave her anything.'

She hurried downstairs and noticed a door on the floor below close softly as she went by. – Too busy spying to do a good turn for anyone, she thought. The air outside was clear and good after the room she had left and the doctor's house looked shining and well-cared for behind a trim laurel hedge. Jane waited impatiently while the maidservant took her message, but the doctor didn't keep her waiting. He came from his dining room, pulling on his coat.

'You look worried, Mrs Darwen. Sit down and tell me about it.' He motioned her to a chair but Jane stood and shook her head.

'There isn't time, Doctor Barnes. It's Maudie Dove's child. She's very ill and I think she has diphtheria.'

He glanced at her sharply. 'You've seen it in other families?' Jane nodded and he seemed satisfied to trust her judgment. 'Run back and get these boiled up,' he said, giving her a packet. 'Take these, too, they never have enough light,' he said, and Jane tucked three candles into her bag. 'I'll bring the rest.'

She ran back to the sickroom and Maudie was in tears. The child was a very bad colour and her breathing was painful to hear, but Jane cleared the only table and pushed clothes into the other room, and a chair out on to the landing to make more space, ignoring Maudie's pleas that the landlady would turn her out.

'Put the candles on saucers if you've no more candlesticks,' Jane told her, 'and fill that saucepan with more water. We shall need as much hot water as you can boil.'

A face appeared in the doorway and a whining voice asked what the noise was about. 'You can either come and help or get out,' said Jane, crisply. 'If you're the landlady, I'll have a few words to say to you later about this room. It isn't fit for a dog.' The face vanished and a door slammed below them, as the woman just avoided meeting the doctor on the stairs.

Dr Barnes opened his bag and put a clean towel on the bare table. Jane picked up the bowl of boiling water into which she had put the scalpel, some forceps and a tracheotomy set of silver. She poured the water into a bucket and tipped the instruments on the towel to cool. The doctor opened the child's mouth gently and placed a metal spatula on her tongue. He could see the grey membrane that had nearly closed over the pulsating throat, and the child's breath came in ugly, shuddering sighs as she struggled for air. Her terror mounted and her face was livid as she gagged on the spatula.

34

Jane tore up some old linen into strips, then stood back as the doctor arranged his tools and saw that everything was ready. She was torn between her desire to stay and help and the dread that Walter would have left for the Barracks before she could say goodbye.

'I shall need some cotton tape tied to the outer tube of the set,' said the doctor. Maudie stood looking helplessly at the child, oblivious to all else. 'Maudie? Do you hear me? Come on, girl, tape.'

'Don't,' said Jane, gently. 'I'll stay. She's too young, to frightened to manage this.' She opened a sewing box and stirred a mass of tangled cottons and tape until she found a fresh hank of white tape half an inch wide. 'How much do you want, Doctor?'

'Enough to put in the holes at the side and tie at the back of the neck, or better still make them long so that we can tie them at one side or the other, and not have a knot at the back.' He looked at the tape and saw that it was strong. 'Good. Now if the mother can't help, you will have to help, Mrs Darwen. I must have someone to hold the child quite still.'

Jane blenched. 'She will see you. She'll see the knife in your hand and she's old enough to know what you are going to do. Oh, Mother Mary, she'll know it's going to hurt!'

Dr Barnes turned away and took off his jacket with slow deliberation. He folded it with fastidious care and hung it on the brass bed rail where it couldn't touch the grubby bedclothes. 'I can do this, but not unless I have your help. If we do not insert this tube in her throat now, she will die.' His eyes were hard. 'She *will* be frightened, she *will* be hurt but I have no way of deadening the pain. She is unable to swallow, so laudanum is out of the question. I have nothing more that could help, and we have very little time left.'

He smiled and Jane sensed his anxiety under the stern manner. She rolled up her sleeves and nodded. She found that she was no longer trembling although her face was tense with fear.

'Put a pillow under her neck and a towel across her chest,' he ordered. 'Now, take her hands in one of yours and use the other hand to keep her head still. If she struggles, keep her hands down at all costs and leave the head to me.' He looked at her sternly and seemed satisfied. Jane was unable to speak as she fought for self-control. He turned to the table and picked up the bright blade, keeping it from the child's vision. Jane was surprised and

35

somehow comforted to see beads of sweat appearing on the doctor's brow.

The small body went rigid under her hands and it seemed suspended without breath or life. A rushing intake of breath, and another, then a convulsive sigh and the child struggled to free her hands. A strangled scream died and gave way to a hissing, bubbling sound as if air was being released from a balloon. Jane's fingernails dug into the soft flesh of the tiny wrists but she dared not let go. She turned her head and saw the bleeding gash in the tiny throat and the shining silver tube sliding in through the gap. She raised the now relaxed head while the doctor tied the tapes and made sure that the tube was held firmly in place, then watched as he inserted strips of clean linen under the silver plate to cover the skin edges.

Only then did the doctor allow himself a moment of relief when his eyes closed and his hands quivered. Maudie came to life. 'She's dead, Doctor! She's too quiet. You've killed her!'

'Silence, woman! Killed her? If it hadn't been for me and your good neighbour, she would certainly have been dead within the hour. The child is breathing through this tube and she must go up the hill to the Isolation Hospital as soon as it can be arranged.'

'Oh, no, you can't take her away from me!'

'We must. It's diphtheria and very infectious.' He touched Maudie on the arm. 'You must do as I say, but try not to worry. I think she may do now.' He peered into the dingy corners of the room, the dirt showing in the improved candlelight. 'Even if we didn't take her to hospital, you couldn't nurse her here. This room is dirty and damp. It needs a good scrub. Do you hear me? As soon as the child has been taken away, you must get that window open and put the mattress over the sill. Scrub the floor and wash all the bedding and clothes. Anything that can't be washed must be burned. I shall come back tomorrow to see that you have done this and I shall bring a sulphur candle to burn here. You will not see your child in this room until she is well and the room is wholesome.'

He washed his instruments in the bucket of hot water and dried them carefully, before packing each item separately in the leather case, and then he added the green baize roll of spare tracheotomy tubes. He closed the bag with a snap. Maudie tried to speak, the tears of utter thankfulness rolling down her cheeks. 'Try to keep it clean,' he said, more gently.

'Doctor. Oh, Doctor, I can't pay you.'

The elderly man looked at the distraught face. He turned to the now peacefully sleeping two-year-old child and he coughed. 'I don't want money for this,' he said, brusquely. 'If you make a proper home for this little one, if God spares her, you will have paid any debt there might be.' He put up a hand as if to convince her that he was not being kind. 'But if you carry on as you have been doing, taking no pride in yourself or the child and living in a pigsty, then I'll see you end up in the workhouse.'

'I'll try, Doctor.'

'I think you will, but that isn't enough. You have to make a home for your man when he comes out of the army. He'll want to see a bonny child and you healthy and smiling.' He took Jane's hand. 'Thank you, my dear. I could use you as my permanent assistant.'

Jane smiled and waited until he had clattered down the wooden stairs then turned back to the room and forced the window open. The cool air flowed in, freshening everything and Maudie brought more water from the tap downstairs. Jane put it on the stove and noticed that the metal was grey and mottled with rust, offending her ideas of what was neat and good.

'Maudie,' she said, 'I'm going home now. As soon as they've taken the baby to the hospital and you've hung out the clothes, come to the shop and I'll give you a bar of carbolic soap and some blacklead for the grate. Bring a basket and I'll find a cabbage and some fish for you.' Maudie looked at the sleeping child as if frightened to be left alone with her.

'Will she be all right, Mrs Darwen? What can I do if you go and she stops breathing?'

'She's not going to do any such thing,' said Jane, firmly. 'The hospital cart will be here soon, but you mustn't leave here until it does. If the tube becomes blocked, you are to clean it out with one of the duck feathers that the doctor left. Now do you understand?'

Jane patiently showed the girl again how to insert the feather, enough to twist inside the silver tube, but not far enough in to stop the air flow. She brought it out, covered with mucus and tossed it into the fire. 'Do this if she sounds bubbly and make sure you burn the feather.'

'I don't know how you know all these things, Mrs Darwen.'

'By using my eyes and helping people,' said Jane briskly. 'As you will have to do if you want to be happy, Maudie.' She looked

37

round the room and at the peaceful infant. 'Can you manage?'

'I think so, Mrs Darwen. I don't know how I can ever thank you. I thought I was going to lose everything. First Ben going away and then the child.' She brushed her untidy hair away from her eyes. 'And this place is so drab, but I will try to make it better, really I will. They wouldn't keep her for long or take her away from me, would they?'

'The Good Lord knows, Maudie. Pray she'll be well soon.' Jane paused. 'I've never heard you call her by name.'

'She hasn't a name. She's never been christened, so she hasn't a name.' The tears fell again. 'I wanted to call her Lucy but Ben doesn't hold with church and somehow I never managed to take her.'

'When the cart comes, tell them that she hasn't been baptised. The hospital chaplain will want to know and he can christen her, just in case... I mean to be safe and to give her a place in the Church,' added Jane, hastily. 'You will have to walk up and see the chaplain later, but there is no reason why you can't call your little girl by name now.' Jane smiled. 'I had names for all of mine even before they were born,' she said. She tried not to think of the day when the vicar had come to her bedside to baptise Caroline, the day before she died.

'You are so good, Mrs Darwen. I get so mixed-up with things. I know I'm not a good mother but I've learned a lesson today. I'll stay with... Lucy until the cart comes.'

Jane hurried home, feeling as if she carried the plague with her. It was good to see the gleaming stove and the whitewashed surround to the hearth. The house was empty and she stripped off her clothes and washed at the bedroom washstand, and dressed in fresh garments. She hung her red stuff dress on the clothes line to air thoroughly and felt more normal. She looked out old clothes for Maudie and for the child and when she heard the hospital cart creaking past the house, she didn't look out as it went up the hill to Fairlee. It was too much like the time Emily had been taken away with scarlet fever.

Jane unbolted the shop door and two women were waiting outside, their eyes glinting with curiosity.

'I said to Mrs Ralph here, I said, I wonder what's wrong? Mrs Darwen always has the shop open at this time,' one of them said. Jane ignored the implied question and smiled pleasantly. It would be common knowledge soon enough that Maudie Dove's baby had diphtheria.

'My husband had to go to the Barracks,' she said, and was conscious of the empty back room as she had never been during all the years she had lived there.

All the time she served in the shop, she heard little of the chatter. Walter had gone without saying goodbye. He had gone for she knew not how long, perhaps forever. Her heart was heavy with dread and misery, but what could she have done? She couldn't leave a child to die, with its incompetent mother. If only Maudie had come ten minutes later, it wouldn't have mattered. They could have said goodbye and Walter would have kissed her in the way he did when they were free to love. Would he go away immediately? Was she to let him go without touching him again?

She wished now that she had given him all the tiny gifts that the family had prepared to slip into his kit as surprises on the voyage. He might never unwrap the grubby, handmade penwiper from Janey nor the carved wooden spoon that Sidney insisted he would need in South Africa. The shop cleared and Jane went to the outhouse. The crabs had been boiled and the boiler was still hot. The cage of lobsters had gone, as were the baskets of fish and oysters for the officers' mess.

Jane sighed with relief. He'd taken the cart and they'd have to let him bring it back again, after he made his last delivery. That is, unless they commandeered the cart, and poor old Bess with her ambling walk that would make any soldier unlucky enough to ride her want to join a foot regiment. Jane smiled in spite of her anxiety. She went to clear the fish slab and worked hard, and a few minutes later heard Walter's familiar whistle.

She rushed out, her face glowing. Walter gave her a quick hug. 'I thought you'd gone for good,' she said.

'Not for a few days yet. I took in the fish and they told me to report in uniform in three days' time. They've had trouble with the victualling, and they need more horses.' He laughed. 'I told them they could have Bess to serve her country, but they jibbed at that. They took it for granted that she was all I had and didn't ask any awkward questions, but I met Bert and he's sweating in case they take his stallion.'

'Serve him right if they did. And that black beast is wicked. Best place for him, the army,' said Jane.

'I wouldn't mind him under me,' said Walter, 'but I need Bert's goodwill just now. I advised him to keep the beast in the stable until the barges leave and I'll do the same with Blackie. They're offering next to nothing for mounts and I want to keep him. If they come sniffing round here, tell them the army has already said you can keep the horse that drags the cart. That should settle them.'

Jane poured more tea and added water to the thick brew that had been stewing on the hob for hours. She stirred in sugar and Walter gulped noisily. She hoped they'd give him good strong tea where he was going. A man got used to creature comforts, she thought, and sat watching him although there was work to be done.

Janey and Clare pushed back the bead curtain that separated the shop from the passage to the living room when the wooden door wasn't closed. Janey put a basket on the table and the smell of freshly-baked bread came through the white cloth. Jane took the three large loaves and put them in the bread crock where there was a piece left from yesterday that ought to be used first, but she took one of the fresh loaves that were still warm and tempting and sliced it on to a dish. Clare fetched butter from the larder and Walter scooped up a quart of shrimps into a wide blue Delft dish and put them before the children who reached for handfuls of the glistening fish, but Jane stopped them.

'Wash first,' she said, slapping Sidney on the wrist. 'And you can all stop chattering and giggling and tell your father what you did this morning.'

Sidney came back first and sat looking too good to be true. Jane poured tea and looked at the girls who were prim and trying to be very ladylike. 'All right, now what did he do this time?' said Walter, knowing the signs.

'Nothing, Father.' Sidney stuffed his mouth with shrimps and bread, making any attempt at speech impossible.

'He poked his tongue out at Miss Martin,' said Lizzie, with an air of self-importance. The children sniggered and Edward tried to kick Lizzie under the table.

'Tell-tale!' he hissed.

'That's enough,' said Jane, sternly. 'Your father doesn't like rude little boys.' Walter grinned, and Lizzie smirked, sensing his approval. 'And I don't like girls who tell tales,' said Jane. Lizzie pursed her lips and pretended she wasn't listening. She took a small shrimp and peeled it with care, looking down at her plate.

'Why were you rude?' asked Walter. Sidney swallowed violently and coughed. 'SIDNEY! If you bolt your food like that, you'll have your mother up all night giving you medicine for stomach-ache.'

40

'Miss Martin said I smelled of horse manure. I didn't smell so I put my tongue out at her and she saw,' he said, defiantly. Walter got out of his chair and came round the table and sniffed. Sidney tried to sidle away.

'You've been down to Bert Cooper's stable again. Did you ride his new one?' Walter looked very serious.

'No, I only went to look at him. I talked to him over the door and he licked me but I didn't get on his back.'

'You know what I think about that horse, Sidney. I forbid you to get on his back, even in the stableyard. He's a brute and it will take a man to handle him. Whoever broke him ruined his mouth and his temper which is why Bert bought him cheap. He's got a hard mouth and if he bolted with anyone less than twelve stone on his back, he'd kill him. He's as much as I can handle when he's fresh and I can't see Dan or a boy riding him. Bert's half-scared of him. Can't think why he bought him. He ought to sell him to the army and cut his losses.'

'You heard your father,' said Jane, giving Walter a grateful glance.

'You just give me your word that when I go away, you will never try to ride him,' said Walter. 'I want your solemn word and no fancy tricks either with any other horses.'

Sidney nodded. 'I promise. I really didn't ride him, but he's different. Bess is so slow and you don't let me ride Blackie very often. I think he likes me,' said Sidney.

'You must understand,' said Walter. 'It wouldn't be fair to your mother if I go away.'

Emily began to cry. She opened her mouth and shut her eyes, treating the family to the sight of a wide open mouth full of half-chewed shrimps. She looked as if she was about to choke.

'Emily!'

'You *are* going away and it's further than Portsmouth. You'll go away and be killed and we'll never see you again. Miss Martin says that soldiers get killed.'

She choked and Jane slapped her on the back until her colour changed back from puce to her normal pallor. Walter sat by the fire and took her on his knee. Emily clung round his neck but her sobs grew less.

'Listen,' Walter said. 'I have to go across the quay and up to the Barracks and then away for a while. They say the war will be over before I reach South Africa, but we can't know for certain. While I'm away, you must all look after your mother. Help her with the work and the boys must do the deliveries.'

'Up at the Barracks?' said Edward.

'Yes, you'll have to do a man's work, Edward. I think you're able. You must make sure the beasts lack for nothing. Ask Bert Cooper or Mr Walmsley if you need advice and Dan will help out if you ask him.' He put Emily on her feet and eyed the girls with speculation. 'You girls will have to do your share, too.'

'We help,' said Clare, tossing her head.

'Sometimes,' said Walter. 'I know just how much you help. In future, you must serve in the shop when you are not at school. I know you don't care for it, but that is your own personal sacrifice now. It will do you no harm to take some of the burden and you'll spend less time with Ethel Sheath down the river fields.' He took out his big handkerchief and wiped Emily's nose. 'And Lizzie must learn to mind house and cook and give your mother a rest. I want no sulks and tantrums when you are asked to do things.'

Jane cut wedges of bread pudding that had been cooking slowly in the side oven. The crusted sides were glossy and raisins clustered rich and dark inside. Walter took his to the desk at the side of the room and opened his account books. The girls took it in turns to serve the last of the customers while Jane washed up and returned the few uneaten shrimps to the shop.

There was an atmosphere of unrest. Everyone glanced at Walter anxiously, as if he would disappear in a puff of smoke, and Jane dreaded being left with the children for the evening. She was sure that he would go to the Wheatsheaf as soon as the books were finished. Lizzie and Emily still seemed on the edge of tears and Sidney was being difficult.

It was as if they all waited for an inevitable calamity, the realisation of which might be a relief. When Walter had gone, it would be easier to adjust, to plan and to have matters settled. It was wicked, Jane knew, but she wanted everything to be settled and wondered if she could bear the next day or so, or if she had the courage to act normally while he was still there. She recalled how Walter laughed at her whenever she said. 'It's always better when you know the worst has happened.' She smiled and Walter saw the smile and was glad. The books were balancing nicely and he had more money than he supposed.

Jack was teasing the cats and getting restless, whistling between his teeth in a way that irritated Walter.

'Go up to the *County Press* and see what the latest news is,

Jack,' said his father. Jane looked up sharply. 'I thought I'd stay in, tonight,' continued Walter, casually. 'Send Edward round to the Jug and Bottle and we'll have a drink here and a bit of music.'

Jane cleared the top of the harmonium of an accumulation of books and oddments and the tapestry runner. The lid was stiff as it hadn't been lifted for nearly a year. She lit two lamps and placed one so that a circle of warm light fell over the sheet-music stand.

Walter leafed through the pile of music kept in the seat of the music stool and selected a few music hall songs, a hymn with a rousing tune, one or two romantic works and lastly, 'The Lost Chord'. He loosened his tie and tried a few notes, avoiding the one that stuck.

Jane put some coal on the fire so that it burned clean and bright, instead of giving off the dull redness that everyday coke produced. As soon as the room absorbed the heat, each member of the family settled down. Janey spread newspaper over the chenille cloth before giving Sidney a pile of cards and a bottle of ink. He sharpened a wooden meat skewer into a wedge shape at the thick end and sat back.

'What prices shall I do, Mother?'

'Just two for one penny and one tuppenny. Perhaps we could do with another for dates. The last one fell in the box and is too sticky to use.' She smiled. 'Nice big thick letters that everyone can see.'

Sidney bent over the cards. He dipped the wedge end into the ink and carefully wrote in very thick lettering, ONE PENNY. He examined the result and underlined the words. He drew another line over the letters and finally enclosed the lot in a box of dark ink, like a mourning card, Janey thought. There was nothing more he could add, so he propped it up on the sugar bowl to dry. The other cards were quickly done and he had left the big one till last. This might give him more artistic scope.

'Is that for dates?' said Janey. 'Do you know how to spell dates?'

'Of course I do,' Sidney said. 'And I've seen a picture of a date tree.'

'They don't grow on trees, they grow on palms,' said Clare.

'They do. They grow on palm trees. I know. I saw a picture,' said Sidney.

'Take no notice of Clare,' said Janey. 'Draw me a palm tree.'

Sidney frowned. He thought he knew. He'd read that dates come from Africa, so he wrote 'Dates' in the middle of the card

43

and absentmindedly licked the inky end of the skewer. Palm trees? It was funny that he thought he knew but Clare would laugh at him if he was wrong. He tried to recall the picture he'd seen. The edges of palm fronds were feathery. Perhaps if he turned the skewer round and used the pointed end, he could do it. He stuck out his tongue and concentrated. The ink ran down and settled in a dark stain at the base of his thumb. He drew the first leaf and found it easy, so he finished the tree and added squiggles underneath to represent sand, then placed the card away from him to dry.

'You've got ink all over your face,' said Janey. She smiled and looked like Jane must have done as a young girl. 'Come outside to the scullery before Father sees you. I'll wash your face and hands.'

'Why do I get dirty when I'm enjoying myself?' Sidney asked.

The girl dried his hands on an old towel. 'It's not on your shirt like last time,' she said. 'You can hide the mark on your thumb. I can't scrub that or you'll be sore.' She hugged him. 'I think you do lovely pictures.'

'One day, I'll paint real pictures,' he said.

'One day,' she said, soothingly. 'But you'll have to work hard and earn the money to buy paints before you start. You know that Father doesn't think artists are worth anything, but I like pictures.'

'I don't want to wait for years and years,' said Sidney. 'I'm almost grown-up now.'

'Almost,' said Janey and took him back into the warm.

Jane turned the pages while Walter played. She let the music flow over her and the girls knitted and Edward and Sidney played Halma. Jane was happy. It was strange that a man like Walter could love music so much. As soon as he sat down to play, and his hands tried the old tunes, he became softer, gentler. She looked at his relaxed mouth. – Perhaps that's the reason he hasn't played for so long, she thought. He's had to harden his heart and do without sentiment and love and to concentrate on the company of men, playing the harmonium only at Christmas and when visitors come.

This evening was like the old days when they were free to go to bed after the singing, to love and be loved and to be perfectly natural with each other. Jane leaned against him as she turned the page and his shoulder was firm against her breast.

Emily lay on the rug, her knitting forgotten. She saw caves and dragons, men with flaming swords and beautiful ladies in red robes that shimmered and undulated against the black rocks in the fire. The warmth comforted her and she forgot that her father was going away. This was home, with Father and Mother, warmth and good food and kindness. This was complete security that could never change and which she would never, never leave.

A wreath of dark smoke came from the lamp and Jane trimmed the wick. She poured ale and brought out a seedy cake from the larder. The wooden clock in the corner came up to the hour and struck nine times. Clare mixed a jug of cocoa and added hot milk and water.

'I don't want to go to bed,' said Emily.

'It's time you all went,' said Walter firmly. 'Drink up your cocoa.'

'We can't all go,' said Clare. 'Jack's still out.' She smiled. 'I want to stay until he comes in and hear the news.'

'No, you don't, young lady. You go up with the rest.' Jane looked annoyed. 'I'd forgotten Jack. Where do you suppose he's been all this time?'

Walter took a large slice of cake. 'You worry too much, Jane. He's a bit restless but so was I at his age.'

'The others aren't, and Edward's older than Jack.'

'They'll be waiting for a bulletin.'

'Or up to no good under the Town Hall arches with all the Sea Street riff-raff.'

'He'll come to no harm. The town is full of people and he wouldn't go far away.' Walter drank his ale and turned back to the harmonium, improvising and humming to himself. Nothing was going to upset him tonight. He wanted to store this away to fill his mind in Africa.

'Off to bed,' said Jane and Emily dragged herself away from her fantasies. She picked up Sidney's work of art and showed it to her mother. The palm tree had dried out nicely with no blots. 'I don't know where you get the talent from,' said Jane. 'Put it in the shop on your way to bed.'

The girls stayed long enough to brush their hair in the warm room, and to squabble over the ownership of a hair ribbon, until a sharp glance from their mother sent them meekly up the stairs. Walter checked the shutters and made up the fire, and suddenly they were alone.

Jane sat on the stool by the fire and Walter tried a few chords.

He looked quizzical and played the first notes of one of her favourite pieces. Jane stared into the fire as Emily had done, but saw no princesses. She crooned softly, then as her confidence grew, she sang, her sweet contralto lending depth to the old Irish love song. Firelight played in her hair, bringing out the blue-black lights. - Like the wing of a raven, thought Walter. She removed a hairpin that dug into her scalp and shook one side of her hair free. Absentmindedly, she took out the other pins until her hair was a loose silk veil, below the shoulders of her dress.

They went from song to song, with Jane singing alone or with Walter joining in with a low baritone. There were half-recalled Gaelic songs and snatches of popular ones and they were content.

If only it could go on for ever. If only the war was nothing but a bad dream and if only she could go to Walter again as a true wife. Jane sipped her ale and Walter looked for more songsheets and the house was still. Walter folded the music and put it back in the seat. He stirred the fire and sat on the hearth rug at Jane's feet. The firelight was less bright now as he looked up into her face and he couldn't see the depths of her eyes. He took her chin in his hand and turned her face towards him.

'You're happy,' he said.

'And why would you be thinking that?' Her smile was tender.

'When you are truly happy your eyes have a greeny tinge in the brown like green shamrocks trying to grow.' He was teasing her as he did long ago, knowing that her eyes were dark brown. She looked towards the shamrock growing in the bowl on the dresser. The plant had been there for years and flourished, although her family in Ireland had told her that neither the shamrock nor she could thrive in England.

Walter bent his head and kissed her mouth. She trembled with love and a desperate fear. Half of her mind wanted to scream, 'Get away! Leave me alone! Do you want to *kill* me?' and the rest of her her wanted to take him in her arms, to cradle his head on her breast and to murmur that it was all right, she would love him whatever happened to her.

He unpinned the cameo brooch from her neckband and opened the buttoned lace at her breast. He pushed all thoughts and conscience from his mind and allowed his desire to grow while Jane sat beside him, hypnotised. This had nothing to do with her. This was another Jane Darwen who had no powers of resistance. Walter kissed her again with increasing passion and she knew

46

that the last vestiges of her will were dissolving.

'No!' she said, but his arms tightened, his hands fumbling with her skirt. Jane gave a sob and sank back with him on the rug just as the shop door banged.

Walter sat up as if recovering from a dream. He shook his head violently and then buried his face in his hands. Jane buttoned up her bodice and stuck pins in her hair at random, regaining some of her poise. 'Who is it?' she called and was answered by a sob from the dark shop. She took a candle and lit it, holding it high above her. In the shop, she saw a figure bent double by the counter.

'Dear Mary, what now? Come into the light and let me see what's wrong.' Jack limped into the living room, holding a handkerchief to his face. His shirt was torn and there was road filth on his trousers.

Walter regarded him with curiosity mixed with amusement. 'So, you took on someone bigger than yourself?'

Jane filled a bowl with warm water and found an old, soft rag. She bathed the blood from his face while he groaned, hoping for sympathy. 'Praise be,' said Jane briskly. 'There's more mess than damage. You'll have a black eye tomorrow and a few bruises but no worse than the last time.'

'Was it Percy Cantor again?' said Walter. Jack nodded. 'And now you can't remember what it was that was important enough to fight over.'

Jack grinned through swollen lips. 'I think it was about the war, but it's never one thing with Percy. He riles me and we say things and it starts. We just go for each other, hammer and tongs, until one of us gives up.' He wiped his nose on his sleeves. 'He had to give up tonight.'

Walter went out to bring in the coke for banking up the fire. 'Why don't you keep away from Percy?' said Jane. 'Your brothers never fight, and I'm sure your father never did when he was a boy.'

Jack shrugged her hand away from his arm. 'He's going away to fight now, and it isn't just fists he'll use on the Boers,' he said, defiantly.

Jane shook him. 'That will be quite enough from you, young man. Don't you ever say such a thing to your father or he'd...'

'Strike me?'

Jane took a deep breath. 'Slip out of those trousers and I'll

47

sponge them,' she said. 'And take your cocoa up with you. Better be out of here before your father decides that it's not all that amusing, after all!'

Jack opened the door to the stairs, and took the candle she handed to him. He kissed his mother's cheek and whispered, 'It's all your fault. I get my Irish temper from you.'

'Get along with you,' she said, giving him a playful push. 'You wouldn't find me fighting Percy Cantor.'

'But you can fight when you have to,' he said, and closed the door behind him.

Walter made up the fire and took the cold crabs into the shop and closed the door. 'I don't want the cats getting at them,' he said. 'Micky and Ike won't leave the outhouse alone while there's fish about and the window catch has gone. I'll mend it tomorrow.'

Jane went upstairs and Walter busied himself with putting away the harmonium, the books and the runner and the vase of leaves that Jane had arranged. He stayed down until Jane was in bed and when he came upstairs he undressed in silence. In bed, he made no attempt to touch her and Jane was torn between frustration and relief. Once more, it was as if she was in bed with a stranger.

The hour struck and she knew that Walter was awake, too. She turned away from his side of the bed and stuffed her hand in her mouth under the bedclothes. – I dare not cry . . . I mustn't sob yet until he is asleep.

Another hour passed and at last he was asleep and the hot bitter tears ran down and soaked the pillow and when she woke, her cheeks were stiff with salt tears.

Chapter 5

Jane Darwen caught up her basket and hurried out, locking the door behind her. The card saying 'Back in Five Minutes' was hanging straight and she hurried to the grocery store a few houses away. Most women were still at home, straightening up after the children left for school and Jane hoped that she was early enough to be served first.

'Good morning, Mrs Darwen,' said Mr Foster, wiping his hands on the coarse apron covering his dark trousers. He swept aside spilled sugar from the counter. 'And what can I do for you?' Jane handed him the list and put the basket on the small cane chair. The shop was empty as she had hoped and Jane went from one open sack to another, enjoying the different smells. This shop never failed to delight her.

'I wish that our shop smelled as sweet as this one, Mr Foster,' she said. She could detect the scent of cloves and coffee and she admired the gleaming black and gold tea chests on the shelves. A handful of lentils running through her fingers reminded her of sand on the sea-shore at Cowes and the crushed oats made her think of feed for the horses. She cut a sliver from a cream cheese on the tasting board.

'I knew you'd go for that one,' said George Foster.

'Folley Glebe Farm?'

'That's right, me dear, Folley Farm. I could sell twice as many again that Mrs Attril can make. Makes them nice and close and with a good flavour. That batch is perfect. Can't think why she don't go in for the Agricultural, but I suppose there'd be even more after her cheese and she can't supply me with all I want now.' He gave Jane a dry biscuit and she took a slice from the next one.

She nodded. 'I'll make sure of that one for Walter.'

'Will he be here to eat it?' said George and could have kicked himself when he heard his own voice.

'Why? Has there been another bulletin?' Jane looked anxious. She knew that Mr Foster walked up to the *County Press* window early each day while his assistant cleaned the shop. He liked to be first with the news so that he could pass it on to customers who came from the other side of the bridge.

'They haven't wasted much time,' he said. 'They've already wrecked a train taking supplies to a place called Mafeking. Never reached the place! I wrote down all the names, like I do, you know. People come in who might know someone out there. You never know who might come in and ask.' He looked embarrassed. 'It might be you, my dear, wanting the latest news, but I don't think Mr Darwen will be sent away. He won't be sent overseas at any rate,' he added, as if he knew more than the bulletins reported. 'It's bound to be over soon, but this being a garrison town, folks like to know. A good number of women in Sea Street and Little London have men in the Regulars and half of them can't read newspapers. I've started a list of happenings, and names of my customers who have men in the service.'

He reached down under the counter and brought out a school exercise book. He ran his finger down one list. 'There's six families on Hunney Hill alone.' He turned a page. 'The place where they took the train was Kraaipan. What names, Mrs Darwen! They call them Outlanders, but I call them outlandish!' He laughed at what was fast becoming his standing joke, then became serious. 'They're an ugly crowd of ruffians in my opinion. Do you know, they fired on a Red Cross train which went to help the wrecked arms train! Fired on the Red Cross! Now if that isn't the work of *animals*, I'd like to know what is.'

Jane gasped in horror. 'But the Red Cross helps all sides. Their flag is sacred. Nobody fires on the Red Cross or the white flag of truce.'

The grocer smiled. It was going to be a good day. The shop would fill once they heard he had the early news, and as the day progressed, with fresh bulletins replacing the earlier ones, his would be the only firm record of all of them. Even the people from Hunney Hill who usually did their shopping at Parkhurst would have to patronise his shop. 'You'll take the cheese?' he said.

Jane hesitated, then nodded. Everything must carry on as though Walter was staying in Newport. She must continue as if nothing had changed. 'Yes, I'll take it and a piece from the block.'

George Foster made a stiff cone of blue paper and emptied the contents of the brass bowl from the scales into it. He tucked in the ends. 'One pound of Greek currants. I don't know when we'll have more if the war goes on. You'd better give me your order for Christmas soon if you want to be sure of it.' His fingers were busy, weighing up brown sugar, loaf sugar, tea and cocoa. 'I'll weigh up the flour later and send it down if you don't need it now,' he said. 'Tell me what you want to take with you now.'

'I'll take the saltpetre and salt as I have a pig's head ready for brawn,' she said. 'I'll take the brown sugar and tea and a bag of broken biscuits.'

She put a hand into the tin open on the counter and the piece of biscuit broke without a sound. – Baggy, she thought. George saw the look and reached under the counter. 'Not those for you,' he said. 'I give them to the children.' He ripped the paper sealing the edge of a fresh tin and the brass scales swung and tipped as he piled broken biscuits into the scoop. The shop-bell rang and Jane glanced up to see who was coming in.

Annie Cooper stood in the doorway as if she hoped to see something she shouldn't. She watched Jane take out her purse as if suddenly in a rush to be away, then came closer to see what Jane Darwen was buying.

'I'll pay for these and perhaps you'll put the bill for the rest with the other things,' said Jane. 'By the way, I'll be needing some more carbolic soap.'

'You must be washing your house away, Jane! I was in here last week and you bought three bars.' Annie Cooper stood by the counter, her beady eyes searching Jane's pile of groceries.

'I had to lend to a neighbour,' said Jane and stacked the items she wanted to take with her in the basket, very quickly.

'I suppose it was that Maudie Dove?' Annie sniffed. 'You'll be lucky to see that again. I think you're very foolish to dare to go into that house. It isn't respectable in the first place and think of all the diseases they have in Sea Street.' It suddenly occurred to Annie that Jane had been in contact with diphtheria and she drew back.

'If everyone felt as you do, there'd be little human charity left in the world,' said Jane, sharply.

Annie went red. She looked at the bundles in Jane's basket. 'It's disgusting,' she said. 'Giving things away and feeding your own children on broken biscuits!'

Jane felt her temper flaring. Annie always picked on the one thing that could rile her. A sharp retort came to her lips but she bit back the words and made for the door. 'Will you please put it all on the bill, Mr Foster? I haven't time to waste here.' The doorbell jangled with rage and Annie looked smug. George took her order and noted with satisfaction that Annie Cooper also wanted broken biscuits. He carefully weighted out exactly a pound from the soft stale ones on the counter and handed them to her.

Jane was still ruffled when she opened the shop. There was a lot to do and Annie had thrown her off balance. She took the big roasting tin from the pantry and in it laid the two ducks, potatoes, carrots and slices of swede and turnip. She grated rock salt and coarse pepper over it all and topped it with a lump of dripping. The bakery was two doors away and they agreed to have the ducks ready for dinner-time when Walter would be back from the country and the children home from school.

She was feeling better now as she thought of the pleasure the children would show when they saw what was to eat, and the morning was too busy for thoughts of Annie and her like. The shop filled with women out to hear the latest news and the rumours grew as the morning progressed. Jane heard snippets of truth and half-truth; that a gold mine had been taken and all the people were killed, that the Boers were showing the white flag already and yet another rumour that women would be called on to go out to nurse the wounded.

'Mr Foster came back with more news but he hasn't put it all down in his book yet,' said Mrs Fry. Jane smiled. George Foster liked his moment of power. 'Asked him if it was true that the Queen herself is coming to talk to the people of Newport from the *Country Press* office.'

'And what did he say about that?' asked Jane. 'Everyone knows that the Queen isn't at Osborne just now.'

'He said he'd let us know when anything was arranged,' said Mrs Fry. 'I hope he tells us in time to get up there to see her close up.'

'Whatever next?' said Jane, who believed less than half of what she heard, and more that she didn't want to consider as true.

There was the troopship sunk off the coast of Africa and the news of thousands of refugees flooding into Cape Town . . . that had the ring of truth in it. If only there were more reports and fuller accounts in the bulletins and less of the armchair pronouncements that confused everyone, it would be better for all concerned.

She wished too, that the women would gossip elsewhere, but it was good for trade as they couldn't stand in her shop without buying something.

'I'll have a packet of herbs and some dried peas, Mrs Darwen,' said Mrs Fry. Jane handed them over and wondered if poor Peter Fry would live on herb dumplings and peas for the next month as his wife had requested the same three days running, as the cheapest things she could buy in the shop.

Between serving, Jane made batches of pancakes and stacked them in layers in a closed dish in the side oven, and as dinner-time came near, and the women had to go home to get food ready for the children as they came out of school, she washed a cabbage and finished cooking the pancakes. She laid the table and cut bread and when Walter hitched the horse outside, she was ready with a piece of thick hessian in one hand and a handful of broken biscuits for the horse in the other.

'Something to fetch?' asked Walter. He took the hessian and went to the bakery while Jane fed bits of biscuit to Bess. She watched the road leading to the Barton until she saw the children racing down the hill, laughing and hungry, and Sidney got home first and leaned against Bess to get his breath back.

'Can I take her back after dinner?' he said.

'You'll have to ask your father,' said Jane. 'I don't know if he wants her again.' She gave him an affectionate slap. 'Get washed if you want any dinner.'

'What is it?' Clare rushed in to be first to see what was in the oven. There were no pickles and cold meat on the table, no stew in the big pot by the fire, and only pancakes in the side oven. Walter came back carrying the cooked ducks and placed the tin on the table. He tossed the hessian to the back of the stove and began to carve.

'It's like Christmas,' said Emily. Walter tried to sound as if he felt as festive as the children, but his humour was forced and hollow. Jane filled plates, put jam on pancakes and made tea but ate very little, and was glad the children never ceased chattering.

Walter took his tea to the desk and lit his pipe. He nodded when Sidney asked if he could take Bess and the cart back to the stable, and Clare demanded to go too. Walter hardly seemed to hear her and she ran after Sidney in case her father changed his mind.

Sidney let Clare climb on the driver's seat beside him, where she spread her skirt and put her nose in the air as they passed Ethel Sheath's house. Sidney drove slowly until they came to the turn in the road, then jerked on the reins sharply to make Bess trot. Clare, taken by surprise, fell backwards, her legs threshing in the air and her long drawers on view to the children who sat on the parapet. Ethel Sheath nearly fell in the water for laughing, and Clare was speechless with fury. She pummelled Sidney's back with her fists.

'That'll teach you not to be stuck-up, Miss,' he said. 'You know that Mother doesn't like you showing off,' but he found a piece of only slightly fluffy toffee in his pocket and gave it her as a sign of truce.

They stabled the horse and dragged the cart under the shed. Blackie was restless and Bess whinnied to him, but Blackie trampled his straw, badly in need of exercise. Sidney slipped a halter over the horse's neck and led him out along the river bank. As Blackie grew quiet, Sidney mounted him. 'Come on,' he said to Clare. 'We'll go as far as the gypsies, and walk him back.'

Clare climbed on to a log and then up behind her brother, hitching her skirts up round her waist and clinging to him as Blackie started off along by the river. She forgot her bad temper and she could see the gypsy encampment across the river as soon as they reached the bend.

'Some day, I'm going over to see them,' said Sidney.

Clare gasped. 'You can't! Oo – er, you mustn't do that. You know what Father says about them.'

'He only says we must never buy from them without asking him first.'

'Granny says that they run off with children and their fathers and mothers never see them again. They sell them on the mainland and make them work in the mines.'

'Don't be silly. They can't do that. They make pegs and baskets and tell fortunes. They come in the shop and Mother always finds something to give them, like our old clothes. She gives them bits of fish, too. I think she likes them.'

'I go and hide when old Mrs Lee comes into the shop. She's got

54

funny eyes and seems to know what I'm thinking,' said Clare.

'You ought to hide, then,' said Sidney. 'We all know that Clare Darwen has bad thoughts.'

She clung tighter, knowing that Jack and Edward would never let her ride with them as Sidney did. 'I don't want them to run off with you, Sidney.' She slid down over the tail as they came back to the stable and Sidney put Blackie in his stall, with a few apples to crunch and fresh water.

They ran back and followed the other children, arriving at school in time for the bell, laughing at the satisfying thought that the gypsies might run off with Miss Martin.

Walter banged his thumb with a hammer. He'd spent the afternoon repairing the window catch in the outhouse and putting up two shelves – a job he'd intended to do for several years. The last nail went in and he put away the tools as Jane called him for a cup of tea. She brought out his mug, to see how he was doing. Walter sat on the edge of the boiler to drink it and Jane looked round at his handiwork.

'It's grand, Walter. Really grand. I shall find that really useful.'

'Is there anything more I can do?'

'Nothing. You're a dear man and you've done wonders.' She smiled, reassuringly. 'We'll manage.'

'Tomorrow, I get into uniform,' he said, almost to himself, as if he didn't believe it could happen until he saw his own tunic in the mirror.

'And you'll be very handsome!' she forced her voice to be light, but her eyes showed her pain, and they shared their suffering, without the need for many words.

'Last night...' he began.

'It didn't happen, so there's no harm done,' she said briskly. 'You have no cause to be blaming yourself, now.' Her voice deserted her. 'I'm glad,' she whispered, 'I'm glad that you still – that I am not ugly yet. I am glad that you wanted me.'

He gathered her into a comforting rather than a passionate embrace and wiped away her tears. Jane smiled, shakily. 'For all that, maybe you'd best be at the Wheatsheaf tonight to say goodbye to your friends.'

Jane walked to the bridge to see if Aaron had brought home the catch. She looked across the bridge and heard the bugle call from the barracks at the top of the hill over the river. It came as pure as

55

silver and she shivered. The bugles had called often that morning, the children had heard them on the way back to school and early the next morning, as they ran up the hill to the Barton again and Walter had to be ready.

'I don't think it can be today,' he said. 'They weren't ready when I took up the last load to the Mess. They said they had a troopship late from Liverpool and it isn't standing off Cowes yet. They still have to wait for supplies and they can't load the horses onto the barges until the last minute. The barges for the men are ready down by the Mill and we've been told to muster our kit, so I'd better be ready even if there is a delay.'

'You'll go with the men?'

'Not on the first barges. I go with the horses.' He pulled out an old kitbag that had been in the cupboard since his army days. It was the one he had used in Ireland all that time ago but was still serviceable. Jane checked his hussif, the waxed thread and needles, beeswax and an awl, and Walter honed his pocket-knife and packed bootcleaning materials. He found a button stick and a tin of metal polish which he wrapped in spare rags. Jane polished the leather case containing his cutthroat razors and strop and the scissors for trimming his moustache and sideburns, and a pair of silver-rimmed hairbrushes.

Jane made a parcel of pies and fruit and Walter kissed her. 'Don't cry,' he said. 'I'm not gone yet. I'll be like a bad penny, you'll see. They'll have to let me bring Bess back as it was they who asked for extra fish today and I can't leave the cart there.'

It was nearly two o'clock when Jane heard the cart returning. The children had gone back to school after dinner and she was tidying the shop. She looked up when she heard the cart and the clatter of army boots as Walter jumped down to the road. He stepped through the doorway, looking taller and bigger, yet slim and well-shaped, in the full uniform of the Royal Horse Artillery. The cockade at the side of his fur hat gave a dashing finish to the uniform. The tunic sat well on his shoulders and the frogging on the chest was smart and fresh.

Jane stared. Uniform changed his whole bearing, from Walter Darwen, local businessman and shopkeeper, to that of a non-commissioned officer in Her Majesty's Forces. She glanced at his boots and smiled. He hadn't said that he intended taking his spurs, the ones with silver mounts that he won for horsemanship during the Irish Troubles. He saw her smiling, and flushed.

'How do I look?' he said.

'You look like the man I married,' said Jane. He stood by the flyblown mirror over the mantel, his confidence growing with her approval. 'You're like a warhorse,' she said. 'You can smell battle and you can't wait to get there now it's settled.' He shook his head but made no attempt to deny it. 'Is it today?' she asked.

'Yes. I have to go to Barracks and stay there. I'm fortunate to live near enough to come home and say goodbye, but I must be back by four.'

'You'll miss the children! Oh, Walt, what will they think when they hear you did come back and they couldn't see you again?'

'I have to take Bess back to the stable.' He frowned.

'Go now. Take Bess back and ride Blackie up to the school. Tell Miss Martin that you are going off to the War. She *must* let you speak to the children.'

Jane's colour deepened, and her eyes flashed. 'She should be pleased! You are going to fight to protect people like her. You are giving up a lot to fight for your country!'

Walter kissed her. 'I'll go.' He laughed. 'But I won't take you. Poor Miss Martin would be in real trouble from you if she refused me permission to go into the school!' Jane buried her face in the rough tunic. 'I thought I was fighting for you and my family,' said Walter. 'If I'd known it was for Miss Martin, I'd never have volunteered.'

He strode out to the cart and Jane was amused to see the slight swagger in his bearing and when she saw him on Blackie a little later, she felt very proud.

The dark brown horse was fresh and eager to go. 'Steady, Blackie,' Walter said and rode him gently along by the withy beds before putting him to the hill leading to the school. As he approached the door, the hooves crunching the gravel, the bell for change of lesson rang. Walter rode up to the porch and the boy ringing the bell stopped and looked up.

'Tell Miss Martin that I'd like to see her.'

The boy dropped the bell with a dull clang as it hit the gravel and ran through the doorway. A minute later, the headmistress, Miss Martin appeared, flustered and pink, smoothing down her mousy hair. Walter dismounted and advanced, smiling with considerable charm. 'It's Mr Darwen!' she said.

'I'm very sorry to disturb you, Miss Martin,' he said, 'but I am leaving for Africa and would like to say goodbye to my family.' He

57

went on to say that he didn't know when he would see them again and he was sure that she would understand a father's feelings.

Miss Martin looked overwhelmed. 'Of course, of course,' she kept saying. She *did* understand and he was brave and yes, he must see the children. The boy who rang the bell hovered, trying to take in every word.

'Go to the classes and fetch all the Darwen children,' said Miss Martin. 'Then ask all the mistresses to assemble their classes in the main hall.'

Emily came first and flung herself on her father. He kissed her and told her yet again that she must help her mother in the house and be a good girl. She gazed at him in awe. Was there anyone in the whole world as handsome as her father? Janey and Lizzie were close to tears, but Clare made the most of the situation and posed, head in air, next to him. She was delightfully aware of all her friends, and most important, all her enemies, looking on, green with envy. Ethel looked deeply impressed.

Sidney smoothed the soft flank of the horse and regarded his father, wide-eyed. – I must draw him like that, he thought. It was the first time he had seen his father in uniform.

Edward and Jack tried to appear nonchalant, as if their father came up to the school every day, wearing silver spurs, but they couldn't hide their pride and delight. They shook hands with him when he had kissed the girls, feeling very manly as he gravely held out a hand to each boy in turn. The family waved to him from the porch and then followed Miss Martin, rather apprehensively, into the hall.

Miss Martin called them in and lined them up in front of the entire school. Her face was flushed as it was when she was angry or deeply moved and she was very conscious of her own generous part to play in the small drama.

'You have seen,' she said, 'a brave man about to go and fight for Queen and Country and for us!' She paused for effect. 'He will be leaving his dear wife and children for a long time.' She considered the rapt and upturned faces. 'Because of that, I intend to allow the children to come to school an hour later each morning so that they can help their mother in the storeroom before they come.'

A buzz that could have been approval but was more likely envy, filled the room. Miss Martin smiled and looked at the Darwen children, secretly wishing that they would appear more impressed and grateful, but she attributed their embarrassment

58

to the fact that they must be quite overcome by her generous gesture. Only Clare smiled happily at her. That would show them! She saw Ethel's red hair and freckled face in the crowd. Nothing like this ever happened to her. Her father would go no further than Portsmouth or Southampton, with trips up the Hamble river.

The children filed out of school and grouped round the Darwens. 'We have to do all the deliveries,' said Edward, casually. 'We even have to go to the Barracks.'

Percy Cantor put a leading hand on Edward's arm. 'Let's have a ride sometimes, Edward.'

Jack pushed him away. 'Not you, Percy Cantor. Only *we* are allowed to ride on our cart. Us and our friends, and you're not a friend, not by a long chalk!'

Percy clenched his fists. 'If Edward says I can ride, then I *will* ride in your cart. He's older than you and he'll be in charge, not you.'

Jack spat on the ground and swore. 'That's what I think of you, Percy Cantor. And *if* I catch you on our cart, you'll get more than you bargained for.'

Edward was suddenly like Walter. 'If you fight, neither of you will have a ride. You ought to know better, Jack. The last thing that Father said was that we mustn't worry Mother.' Jack looked discomfited and ran away down the hill. The others followed slowly and when they reached the shop he was sitting on the counter eating a date, having forgotten that he might be in disgrace again.

'Come on,' he said. 'Mother wants tea over early and done with.'

'Why is she in a hurry?' asked Janey.

'There's a rumour that the barges will take the horses and mules out to the troopship. It's arrived at Cowes and the barges will come up the river close to the lane from the Barracks.'

'They might go by train,' said Edward. 'Mother might go up to Parkhurst and miss them.'

'If she walks up Hunney Hill, she'll see them anyway. Aaron said the barges are drawn up by the mill.'

Jane ate little and heard nothing. She watched the steam rise from the kettle and wondered where Walter would sleep tonight. She couldn't imagine the house without him. – Will life ever be the same again? she thought. The children had finished eating before she had spread her first piece of bread and butter and jam. Sidney picked out the caraway seeds from his cake and arranged them in a pattern round the plate. He made extra leaves of grey from the seeds that went well with the blue design on the china.

'Eat up your cake, Sidney.' He crumbled the rest of the cake and gathered it up, watching to see when Jane looked away, then lowered the mess on the floor for Nero, the black labrador, to lick up.

'Will you do the horses?' said Jane to Edward.

'If I take Jack with me, we can feed the ducks and clean some harness, too,' said Edward. 'It will help in the morning.'

'That's a grand idea. Janey and Lizzie can take the swill to the brickyard and Clare must tidy here and see to the shop. Come along, you two, I want to see if the men are leaving and you'll only get up to mischief if I leave you here.' Emily followed her, excited at the prospect of seeing her father again, but Sidney went reluctantly, wanting to stay with his design and perhaps stick the seeds on paper and make a proper picture.

Outside the shop, they turned towards the river. The quay cut across the two main roads of the town and using the short-cut saved ten minutes at least. As it was still quite light, Jane didn't mind walking by the warehouses and iron cranes, and in daylight with other people about, they held no menace. In spite of this, she quickened her steps as she left the road. They crossed over the cobbles by the swing bridge and entered the narrow, overhung lane that was Sea Street. Other people had heard the rumour and many were taking the same path to the Barracks at Albany. In minutes, the snaking rise of Hunney Hill was teeming with relatives, friends and idlers, all going in the direction of Albany.

A pedlar, taking full advantage of the situation, sold liquorice sticks and brandy balls from a pitch under the porch of the Cock and Hen.

Dogs barked, children chased each other up the hill, and the bugles called. Jane had heard bugles all her married life since marrying a soldier and now living here. She had heard them early that morning, and now again, with a sound of greater urgency – a gathering call that was like the call of birds waiting for winter migration. But these bugles called of going, of leaving all that they loved and to Jane, there was only sadness. She could hear no promise of return with the spring.

Dark leaves touched with gold, marked the forest on the left, stretching along the straight road to Gunville. Fallen leaves lay light and dry on the banks at the roadside and the Barracks appeared through the trees, scrubbed and austere in the evening sun. There were men on the Square, too far away for Jane to see if they were Regulars or volunteers, Sentries prevented the onlookers from passing the gates and waved them to one side to look through the railings.

The children were tired. They could see very little and the crowd pushed and shoved them against the roughcast wall. 'Where is Father?' Emily asked for the third time. She was torn between her longing to see him and her intense boredom. What had begun as an exciting outing had become just another long walk with nothing to see and the prospect of yet another long walk home. Sidney said nothing, but watched the faces in the crowd, and turned towards the next fresh sound.

'Look, Mother!' Sidney pointed to the main driveway and his clear voice made many heads turn to see where he was looking. Men in uniform were gathering, holding musical instruments that glinted as they formed ranks.

'It's a band!' A ripple of excitement went through the crowd. 'It's a band. That means they'll be out soon. They always march out to a band. You'll see, they'll play them out to the barges.'

Behind the band came horses with men sitting high on the saddles, leading strings of horses and baggage mules with grooms. The row of poplars, dark behind the men, was aflame at the edge of the setting sun, and the theatrical scene formed and consolidated, the horses pulling at their bits, the men curbing them until the drum major raised his arm and the band stuck up a march. The sentries opened the gates and stood at the salute.

The crowd scattered and re-formed to line the route and one or two women sobbed. Jane stood silent and pale, holding Emily's hand and her other hand rested on Sidney's shoulder. She had stood back with them in the first surge from the railings and they stood on the raised bank and looked over the heads of the others.

It was there that Walter saw them, making a picture for him to take with him to Africa. Emily waved, but the others stood still. For a moment, Walter raised his riding whip in salute and smiled, then obeyed a sharp command of 'Eyes Front!'.

The swaying backs of the horses moved along the lane leading to the barges. The strings of mules were followed by the ragged assortment of children and dogs that seemed an integral part of

61

such processions, but Jane turned back along the road to Newport, passing latecomers who hurried after the sound of the band through the dusk. They went back through the town, avoiding the dark quay and the riverside. It was enough that he had seen them once more. It was enough to know that he was well.

– Now I can plan, Jane thought and there was serenity in the conviction that she could take on the burden of the family alone. God willing, she would manage, and have everything in order against Walter's return. She gave a deep sigh and as they turned to go down the High Street, she said, 'Run on home and get a basin. We'll go up the road and buy faggots and peas for supper.'

She gave Sidney the money and left the two children to bring the warm basin home. She stopped by the *County Press* window. Already, Newport was a town without men and the handful of folk reading the latest news was made up of women like her. Jane called in on Maudie and saw that she had clean curtains at the windows.

'It's all your doing, Mrs Darwen. I'll never be able to thank you. I went to the hospital and saw Lucy. The parson baptised her and she's much better.'

'Is the tube out?'

'Not yet. Not until she's stronger, the Sister said, but she smiled at me and I know she'll get better.' Maudie laughed. 'I've got other good news, too. Ben is coming home to see Lucy before he goes overseas.'

Maudie was radiant, and Jane was suddenly lonely. Lucky Maudie. In spite of her poverty and having a sick child, she would have two precious days, and nights, when she could give herself with simple love and enjoyment. She was healthy and would have more children.

Jane stifled something akin to envy. Envy? That was ridiculous. She didn't want to change places with this little slut. She pulled on her gloves. 'I'm happy for you, Maudie, but now I have my own family to look to.'

Chapter 6

Jack blew on his fingers. It was warm in the stall with Bess after feeding the ducks. The December sky was clear and the afternoon was chill, with a cold moon rising. Bess moved comfortably, pulling at hay in the wicker rack above her head, and the smell of animals and the lantern's glow worked a soothing magic on the boy.

Edward had gone for fresh water for the trough and the other chores were finished. The latch was lifted and water gushed into the trough. Jack took up the lantern. 'Everything's done, Edward.' He held out the basket of duck eggs. 'They laid in the run today. Don't wander about this weather.'

They locked the stable and pulled their caps low on their ears. The river was a stream of black lead overhung with mist that swirled and dispersed in the rising wind. The boys came out onto the bridge as Aaron Sheath threw fish-guts into the water.

'Any news of your father?'

'Nothing,' said Edward. 'One or two have heard but we haven't.'

'Long time. Getting on for six weeks. You should hear soon.'

'Father said it would take time, Mr Sheath. It took three weeks by sea to get to their first landing and he didn't know if he would be allowed to post from there. So even if he does post from there, it's three weeks there and three weeks back.'

'You'd best take the rest of the fish.' Aaron lugged a huge basket onto the stones. 'You can carry it between you. Get home now. You look shrammed.'

The boys struggled back with the fish and set the basket on the shop counter. The back room was lit by just one candle and Edward went out to the yard to find his mother. 'You aren't doing laundry tonight, are you, Mother?' he asked, anxiously.

Jane looked up from the bundle of twigs she was pushing under the boiler. She smiled. 'Not tonight, so don't look so worried. I'm not too tired this evening and I thought I'd do the crabs for the order up at the Mess. They'll be ready to go on the cart with the rest.'

The boys washed under the cold tap in the scullery and ran back to the warmth of the boiler in the outhouse. The water was now steaming when Jane lifted the wooden lid, but she put it back with an exclamation of impatience. 'Hurry up and boil!' she said. The crabs lay still, as if oblivious to their fate or already dead. They were grey green and fresh from the sea and tiny bubbles appeared on the surface of the water.

'I'm hungry,' said Jack.

'Put the kettle over the fire. I must wait here until this water seethes before I put in the crabs.'

'Can't they wait until after tea?'

'No, Jack. You'll have to be patient. I haven't enough brushwood to bring it to the boil again if the fire dies, so I must do them now. 'Jane looked anxiously at the boys, hating herself for not having a good hot meal ready to put on the table. – They work so hard, she thought.

'Let me do them,' said Jack. 'I can if you want to get on.' Jane looked uncertain. Jack was such a scatterbrain, but his intentions were good. Walter had insisted that he must take his share of the work and must be made to grow up. There were mackerel to fry and the water under the pudding might be boiling dry.

'All right, but be sure the water is really boiling. It has to boil really fast before you put them in.'

Edward went to the coalhouse that was between the shop and the back room, where they kept the best coal used only in the evenings. It kept it away from the cheaper coke that was heaped in the yard. He filled the hods and made sure there was enough kindling in case the range went out. This was a family anxiety, although Edward couldn't recall a time when this had happened, unless the chimney was due for sweeping. Ikey the cat was in there, looking for a place to have her kittens, on top of the coal on an old sack.

He took her to Jane. 'Look, Ikey's nearly due, Mother. I found her in the coal.'

'Holy Mary, not more? It seems only yesterday that we took

64

two up to the piggeries to keep down the mice.' Jane went on filling the pudding steamer. 'You'd better get some more buckets filled and put them in the yard. I'll put a clean sack in there. It's no use trying to make her have them somewhere else. Leave the coalhouse door open a thread.' She turned to the table and put a bowl of mealy potatoes in the middle. 'Call Jack and the girls, and I can't think what's keeping the boys.'

The back door opened and Jack and Sidney came in with clean damp hands. Jack sidled into his chair and studied the bowl of potatoes as if he had never seen such strange vegetables. Jane dried her hands vigorously on her apron. She looked accusingly at Jack. 'Well, what have you done?'

'It wasn't my fault,' said Jack, angrily dashing away the tears that he could no longer control.

'You didn't lose the claws?'

Jack nodded. 'I was sure the water was boiling. I saw bubbles but it was so full of steam that I couldn't see. I put more wood under the boiler and then put the crabs in. There *were* bubbles.'

Edward looked shocked. 'You know that Father says you never add more wood before the crabs go in. It goes off the boil until the fresh wood catches.'

Jane gave a short laugh. 'I might have known,' she said. 'But what's done is done. They're spoiled and we can't deliver them to the officers' mess like that.'

'Why not?' said Sidney. 'It's all good crabmeat. They take off the claws as soon as they get them.'

'No matter. They want to see good complete crabs, not pieces! I'll have to dress the crabs for table and that takes time. You know how long that takes.'

Janey and Lizzie sat down. 'I don't want to spend all the evening dressing crabs,' said Lizzie. 'I want to knit. If Jack made them all throw their claws, then Jack ought to do the work. He ought to take them to the Barracks, too, in case he gets told off.'

'Nobody asked you to help, Lizzie,' said Jane, caustically. She ladled out potatoes with the fish. 'Eat up,' she said in a voice that discouraged further discussion.

Ikey licked the last piece of fish-skin from the saucer and Sidney put down the bowl of milky tea for Nero. It was one of Walter's firm beliefs that strong tea was a preventative of distemper in dogs and he gave it to Nero every night. Jane was touched to see how Sidney made a point of doing the same and had not forgotten once since Walter left for Africa. Her temper cooled. They were good children. There might be too many mouths to feed, too much work to do, but they did try to help all they could and they were very young. She piled more food onto Jack's plate and he smiled, knowing that the worst of the crisis was over.

'Can't we do as Father did?' he asked, with a sidelong grin.

Jane's lip twitched. The memory of Walter's discomfiture when he'd done the same and made the crabs clawless, was very funny. His face, when he'd found two dozen crabs without a leg or a claw between them had been a study in anger, shame and disbelief. 'I don't think we could. We're not as clever as your father,' she said.

Jack bolted the last of his pudding and made for the door. 'We can try,' he said.

The girls cleared the table and spread clean hessian on the deal table-top. The crabs were cooling in the tray as Edward and Jack brought them in and they graded the thrown claws. Janey made splinters of wood from a piece of kindling and Jane inserted one into each claw. Jack carefully placed the other end of the splinter into the body of the crab and soon, the crabs were assembled and laid in the basket lined with white linen, looking as good as new.

'I don't like to send them like that,' said Jane. She picked one up and it stayed complete.

'They'll never notice the difference,' said Jack. 'The officer just lifts the cloth and sniffs and waves us to the cookhouse. The cooks don't mind as they crush the claws to get out the meat.'

'Well, I'm glad I haven't to take them! Jack – you must be the one to take them in, and if anything is said, it's you who takes the blame, remember.' Jane looked at the wooden cuckoo clock on the wall. 'You'd better get up to bed. You'll have to start early, tomorrow. There's a lot to do.'

For the first few days after Walter left, the boys had been up early to help with the work and to lift the sacks of vegetables from the storeroom. The girls cleaned and tidied and made beds before putting on clean pinafores for school, hurrying up the hill in time for the second bell, but gradually, although they did all their work, they went to school more slowly. The road seemed longer, more steep, and the bare withy beds were damp and full of interesting insects and small creatures.

The boys played games and picked long canes from the withy

66

beds and peeled them for swords. On the fourth day, they arrived ten minutes late and after a week, they were just in time for the playtime break. Miss Martin saw them all coming up the drive as the other children spilled out into the yard, and she was very cross.

Jane still smarted when she thought of the sharp note Miss Martin had sent her, saying that the family had taken advantage of her generosity and the children must attend school at the normal times in future. She sighed. Jane could understand the point of view of the headmistress, but apart from insisting that each of them apologised to her, Jane didn't punish them further. They worked hard at home and did their utmost for her. Were they more difficult than other children? She treated them as small adults, not a race apart, to be seen and not heard. They were her friends as well as her children.

Miss Martin expected miracles and yet treated them as if they had no intelligence.

Jane woke early with the feeling that there was far too much to be done. She poured cold water from the jug into the basin and shuddered as she washed in it. Her breath hung in the unheated bedroom and she wiped a film of frost from the window. She went downstairs, still pinning her bun and was glad that she had looked out a warm camisole to wear under her dress and the thick handknitted stockings she kept for very cold weather. The living room was warm and it took courage to leave it to scrub the marble slab in the shop window.

She raked the ashes and built up the fire, turning to the ironing, left unfinished from the night before. The gophering iron charred a piece of paper and Jane blew on it gently. A bubble of spit hissed on the iron and it was ready to use. She took the freshly-starched pinafores and crimped each frill with the iron. As each one was finished, Jane hung it over the back of a chair to harden. She called the children.

'If you're quick, you can take warm water up to my washstand from the table.' She could sympathise with the children. The scullery was draughty and cold and impossible to bear without shivering. The boys took long mufflers and wrapped them round their heads, covering their ears and Jane put the thick serge wraps lined with red flannel that the girls needed to wear and warmed them by the fire. She wiped the mist from the shop window while the girls cleared away and Jane watched the road for the post, hoping that today there would be news from her husband.

On the day he left, Walter had scribbled a note and passed it to a friend of Aaron's who was watching the barges taking on fodder from Cowes. He had managed to toss it into his fishing boat and Jane had received it the next day when the boats came in. Since then, there had been silence. – It's no use wondering, she told herself. It will come soon. The island was such a long way from Africa a distance quite beyond her comprehension. To be at sea for three weeks with no land in sight seemed an impossible nightmare. She recalled the journey from Ireland when the sea had been rough and she couldn't see the land. She'd been seasick and felt that she was on the edge of eternity. Africa? It was another world.

She wiped the soapy water from the counter and arranged the boxes neatly. She nibbled a date from the block and wondered if Walter would eat dates where he had gone.

The bell jangled and Jane took the letters with trembling fingers. The one from Ireland she set aside, then tore open the other, barely able to read through her tears.

He was safe and well, thank God. It was a bad journey, with the horses suffering through the Bay of Biscay and in the wet heat south of the Equator, when the ship was like a foul-smelling Turkish bath. Some of the men had been off-colour, too, Walter said. Jane smiled. Trust Walter to tell her about the horses first! She knew that he was never seasick and considered it a weakness, but horses had no choice and weren't built for sailing in boats and needed all his sympathy.

Jane read on impatiently, eager to find out how he was faring. He described their first camp. Jane looked out at the bleak sky and shivered. He was under canvas. But of course, it would be summer out there. They would be warm and each camp took them further south to a good climate, but nearer to the training camps.

'By the time you get this, we shall be mustering and training and even relieving some of the Regulars. Now that General Buller has arrived in Cape Town, the men are in good heart and eager to engage the enemy. Already, they call him "Buller the Deliverer". I shall write as often as I can, but don't fret if you hear nothing for some time. War news will reach you direct by telegraph and the Press, but our letters go by sea and overland.'

She read on about skirmishes at the Kimberley mines where the Boers were driven back with a few British killed. 'Be of good cheer, the war may soon be over, as soon as it began.'

Jane ran her fingers over the cold marble slab. She didn't feel the chill of it as she was almost turned to stone with the words running through her head 'a few killed'. If he was one of the few, could she be of good cheer? She pushed the letter away in her pocket, forcing a smile as the cart stopped by the door.

'I've heard from your father and he's well.' She told them about the horses and the camp but didn't mention the training or the fact that he hoped to relieve the Regulars. 'You must write to him now that we have a field address. Even if he moves away, the letters will be sent on.' She helped to load the cart and Edward climbed up, with Jack sitting at the back.

'We'll go by the town,' said Edward. 'There'll be ice on the quay.'

'Be careful on Hunney Hill. Be sure to use the drag on the way down and ask Mr Wray if the shoes are good enough for this weather.' Jane turned back to the house and saw that Emily was crying.

'Aren't you glad that your father has written to us?'

'I'm frightened,' said Emily. 'He's where the fighting is and he might get killed.'

Jane took her on her knees and pressed her face against her hair. 'I know. I know,' she whispered. – If you knew how terrified I am, too, Emily, she thought, but murmured more words of meaningless comfort.

As it was Saturday, Jane could afford to let the children take longer over the chores as they had more to do in the extra time off from school, and she made sure that it wasn't all work for them. She sent Emily and Sidney out with their iron hoops to make them warm, racing along by the withy beds. The only warm place in the house was the back living room with its blazing range, and in the bedrooms, water froze in ewers and the windows had frost pictures. Jane put on a pot of beef bones to stew and added vegetables and herbs and savoury dumplings.

She heard a step in the passage and looked up. Sam Walmsley popped his head round the door and sniffed. 'If you let that smell up the road, you'll have half of Newport in here for a bite,' he said. Jane smiled. 'Makes me feel hungry,' he said.

'Come in, Mr Walmsley. Sit down in the warm a minute.' He sat in the big chair, Walter's leather chair with the high back, and stretched his feet to the fire. Jane handed him a mug of tea and he fished for his flask. He added a good tot to the sweet dark brew and sucked at the mixture with grunts of satisfaction. – How like Walter he is, thought Jane. The same love of basic homely pleasures and the way he sat in that chair, thinking of nothing more complicated than the pleasure of a hot drink on a cold morning. He wiped his moustache with the back of his hand, and gave her a penetrating glance.

'You're pale, gal. Finding it too much?'

Jane smiled. 'No, it's the cold. It gets into me when I go to the outhouse but the boys are lighting up the boiler and we'll soon have a good fug.'

Sam looked at the well-polished brasses, the room swept and clean and he'd already looked in at the horses on this way down to the barges and saw that they were in excellent condition. He nodded, approvingly. 'I said I'd keep an eye on you for Walter, but you haven't asked for help yet. I don't think you need me.' He pretended to be hurt. 'If you don't ask a favour soon, I'll think there's others you'd rather have helping.'

'And who is asking for compliments? It isn't true that you haven't helped us. I heard how you rescued Jack the other day when the wheel locked, and I haven't thanked you.'

'It was nothing. There's little enough you let anyone do, but I've brought along a load to save them one journey. I'll take some fish while I'm here.'

'Have the oranges come in yet?'

'I've brought plenty. This is the Christmas lot, so you need plenty. The first batch of apples are out of store at Wootton and they look good.' He took an apple from his pocket and cut it with his clasp knife, handing one half to Jane. It was crisp and sweet and had the waxy, dense skin of fruit stored in a cool loft.

'I heard from Walter,' said Jane, She handed him the letter, and watched his face as he read it.

Sam carefully kept all expression hidden, but he thought, – pity he told her he's going to the Front, but that's like Walter. He's proud of the fact and thinks she'll be pleased, too. Should know he'll worry her half to death. 'Well, he seemed to be thriving,' he said, heartily. 'Now to important things. Have you ordered your Christmas dinner?'

'The goose is coming from Folley as usual, and there's carol-singing and the Church Social and I expect one or two will drop in.' Her voice faded as she imagined Christmas without Walter

70

singing at the harmonium and the children saying their party pieces for him.

Sam pursed his lips. 'I know it will be hard, Jane. The hardest yet, but I'll drop by, and if I know you, there'll be plenty of extra mouths to feed. You'll have so much to do that you'll have no time to fret.' He picked up his hat and buttoned his collar. The air outside made his breath come in clouds as he unloaded the cart, and the cold fingered its way into the shop. Jane closed the door to the living room to keep the heat in and put on woollen mittens to handle the cold boxes of fruit. She covered the bananas with straw to keep out the frost. Her fingers ached and it would be so easy to let the cold and misery flow over her, if she offered no resistance. She was utterly lonely, but she gritted her teeth and prised the frozen fish from the slab for Sam to take home.

It was impossible to keep warm. Edward and Jack came back, bringing the east wind with them. Their faces were blue with the cold and their lips chapped. As soon as they shrugged out of their overcoats, they sat by the range to warm through before going out again. Jack sat rubbing his chilblains as they itched with the returning warmth. Jane tried to tell him that sitting close to the fire only made them worse, but she knew that he would take no notice. For two months every year he endured itching and painful chilblains.

Jane looked up in surprise after serving a customer. 'You'll get cold out here,' she said to Edward.

'I want to talk to you, Mother.'

'Well, hurry up, I'm freezing.'

'I've been talking to Fred Cantor.'

Jane had her hand on the door knob. The shop was empty and she wanted to get warm. 'I don't like that family, Edward. I thought you'd had enough of them. Percy is always picking a fight with Jack and Fred drinks.'

Edward shifted from one foot to the other. 'He said I'll be fourteen soon.'

'I know that! How very clever of Fred Cantor to know it too. I'm freezing out here, so get it out, whatever it is,' she said. She raised her eyebrows. Edward looked like Walter when he had something to say that he knew would make her angry. 'Well?'

'He wants me to work on the railway with him.' The words spilled out, incoherently. He repeated them more slowly.

'The railway? The cheek of it! You still have schooling to finish my lad, and you'll not leave a minute before your time. And what would you be doing on the railway, I'd like to know?'

'They want a boy to help on the station at Cowes and see to the luggage.' He looked at her beseechingly. 'It wouldn't be just yet,' he added.

'And what would your father have to say about that? How can you even discuss it when you know he says you are to work with him when you leave school? There's more than enough to do here, heaven knows. In fact, I don't know how I'll manage when you go back to school after Christmas and the weather is bad.'

Edward almost smiled. 'But the war will be over before I leave school. Father will come home. Everyone says it's nearly over. Fred said...'

'Fred Cantor? I might have known he would fill you with rubbish.' Her eyes flashed and her misery came to the surface. 'What does *he* know about it?' She snatched the letter from her pocket and thrust it into his hands. 'There! You're so grown up, you can read it.' Her hands shook. 'Read that and tell me if the war is nearly over. Tell me if the war will be over by Christmas,' she sobbed. 'Decide for yourself if your father will be back soon, or ever.'

Tears, held back until the children were in bed, stung her lids. Her shoulders heaved and her control ebbed. Edward read the letter and stood watching her, helplessly. His awkward red hand reached out to touch her shoulder. 'I'm sorry, Mother,' he said. 'I didn't know you were so worried. You never say. You never let on. I promise we'll all help and I know he'll be back. He will, you know. Father will come back safely.'

By the time the others were there, Jane was calm and only a slight redness of her eyes and on the tip of her nose showed that she had been crying, but everyone had a red nose in this weather and the others didn't notice that anything was wrong. Jane felt Edward looking at her from time to time and he had a new note of authority in his voice when he told Jack to fetch more coal and the girls to lay the table as it was nearly dinner-time, and they'd better be quick. As they sat round and ate the hot soup and dumplings, Jane decided that she had to go on, that Walter would be hurt if she let Christmas go without doing all the usual things.

Sunday dawned with a red edge to the sky. The wind had dropped and the lowering clouds raised the temperature. Jane met the children from Sunday School and they walked along to Fairlee Cemetery. The ice had melted but mud thrown up from the gutters by carriage wheels made the narrow path slippery. They picked their way with care, Jane firmly holding the wreath of holly and laurel leaves that they were taking to Caroline's grave.

The Websters and the Foster family from the grocer's shop joined them at the gates, each family carrying a similar wreath. There were few families having no tiny grave to tend and visit, and infants' graves scattered the cemetery, with headstones telling of infants dying at birth, within a first year of life or under five years of diphtheria or infantile paralysis.

Jane secretly hated the cemetery, but for most of the parents it made a meeting place, a social outing after a solemn pilgrimage. They exchanged gossip round the water trough where they filled vases and threw out dead flowers. Jane placed the wreath on the green mound and wiped the simple headstone clear of mud.

Caroline Darwen, died in infancy, 1895.

The Websters had lost their only son when he was nine and they'd recently bought a splendid angel, carved in Italian marble, to watch over him. Jane imagined it at night, cold in the darkness, with folded, menacing wings. She never passed it without shuddering and wondered how cold it was for the little ones under the ground, and she ignored all the hints from the other parents that a more suitable stone could be erected to Caroline. Jane preferred the simple headstone, thinking that a green turfed mound was natural and nearer to God.

Walter never visited the place, professing that it was no place for men, but Jane suspected that he shared her horror of the memories it evoked.

Mr Foster was in good form. He'd put on a smart tailcoat and was bursting to tell the latest news from the afternoon bulletin, but most of the mourners had read it as they had leisure on a Sunday to walk by the offices on their way to Fairlee or Carisbrooke. He caught up with Jane. 'Have you heard the latest, Mrs Darwen?'

She tipped some faded flowers onto the rubbish heap and the dark memories receded. 'I heard there was nothing fresh,' she said.

Mr Foster trimmed his step to match hers, and looked important. 'Relief forces reached Kimberley with some success. Lord Methuen has reached the relief column and attacked at the Modder river.'

Jane smiled. The little grocer was so delighted to be the

temporary fount of all knowledge that he was inclined to learn the bulletins by heart and sounded like a gramophone record. 'I heard that one,' said Jane.

Mr Foster was disappointed, but his face brightened as he walked after her. 'But have you seen the Casualty List?' He stopped as he saw the agony in her face. 'I'm sorry, Ma'am, I didn't think. It's all right, though, there were none from Newport.' He smiled. 'But at least twenty British soldiers were killed at the last sortie. That was from Kimberley. It included some Irish, your countrymen! They fought bravely, a credit to Her Majesty,' he added with condescension. 'Major Scot Turner was among them.'

'Major Scot Turner? God rest his soul. He was a brave man and a good leader, and will be sorely missed.' Jane allowed Emily to pull her back to the grave, where Edward was pinning the new wreath to prevent the wind from taking it. The Fosters had left an offering of white wax flowers under a glass dome and the angel looking down from the Webster grave had traces of unmelted ice on his wings. So much cold and white in death.

'May we go back by the river?' said Jack. He led the way to the gate opening onto the river fields where the tow-path was fairly dry and less muddy than the roads. The children ran ahead to the long quay where the grey barges lay asleep.

The younger children played leapfrog over the capstans at the front of the woodyards and Jack climbed up the sides of the stacked planks waiting to be stored or seasoned. 'Be careful,' said Jane, without much hope that he would. She walked on. He knew that if he climbed high enough, he could step out onto a protruding plank and if it was sturdy, it made a good swing, but if it broke under his weight, he would go flying.

Jane tried to ignore him. A little innocent exercise would do all of them good. She could deal with the scratches and bruises later. She had developed a fatalistic attitude to Jack and his accidents, Sidney ran ahead to the stable door and opened it up for his mother to inspect the animals and to make sure that all was well. The horses were warm in their stalls, the hay was lasting well and the bunker of oats was dry and fragrant, free from mildew.

'You are very good children,' said Jane. 'Your father will be very proud of you when I write and tell him how you care for the animals.'

Blackie snorted and Jane ran a hand over his muzzle. He was

healthy but lacked exercise. She'd have to ask Sam what he thought. The family at Wootton would be glad to have him for a while. Archie could ride him on the farm and use him. It would be good for the horse.

'We may have to send Blackie to Wootton,' said Jane.

Sidney was indignant. 'We can't send him away. What would Bess do? She's always lonely when he's not here.' It was true. The old mare had pined when Blackie went to the farm one summer and if he went out for the day with Walter, Bess would whinny as soon as she heard them cross the bridge on the way home. Bess was a good worker, she had no vices and deserved a little consideration.

'I know what we could do,' she said. 'In Ireland, we always kept a stable-mate for old horses.'

'But you don't want another horse,' said Sidney.

'Not a horse. It would have to be a donkey or a nanny goat just for company for Bess.' Jane was touched by the sudden radiance in the faces turned to her. 'It isn't a promise,' she said, hastily. 'It's only an idea. It means another mouth to feed.'

'But with Blackie gone, we wouldn't have him to feed!' said Sidney, and Jane wondered what she had started, as all the way home, they argued. Sidney and Jack wanted a donkey and the girls wanted a goat.

'If we had a dear little goat, we could milk it,' said Janey.

'Take off your coats and set the table for tea,' said Jane as soon as they were home.

'If we had a donkey, I could ride it to school,' said Jack.

'If we had a nanny goat we could make our own cheese,' said Clare. 'It would be better than Mr Foster's cheese from the slab.'

'And who would end up milking it?' said Jane, dryly. 'It won't be a nanny goat, I've enough to do without that.' But as she put out the bread and pickles, the jam and cheese, she thought back to the little white goats on the hills of Ireland and wondered.

Sidney brought out paper and pencils for their Sunday letters to Walter. The children finished theirs quickly and turned to games and knitting, while Jane tried to think what would interest Walter. There wasn't much to tell. Everyone was well, the shop was well-stocked and the boys managed the deliveries and the visits to the warehouse with the help of Dan Cooper, a younger brother of Bert's who was fifteen years his junior and lived with Bert and Annie since his parents' death.

Jane was sorry for him as he had been an 'afterthought' and then lost his parents. He was helpful and the best of that family, willing and honest with a dry wit that delighted Jane and annoyed Annie. He didn't share the Coopers' inflated opinions of themselves and escaped as often as he could from Annie's frugal kitchen and acid tongue.

Jane was still pondering over her letter to Walter when the children went to bed. She managed to tell her husband about Mr Foster and his bulletins in an amusing way. She inspected the children's contributions, each one typical of its writer. Edward had stated, laboriously, the exact number of times he'd been to the Barracks and what he'd had on the cart. Jack merely added 'come home soon' to the end of Edward's letter and the girls had written about Ikey and Nero, the gossip in the shop and the fact that they wanted new dresses for Christmas.

Sidney had managed, in a few words, to convey all that would make Walter laugh and feel that all was well at home, and he'd included some drawings. Jane sealed the envelope and addressed it carefully. She banked up the fire and left the coalhouse door open for Ikey and the kittens and went to bed.

Chapter 7

'The Queen's coming!' Sidney rushed into the shop and called upstairs. 'Mother, I've seen the outriders. They came down Snooks Hill but went back again!'

Jane Darwen looked out of the window. It was Christmas Eve and bitterly cold. 'They must have found ice on the hill,' she said and hurried downstairs. 'Who is in?'

'Jack and Clare and Edward and me,' said Sidney. 'Emily will be mad to miss seeing her again. She's up at Mr Foster's with Janey and Lizzie.'

'Well, you know what to do. Get some buckets, quickly.'

Sidney ran to the outhouse and in another minute, Edward had an old brass coal scuttle, Sidney a wooden bucket that lived under the mangle in the yard and Jack had an old orange box. They went to the bridge and down by the water, shovelling up sand and grit into the containers until they were almost too heavy to drag up the hill. Clare helped a little but stood at the top of the hill as if in charge, holding a spade in what she hoped was an elegant way. The outriders were along the road and came to the small group of children as soon as they saw them.

One dismounted and smiled. Ignoring his smart livery, he took Clare's spade and helped the boys to spread grit on the icy patches on the road while his companion rode back along the road towards Osborne to report that the road was passable. There was one place where the cold wind caught the slope and everyone for miles knew how treacherous it was in bad weather for walkers and riders alike.

'Good lads,' said the outrider, hastily re-mounting when he heard a distant horn. He went up the High Street towards Carisbrooke and the children stood with shovels in their hands, their faces flushed with exertion and excitement.

A light carriage, drawn by four black horses, slowed as it reached the top of the hill. The coachman looked at the gritted surface and saw the children waving. He threw down a handful of coins and waved his long whip in salute and took the carriage safely down the hill.

There was a glimpse of a black, crêpe-trimmed bonnet and an old pale face sunk on bowed shoulders. Two tired eyes lit with pleasure and the Queen kissed her hand. The footmen clung to the swaying carriage as the coachman whipped up the horses to go through the town and sparks flew from the ringing hooves.

Edward counted the money. 'What shall we do with it?' he said.

'Some of it's mine,' said Clare.

'Let's spend it in Parson's,' said Jack. 'She sells crystallised fruit. There's enough here for a very big box!'

Sidney's face went more red than it had been in the cold wind. 'You two think only of yourselves. We ought to buy a nice present for Mother and give it to her, tomorrow. We can buy it on the way back from the Barracks.'

'Did you get there in time?' asked Jane, as they trooped back into the house.

'One of the men helped us and there wasn't a single slither,' said Edward.

Clare went to the door as soon as she heard the other girls coming back from the grocery shop. 'We saw the queen,' she gloated. 'You didn't see her!'

Emily saw the sandy bucket and began to cry. 'I always miss her,' she said. 'It's not fair. Why didn't you run up to the shop and tell me, Clare?'

'I had to help,' said Clare. 'There wasn't time.'

Sidney whispered in Emily's ear and she smiled. 'Can I help choose?' she whispered back.

'Slip up to Tiler's when we come back from the deliveries and we'll all choose it.'

'Wash your hands and faces before the company come,' said Jane. She straightened the damask cloth and arranged the fancy cakes on the glass stand. She glanced at the clock and shifted the kettle over the fire. The brasses and fire-irons reflected the glow of the clean burning coal and she was satisfied. Her hair was coiled around her head in a dark coronet and her dull green velvet dress was her best. She fidgeted until she heard carriage wheels, then went to greet the relatives from Wootton. In her hand were lumps of sugar for Blackie and she made a fuss of him while he nuzzled her hand for more sugar, his sweet breath warm on the frosty air.

'Blackie looks well,' she said. The horse was well-groomed and had shed weight and Jane was relieved that he looked better now than when he was in the stable under the arches. She had had doubts about Walter's approval over the change, not that he disliked Archie or thought he couldn't look after a horse, but because Walter hated not having a say in any decision about his own.

Archie unhitched the two horses and took them over the bridge to the stable, as it was far too cold to leave the animals standing in the frost, even if they were covered with rugs.

Amy, Archie's wife, hurried thankfully into the warm house and shed her cloak and gloves. She too was wearing her best clothes and sat in a straight-backed chair, arranging the dark brown serge skirt with self-conscious precision.

'Where's Rose?' said Jane. 'The others will be very disappointed when they come back and see that she isn't here.'

'She was very tired,' said Amy. 'She's taken cold again and she doesn't thrive in this weather.'

Jane thought sadly of the lovely little face. Rose was like her name, pretty, with pink and white skin and huge blue eyes, but she had one cold after another all through the winter and had coughs almost all the time. She was as light as a feather and looked as if a puff of wind would take her away.

'I must take some lemons when we go back,' said Amy. 'The doctor says that all I can do is to keep her warm and give her honey and lemon for her cough.' She sniffed. 'You can't believe all they tell you. He said that she should have goat's milk but I can't think why. We have plenty of warm fresh milk straight from the cow and full of good cream.'

'If that's all you need, you shall have as much as she can drink. I'll fill a pail for you when you go. Since Blackie went to you, we've kept a nanny as a mate for Bess and we've more milk than we can use,' said Jane.

Amy smiled, politely. Her eyes missed nothing and she was disappointed. A woman without a man about the place didn't need to be as houseproud and shouldn't look as handsome as Jane did now. She wished that she had thought of dark green velvet for her new dress. 'I didn't think Walter liked goats,' said Amy.

'As Walter isn't here, I have to decide a lot of things, Amy. He may not approve of a few things I do, but I can but do my best.' A dangerous sparkle should have warned Amy not to pry.

'Do you tell him when you write? He'd want to know,' said Amy.

'I tell him what I think fit,' said Jane, 'including not telling him that I lent Blackie to Archie for the farm.' She smiled, but her tension showed. 'If you'd feel better about it, I can write in my next letter and if Walter doesn't approve of Archie having our horse, we shall just have to take him back again.'

Amy was silent and Jane busied herself with moving the kettle an inch to one side and pushing the plate of bread and butter to the centre of the table. Amy knew that it was no good trying to interfere, but it was annoying how well Jane was doing.

'I don't know how you manage, Jane,' she said in a placatory tone. She was sure that if Archie went away, she would be incapable of running the farm. She looked down at the two rings on her hand and took courage from the fact that they were a sign of prosperity. It wasn't right for a handsome woman like Jane to be left. It wouldn't take much to make the town talk.

'I expect the neighbours help when you are hard-pressed,' Amy smiled. 'Does Sam Walmsley come in often?' she added slyly.

Jane gave her an old-fashioned look. So *that's* what they thought. Walter away and all the men visiting her? If only Archie would hurry back from the stable, she would be spared his wife's sly tongue. Perhaps she did get on better with men. She could talk to Sam and Dan Cooper and Archie – and even Mr Foster was willing to help her and many had said to call on them if she needed anything. Archie had said it many times, as if he really *would* like to help, and she knew that he had a very soft spot for her.

The men were no problem, but there had been a subtle change in the manner of the women since Walter's departure. At first they were very sympathetic, almost protective, with many enquiries and offers of help. But when she remained cheerful and refused their aid for the simple reason that she had no need of it and didn't want to impose, they drifted away, coming to the shop for fish and news and then hurrying away when they had been served, no longer offering the help of husbands or brothers in a slightly patronising way, but avoiding all reference to them unless Jane asked after their health. They resented any time the men took to linger in the shop.

Jane couldn't guess the reason for the change, but put it down to the fact that her being alone now lacked novelty and they had other fish to fry. However, the wives were jealous of the way their husbands spoke of Jane with admiration and respect for the manner in which she tackled her difficulties. They liked her pleasant optimism and refusal to lapse into self-pity in public, and in a surprising way, they liked her willingness to help women like Maudie Dove.

'Mr Walmsley?' said Jane. 'Yes, he comes into the shop to take the order and to save me a journey. He says that the fruit warehouse is no place for a woman on her own.' She set her lips primly but wanted to laugh. When had it ever bothered her that the quay and the warehouses were forbidden? 'The boys collect the fruit and Aaron brings me the fish. He's very kind.'

Outside, the sound of Archie laughing with the boys made her sigh with relief. She put the kettle on the hottest part of the stove and took a steaming apple and ginger cake from the warming drawer, and the room was filled with a spicy scent. Archie came in, his face red from the cold and hugged her close, kissing her heartily on the cheek. Jane caught sight of Amy's face and chuckled inwardly. – You needn't think I want your husband, Amy Cheverton, she thought, but it was good to smell the woollen cloth that still kept a faint whiff of tobacco and to feel good strong arms about her.

Edward couldn't hide his disappointment when he saw that Rose hadn't come. Jane smiled, tenderly. He was such a strong boy, solid and quiet and it seemed odd that he should have such affection for the delicate little girl. He was often clumsy and had an unemotional nature while Rose was all mercurial high spirits or deep depression, flitting from one confusing mood to another.

Amy laughed, but unlike Jane, she couldn't leave well alone. 'Do you miss your little sweetheart, Edward?'

Edward turned crimson and stuffed his mouth with ginger cake until he choked, the hot spices making his eyes water. Janey rescued him with a drink of tea and by the time he'd recovered, Emily was talking about the new goat and how Bess liked to have her there.

'I am growing very fond of her,' confessed Jane, 'and the girls are very good at milking her. They take it in turns.'

81

They talked of the war and the latest Casualty Lists and Archie watched Jane closely, admiring her courage and self-control when Amy persisted in talking about the wounded with complete disregard for Jane's feelings.

'They say that Lord Methuen doesn't mind how many men die so long as he has victories,' said Amy.

Archie frowned. 'Everyone was for Methuen when he won without too much loss of life or limb, but now they are saying that General Buller should never have given him command. He doesn't know the country, not like Buller, who fought in the Zulu War. Buller should lead the attacks himself, but they say he was unwilling to fight over Kimberley and it was only because Cecil Rhodes was there and him being so famous, that made him agree to fight for it.'

'But Lord Methuen is an experienced soldier, isn't he?' asked Edward.

'He's had plenty of experience, but not to fight these rascals. He's an old army man, used to fighting in line as battles have been fought, but that way of fighting is no good against those artful beggars of farmers who come up out of the rocks to fire and are off before they can be caught.'

'We must all pray that the war will end soon,' said Amy piously.

'That won't win the war,' said Jane. 'We need to do more. They've started to collect comforts and food for the troops. If you give to that, as freely as you can afford, it will do more than praying.'

'Look, Aunt Amy, I've bought a favour,' said Jack. He showed the button on his lapel: *Buller The Deliverer*.

'I bought one for Lord Methuen but I lost it,' said Edward. 'I'm glad I lost it now. I don't think much of him any more, but they say the Royal Horse Artillery are fighting close to Kimberley, so there's bound to be victory soon.'

Jane cleared the tea things and tried not to think of Walter in the Front Line. They dressed up warmly and walked up to the Square to hear carols outside St Thomas' church. A huge brazier burned in the middle of the Square between the church and the Wheatsheaf and patrons from both places stayed to hear the singing and to give money for comforts for the troops. The faces in the light of many lanterns were of women and children, young boys and old men and a few who worked the farms like Archie and men who escaped soldiering by pleading ill-health – like Bert

Cooper, who seemed able to malinger his way out of anything he didn't want to do.

The manager of a hastily-built arms factory was there and Jane couldn't help wondering if Walter wouldn't have done better to make bombs.

The singing was sweet but subdued, lacking the vitality and strength of male voices, and there was little of Peace On Earth and Goodwill To All Men to sing about. Jane was glad to get back to the warm house, to drink mulled ale and eat potato pie before Archie left to collect the horses. While they ate, Amy played hymns, which seemed more comforting than the anthems in the Square. For once, Jane was sad to see her visitors go, and when Archie kissed her, perhaps more lingeringly than was polite or necessary, while Amy struggled with her six-button gloves, Jane had the absurd desire to hug him and to pretend that he was Walter. Now, she had to face Christmas Day without him.

The morning dawned bright and clear and the children finished the work as quickly as they could, not needing to be told what to do. They brought in fresh goat's milk and sat down to a breakfast of porridge and moist bread and jam. Emily nudged Sidney and they both giggled. The excitement grew, the others caught her mood and all the children had the exasperating air of 'I know something that you don't know'.

Jane brought in a basket and raised the cover. Underneath were presents for all the children – gloves and bright handkerchiefs, bags of sweets and figs. Each of the girls had a new hair ribbon and the boys had handknitted ties.

Sidney pushed aside his presents, which was unusual as he liked new clothes. He went to the cupboard beside the fire and fumbled under the pile of clean tablecloths and bed linen airing there. The other children handed Jane the presents they had made for her. It was difficult to seem surprised when she received purses, sewn by the girls and decorated with beads, as she had helped them over the difficult bits. She admired them anew. Edward had carved a pair of wooden spoons and Jack had made a bookmark of leather, while Sidney's was a picture of the Nativity, drawn with care and love and reminding Jane of the days before she married a Free Thinker and left behind even the pretence of her family religion, which had never been strong with her.

She propped the picture against a blue vase on the mantelpiece and picked up the last package that Sidney put before her, and drew out a small box. Her heart lurched with surprised emotion. She had no idea what it could be. A wad of cotton wool came away and she picked up a brooch. It was cheap and gaudy, a thin layer of mother-of-pearl on white metal with a red rose painted on it. Across the base was the one word, MOTHER. It was vulgar and not the kind of ornament that Jane had ever possessed, but at that moment, it was the most beautiful jewel that she could have been given. She pinned it to her dress and admired it in the mirror, while the children beamed with pleasure at the success of their secret.

'Everyone chose it,' said Emily.

'I liked the red roses,' said Clare.

'Your father left presents for you, too,' said Jane. 'You must look for them.' They searched the room and found them under the long chenille tablecloth. From a wicker basket, they pulled out wooden hoops, skipping ropes and a set of ninepins. There was a big coloured ball, a box of paints and a new chequerboard and dice.

The boys stoked the fire under the boiler for the Christmas puddings and put good coal on the fire in the range. The goose was in the baker's oven and Jane made brandy butter and apple sauce. She opened a parcel that Sam had brought in earlier and found a pretty blue and white jar of Chinese ginger and a bottle of Sherry wine. Edward gave her, as an afterthought, a package from Archie that he had left with him last night.

'I'm sorry , Mother, I almost forgot it. Uncle Archie made me hide it so that it would be a real surprise today, and said not to tell anyone but you.'

Jane felt an almost-forgotten thrill as she opened the box with its extravagant wrapping and colourful picture on the box lid. The girl in the picture was dark and laughing, with a sixteen inch waist and a pretty dress of spotted voile, rather as Jane had been in her courting days. 'Sweets to the Sweet,' Archie had written.

Jane bit into the sweet Turkish Delight and wondered if Amy knew about the gift. Her present lay on the sideboard. It was a box of coloured threads and needles, plain and suitable for a woman alone. She tossed the short note into the fire. 'Edward?' she called. 'You can all have one piece each, but no more or you'll ruin your appetites for the goose.'

'Who gave us that?' Clare looked at the box with envy. 'I didn't see it with the others.'

'It wouldn't be a surprise if you saw everything,' said Jane. 'I don't know! Uncle Archie spoils you all.'

'You can have another piece if you like,' said Lizzie. 'I'm sure he wouldn't mind, Mother.'

'I wonder if he would?' said Jane. 'He is a dear man. A dear man,' she said softly.

'Will he ride Blackie tomorrow?'

Jane started. 'Who?'

'Uncle Archie,' said Lizzie patiently. 'He said he wanted to ride to hounds.'

Jane went pink. She had forgotten that she had invited Archie to call in before the Meet up at the Square, and now she wished that she had been less pressing. The present had done nothing to make her forget the look in his eyes when he had said goodbye. – Sure, there's no harm in the man, she told herself. He's just a good friend.

But in the morning, she kept Emily and Sidney by her side until Archie had come and gone, drinking one glass of ale and putting some roasted chestnuts in his pockets. He looked very well groomed and fit and if she was honest, he was as good looking as Walter, although of slighter build. She was glad to see him ride up towards the Square and found that she had not wept for Walter at all after the children were in bed on Christmas night but had piled all the presents in Walter's chair and pretended that he was at the Wheatsheaf.

A hunting horn sounded in the distance and Sidney flung open the shop door. Frost glistened on the shop front and little rivulets of ice formed in the gutters. The horn sounded again and two horsemen rode towards the Square. The Meet of Foxhounds this year was outside the Wheatsheaf on Boxing Day. Jane buttoned up Emily's coat and gave her the new woollen gloves to wear, pushing up the long fingers until they fitted. They walked to the Square to watch the hounds move off. The hunt would pass the shop on the way to Stapler's Copse, but it was traditional to go to the Square first, or even up to Carisbrooke if the Hunt started from Gypsy Hollow.

Most of the shopkeepers were out and the shops in the High Street had a shuttered Sunday look. Jane nodded and spoke to friends and neighbours and old customers and exchanged the greetings of the season, but few mentioned the war.

Dr Barnes, mounted on a rangy hunter, drank spiced wine

from a goblet. The local gentry, in hunting pink with their ladies dressed in black habits and riding side-saddle, gathered round the landlord of the Wheatsheaf to take a stirrup cup from the silver salver that Mrs Grace held high. Local tradesmen on their own horses reined in their mounts, slightly away from the richer, full members of the Hunt. It was force of habit, but not necessary today, as all men were equal for the Boxing Day Meet. Anyone who could sit a horse was welcome if he contributed to the Hunt Purse.

A bow-legged man in a cloth cap, sitting a saddle-backed mare tried to look as if he didn't drive a coal cart in the working week and the men from the Bugle Inn were on the hotel's hired hacks. Bert Cooper was on his own, highly-unpredictable horse and appeared very uncomfortable. The stallion might be called Satan, a name that fitted him well, but to Bert he was a white elephant, a beast he hadn't the heart to sell at a loss to the army but was almost too frightened to ride.

Jane watched, a slightly malicious smile making her feel wicked. Bert had asked if he could ride Blackie, or rather had demanded him as if by right and had been very put-out when Jane said he was now a working horse on the farm. With Walter away, Bert took far too much for granted and it gave Jane a lot of pleasure to refuse him. In a way, it made up for Annie's sarcastic remark.

'Bert Cooper's horse is playing up, Mother,' said Jack. 'When I went up with the pigswill, he had him in the yard there and could hardly handle him. He's over-fed and under-worked.'

'He'll be off at the first gate,' said Sidney, and Jane noticed that they copied the phrases that Walter used.

She recalled other Hunts, with Walter, mounted and immaculate in a well-cut jacket and top hat, boots that gleamed and his silver spurs earning the respect due to them. He always finished with the leaders and had once brought her the fox's brush, still reeking of blood and excreta. She waved to a friendly face. That incident was best forgotten. Walter's pride had evaporated as he saw the revulsion in her eyes. He never talked of the kill after that, but confined his talk to who was there, where they found, and who fell at what gate and who played the fool and had the rough edge of the Master's tongue. He brought no more trophies home although he was often in the running.

The Hunt Servant stood to the side of the road leading to the

High Street. The Master whipped in his hounds and cracked the long leather thong over their heads. They moved off, each horseman bending to put a contribution in the Purse. The rich threw in a sovereign and the tradesmen gave what they could afford. Jane stood tall, recalling that Walter would have given a sovereign, too.

As he passed, the Master of Fox Hounds saw Jane and raised his hat high in salute. 'I hope he's here with us, next year,' he called and Jane blushed as everyone looked at her. She raised a gloved hand and inclined her head with dignity and Clare looked round anxiously to see which of her friends had noticed it.

Sidney absorbed the colour and atmosphere, the bright red coats against the grey church and the inn-keeper with his two helpers with silver trays. He loved the horses, their coats like polished silk, and immediacy of the horn and the thud of hooves getting into their stride making exciting music with the hounds, flowing in a white and golden stream, just clear of the hooves. They passed, leaving the smell of hounds and fresh dung on the frost.

One or two faint hearts left the procession at the bridge, saying that the ground was too hard with frost for safety, and went home by the back streets to avoid being seen to leave. Jane wondered if Bert would back down.

'Satan looks in fine fettle,' she called, and Bert looked back. 'Are you following?' Jane said, with a slightly malicious smile, having seen that Bert hung back as if to join the prudent riders and quietly leave the Meet for home.

Bert saw the smile and Archie Cheverton grinning from the back of Blackie, the horse that would have been Bert's mount if he'd had his rights. Blackie looked lean and fit, eager to go but disciplined and Archie swung away after saluting Jane with a gallantry that went with the occasion and would have no place in the life of his farm. Bert Cooper tugged on the reins and followed the hounds, his face set in a grim smile. He'd show her that he was as good as Walter Darwen any day of the week!

Jane took Clare and Janey up to Stapler's. They sat on a gate and watched hounds weave across the meadow, in full cry. Horses jumped the five-bar gate in the other corner of the field, bunching in the gully before gaining ground along the Arreton Road. The pink and brown flashed by, the horn called and the hounds made music. It was a scene of pure visual beauty and one that Walter would have loved, but Jane was afraid to walk higher above the copse in case a kill was made, so she took the girls up to the *County Press* to see what quarry her husband pursued this Boxing Day.

The news was evasive. There were mentions of patriotic speeches about the fight on the Modder River, praising the devotion to duty of the men of the Highland Regiment and the Gordons; and their sacrifice. Jane was cold.

'In spite of heavy losses, the Artillery kept up a fierce barrage,' she read. The Artillery? Which regiment? Was it Walter's regiment? The list of casualties at the side of the bulletin naming local men, was dated 20 December and there was no familiar name, to Jane's intense relief.

The politicians wrapped up the news in fine stirring phrases, but Jane's commonsense told her that someone, somewhere wasn't happy about the way the war was going. Her trust in the newspapers had faded weeks ago and she longed to hear the truth from Walter.

Some journalists praised Lord Methuen and some condemned him as a blunderer. Some stood for his method of conducting a battle, using the conventional frontal attack and depending on great numbers of men and guns to force a conclusion, regardless of loss of life, and others stated bitterly that this was not a European war where both sides had a certain code of conduct. This was an alien kind of fighting which the British would do well to emulate, if they hoped to beat the skirmishing Boers.

The Boers had short, sturdy horses, used to working over rough terrain. They had accurate Mauser rifles and no cumbersome bayonets. They fought, retreated to deep trenches where their guns were hidden, attacking again and again, out-flanking and taking the British by surprise while using fewer men and arms. Some dismissed the Boers as cowards because they ran from a bayonet charge, but at least they stayed alive to fight again, unlike the hundreds of men mown down at the Modder by those will-o'-the-wisps.

'I'm cold,' grumbled Clare and Jane took them home, but she was deeply troubled. Walter seemed so far away and she knew that she would not see him again soon. She sliced the cold goose and made more apple sauce, re-heated the Christmas puddings, and cooked potatoes. She laid the table and suddenly, there was nothing to do until the other children came home. She sat fingering her new brooch for comfort.

'Dreaming, gal?'

Jane startled. 'Mr Walmsley!' she said.

Sam looked at the scattered newspapers and the table ready for dinner. – She can't be on her feet all the time, he thought, and it must be bad when she waits for the children to come in and has time to think.

'I hoped you'd ask me to have a glass of that Sherry wine,' he said. 'Unless you drank it all last night?'

Jane smiled, and warmth crept back. 'I can't afford to be tipsy at this time of day,' she said. She fetched glasses and poured out the wine. 'It was very kind of you.'

Sam held up his glass to the light. He sipped and looked up. 'To Walter and a speedy return,' he said. Jane drank solemnly. 'The war can't last forever, Jane, and he'll walk in that door and expect everything as he left it.' His voice, though light, held a plea.

'I do know it, Mr Walmsley,' she said. 'I wondered if...' she began but Sam interrupted her.

'Why don't you call me Sam? Walter does, all my friends do and after all, I've always called you Jane.'

'I don't know. People are strange. They don't believe in friendship between a man and a woman. If I call you Sam, some will think I'm being too familiar.'

Sam gave a short laugh. 'They've been dropping hints to you too, have they?' Jane raised startled brown eyes that were suddenly huge and she put a hand to the brooch as if it was a talisman. 'Oh, yes, there have been a few winks and nods and speculation. It's best you know, Jane. The fact that I'm old enough to be your father, or well, not quite, but old enough for all that, doesn't count. They'll hint and watch and make it hard for you if you give them half a chance. Call me Sam and take it for granted that they know that you and Walter are equally my friends and business associates, but be careful. Not with me! I wouldn't hurt a hair of your head but there's plenty of vinegar faces who think a pretty woman without a man is fair game.'

'How could anyone think that?'

'Even if they didn't believe it, they'd try to make something to gossip over. At worst, it could harm you, at best, annoy and embarrass you. I promised Walter I'd protect you as best I could from any who forced themselves on you, Jane, but the trouble is that your pretty face and that kind heart of yourn might make some think they can take liberties. A friendly smile from a lovely woman is taken as a sign of encouragement. Understand me, Jane. You are a very lovely woman.'

'But what can I do, Sam?' she said unhappily. 'I can't go through life with a frown on my face or all buttoned-up like Annie Cooper, it's not my nature. I have the children here most of the time when I'm not in the shop, so I can't see where gossip could start. People like Annie are the same about everyone and it doesn't worry me!'

'They go back to school, and you'll be on your own. The barges will be up the river with the coal and timber after the thaw, and they are a rough crowd. They mean no harm but they lack moral standards.'

Jane laughed. 'If you're worrying about the men from the barges, you've no need. They would never harm me. I've never heard one of them say a word out of turn in the shop or to me. Walter has been good to one or two of them, the Dutch families who depend on us for fruit and vegetables while they are on the Medina and the men are busy on the quay. I save some goose-grease for one family who have a child with a weak chest and I've often bound up cuts for them.' Her eyes sparkled, all uneasiness gone. 'If I get into trouble, I'll hang a red flag from the top window and you'll see it from the warehouse.'

Sam relaxed. 'That would really set the tongues wagging. They'd swear we exchanged messages.'

'Stay and have some dinner, Sam. The children are coming down the road and it's all ready. Here, get some cider from next door.' She handed him a jug.

'Mother! Why didn't you stay?'

'Whisht! I've never heard such noise. You know I'm frightened of seeing the fox torn.'

'You should have stayed. We saw the Hunt double back and we watched from the ridge when it came round from Arreton to Cross Lanes. Bert Cooper came a cropper by the copse.'

'That's not funny. It's cruel to laugh at someone's misfortune,' said Jane severely, bending her head over the dish of goose to hide her smiling face.

'But it *was* funny,' said Jack. 'We all saw it, and he came off the horse and the horse bolted. Mr Cooper had to walk home.'

'Was the horse hurt?'

'No, it ran off into the wood after jumping a thorn hedge and stayed there, grazing. Mr Cooper could have found him easily if he wasn't so angry and muddy,' said Sidney. The children giggled.

'Where's the horse now?' said Sam, from the doorway. He put the cider jug on the table.

Sidney smiled. 'When he'd gone, we took a handful of carrots from the barn there and called him. Satan came like a lamb and ate all the carrots. He let me take the reins and we led him home. He was quite quiet, but his coat was in a bit of a lather so we thought he ought to be under cover.'

Sam laughed. 'Some people have useful children,' he said. 'So you took him back to Bert?'

'We tried to take him to the brickyard stable but the yard was bolted with a bar across the gate, so we brought him here and Edward took him to our stable to Blackie's old stall. He was a bit hot so Edward said he'd be late for dinner as he must give him a rub down. He said he'll leave him to cool off under a blanket.'

'Edward's coming now,' said Janey.

'Satan isn't hurt,' said Edward, 'but he's a bit upset. Father would have taken him on a halter down through the fields with Bess for company but I couldn't manage them both and Satan *is* Mr Cooper's horse so I thought to ask him first.'

'You did very well,' said Sam. 'I'd have done the same, but Bert's an awkward cuss. He might even try to blame you if he can't find his horse, thinking you played a trick on him. The last thing he would consider is the horse if his pride is shaken. He'll be in the devil of a temper, especially if you saw him ditched. I think it better if I tell him.'

'But your dinner, Sam!'

'I'll be back directly. I'll catch him at home if he's not at the brickyard. He'll have gone to change out of his things, I shouldn't wonder. Keep my bit of dinner as I don't think Annie will ask me to stay!'

Sam followed the lane to Pan Mill. He passed by the Shoulder of Mutton, and as he rounded the bend, Bert Cooper came out of the saloon bar there and swayed with glassy deliberation towards the bridge, having taken all the comfort he could hold. Sam missed him by a minute.

Jane served the family and put a dish of vegetables to keep hot for Sam. It was a relief to have him near to take over a situation that she wouldn't want to face. She had a feeling that Sam knew just how much she disliked the Coopers and was doing his best to spare her from meeting Bert more than necessary. Since the day in the grocer's shop when Annie had been rude, Jane had avoided meeting them and sent notes to Bert rather than go to the brickyard to see him.

Dan was a useful go-between and took Annie's weekly order of fish and vegetables and the duck eggs that Annie used as they were cheaper than hens' eggs.

A banging on the outer door made Jane hurry to open it, thinking it was Sam again, but as she opened the door between the living room and the passage to the shop, the outer door burst open in spite of the 'Closed' sign outside. Bert Cooper lurched into the shop and leaned on the counter for support. His face was red and his eyes angry and bloodshot as a ferret's. He took up one of the heavy iron weights from the counter where they were stacked in a neat column and pushed the metal scales until they swayed dangerously. As he spoke, he punctuated his words with a series of blows on the counter, the metal of the weight making deep dents in the wooden surface. 'SHOP!' he called. 'SHOP! SHOP! SHOP!'

Jane walked behind the counter and fixed him with an icy stare. – Holy Mother, he's as drunk as a lord! she thought. 'And what might you be wanting? What is so urgent that calls for all that noise? Did you not read the sign? Am I never to have a meal in peace with my children?'

Bert tried to stand up straight, with all the laborious dignity of the very intoxicated. 'I've lost me horse,' he said with pathos. 'Lost me horse. It's gorn.'

'And do you think I keep horses under the counter? I know you lost your horse, but it's quite safe and you can collect it when you're sober.'

Bert stared. 'How did you know? Where is it? What have you done with him?'

Jane tried to smile. 'It's all right, Bert. It's safe, quite safe. He was found and put somewhere safe to cool off.'

He attacked the counter again. 'I know what happened!' He glared at her. 'It's those children of yourn. They stole my horse. I saw them there, sly as foxes. They laughed when I took a tumble. Wait until a man's back's turned and steal his horse.' He leaned over the counter, confidentially. 'There's a law in this land and there's a law in the Good Book, too. Thou Shalt Not Steal, it says. That means your children. They've broke the law.'

'Don't be foolish, man, if it hadn't been for my children, the horse would be in a bad way by now.'

'So they *did* take him! I knew it. I said to myself, "Bert," I said, "those children are there without a father and no one to tell them right from wrong. No one to punish them if they steal." They need a dose of the strap, all the lot of them. They should be taken away and taught that it's a sin to steal. They need a strong hand, with a strap in it!' he leaned further over. 'Do you know what I'll do? I'm going up to Fairlee and tell the Constable that you keep a den of thieves.' His voice was full of maudlin reforming zeal.

'Listen, Bert. Please listen to me,' said Jane.

'They'll preach about them in the pulpits,' he said. Jane didn't know if she was frightened or merely very angry and disgusted.

'Bert! Now listen, will you?' she said. He was a heavily built, coarse-faced man at the best of times, unattractive to a woman like Jane who commanded the respect and admiration of most men, but now, rapidly sinking into a state of tearful introspection, he was repulsive. His breath reminded her of the one time that Walter had come home like this, and had forced her into bed with no tenderness, not a word of consideration and just an act of violent release, that left her feeling sick and Walter suddenly sober and ashamed.

Jane forced herself to speak normally. 'It's all right, Bert. Don't you worry, now. There's nothing wrong. The horse was hot and frightened.' He stared at her and she knew that he was taking in nothing. She leaned forward, in spite of her revulsion and her breath came sharply as she prepared for long explanations and argument. If only someone would come into the shop, but most people took notice of the sign that the shop was closed and there would be no casual customer to rescue her.

'The horse is warm and dry in Blackie's old stall. The boys tried to find you but you weren't in the brickyard. You know how Walter trained them to care for horses?' She smiled. 'Come now, Bert, they were helping you as a friend, and helping the poor beast who didn't know if it was Sunday or Tuesday week!'

'What have they done to him?' he asked, thickly.

'I'm telling you,' she said. 'He's in the stable. Now you go home and take a rest and come to collect him later when you've both cooled off.'

'He's not my horse, that's the trouble,' he said angrily. 'I want to know what those boys have done to him.'

'They haven't done *anything* to him. They've saved him from

93

getting tangled up in the brambles in the copse and they've done what many a man wouldn't have the sense to do.' Her brown eyes glowed with anger and the loose hair from her bun began to curl over her cheeks as she nodded her head to make her words clearer. A thought made her lips twitch. 'He isn't *yours*? You've *sold* him, Bert Cooper!'

'I said I'd ride him today and deliver him after the Hunt.'

'So Mr Webster bought him after all.' Jane laughed. 'No wonder you were worried. I suppose you've already taken his money?'

Bert nodded. He had forgotten his sense of outrage and why he was there in the shop with Jane Darwen. Somehow it had sunk in that Satan was safe and now his gaze was fixed on the woman on the other side of the counter, leaning across to impress him with the truth, her breath coming quickly and her face flushed with concern. He put a hand out to take one of hers. Normally, he was afraid of her and had never dared do more than pass the time of day and to discuss business matters, but now, alone with her in the dim shop, his inhibitions dulled with spirits and he felt bold.

'You're a very pretty woman, Jane.' His voice was even more slurred as the spirits reduced him to the man that Jane had long suspected him to be under the well-cut clothes and the business acumen. 'Very pretty. Too pretty to leave behind. What's a woman like you doing without a man to look after you? Why did Walt go away when he had a woman like you to cuddle up to?' She tried to pull away but he caught at her dress and his hand was hot and hard on her breast, pulling her to the end of the counter where he could be closer.

Jane tugged back and felt the fabric splitting slightly. – It's my second best! she thought indignantly. If she pulled back more, she would have one ruined bodice and who knew what would happen if she was exposed to those shifty eyes, those fumbling, strong hands? So, ever practical in any crisis, Jane relaxed slightly but reached under the counter with her free hand for one of the wooden skewers, split at one end to take the price cards and pointed at the other. Her Irish temper was getting up and under it, she was very scared. Drunken breath fanned her cheek and his moist lips touched her ear, as she brought the wooden spike on to the back of his hand.

Bert howled with pain and rage and released her. He sucked his hand and glared at her as she shrank back behind the counter. – Holy Mary! she thought. There's no way out but where he is. She looked round for some sort of weapon and retreated to the boxes of stored fruit. She held an orange in each hand and prayed for help. She saw the hard eyes and the loose mouth as Bert slowly walked round the counter towards her. He picked up the heaviest of the weights on the counter and passed it from one hand to the other as if testing it for efficiency. He stood for a moment, half-smiling as if he would enjoy his revenge for this glancing injury and all the other, small snubs he had endured in the past from the wife of the one man he envied ... for his easy manner, his looks and above all for the making of eight children with this lovely body.

He raised his arm and threw the weight, just as a shaft of light came across the counter as the outer door opened. Jane threw herself against the wall and the weight missed her by a fraction and chipped the marble slab in the window, losing itself in the mackerel and ice.

Jane opened her eyes in time to see Bert flat on his back, with Sam Walmsley standing over him, his boot raised to kick him, and a look of such fury on his face that Jane was more frightened than she had been of Bert.

'No Sam,' she said, with icy calm. 'He isn't worth it.' She went to him and forced him to look at her. 'No Sam. No more, but thank God you came. I thought he'd kill me.'

Sam jerked the man to his feet. Bert shook his head and put a hand to his jaw. He looked decidedly more sober, but unsteady. Sam took a deep breath and Jane knew that the worst was over. She watched him take the man by the front of his shirt and push him against the wall. Bert cringed as he was shaken hard.

'Now, I think you have an apology to make to the lady,' said Sam, softly. Bert said nothing, so Sam knocked his head against the wall.

'Sam!' whispered Jane. 'Careful Sam, I want no trouble.'

'Apologise,' said Sam patiently. 'Or I'll frog-march you up to the Station and charge you with assault and battery.' He accompanied his words with a casual but hard slap to the man's cheek. '*Well?*'

'I didn't mean to hurt you.' Bert glanced at Jane with a hint of genuine regret as he sobered. 'It was the drink in me. I never could hold my drink without it making me want to pick a fight or to ...' he looked away. 'I'm sorry, I *am* sorry.' The self-pitying tears coursed down and his nose began to run. 'It was the horse, you see. I sold him and I thought I'd have to give the money back.' He began to beg her pardon over and over again.

'Please get him out of here,' said Jane, faint with disgust.

'We'll take the horse back,' grinned Sam. 'It's a fair walk to the Websters. A walk is just what this one needs.' He pushed Bert out into the street and steered him in the direction of the stable. Jane stood in the doorway until they crossed the bridge then she went to clear away the dinner things.

So she missed the sight of Bert Cooper walking behind the horse that Sam was riding; a Bert with shuffling feet and an eye that promised to be all the colours of the rainbow the next day. She missed the twitch of lace curtains as the little procession went up Church Litten and out to the stable near Oyster Shell Cottages. By dinner-time the next day, everyone in Newport knew that Bert Cooper had been dead drunk after the Hunt and that Sam Walmsley had given him a black eye.

In the grocer's shop, there was endless speculation and Mr Foster came second-best in the news interest. 'I can't think what happened, can you, Mrs Darwen?' said Peter Fry's wife.

'Men do funny things when they take too much,' said Jane and brought some good smoked bacon to boil. Sam liked cold ham with some of her pickled onions, and the dear man deserved a good dinner once in a while now his wife was an invalid.

In the Wheatsheaf, there were hints and questions, but neither of the men would be drawn. Bert was silent from shame and fear that Jane would write to Walter and tell him about it and Walter would be back from the war some time with this boiling up inside him.

Sam said nothing and knew that the war news would veil the small local scandal as soon as the news was bad again, and he had no intention of subjecting Jane to more embarrassment, because of his deep respect for her, and his love.

'All right, gal?' he said, from the shop door the next day.

'Yes, thank you Sam,' said Jane. 'I wrote to Walter and told him about the Meet and what the Master said about him.' They looked at each other. 'It was good to have something that would interest him, as I could think of nothing more of importance.'

'No good writing for the sake of it,' said Sam. 'And you aren't the one to worry him about trifles that we can sort out.'

'That's what I thought,' she said, and smiled. 'You didn't have your dinner, Sam. Come in tomorrow when the children are home.'

Chapter 8

Jane Darwen watched the local odd-job man pass with his barrow of ladders and paint pots and saw him look at the shabby paint on the shutters of the shop on Coppins Bridge. He went on and she flaked off a thin layer of green with her fingernail and wondered if she should ask Mr Damer to let her know what he would charge to freshen the woodwork. Walter hadn't bothered to have the place painted for years and it irritated Jane to see the building lacking care.

She braced herself to make another decision. There was no sign of an end to the war and letters from Walter were few and unsatisfactory. She had hoped to hear about the war in greater detail, but he'd never been much of a writer and all that his letters contained were references to the horses and the terrible suffering of them when wounded. Of the men he said little, although he had written after the disaster at Magersfontein, when he'd seen men of the Highland Regiment and the Gordons mown down, after the British had tried a frontal attack on the Boer defences.

He wrote also of a treachery of Boers who hoisted a white flag over a house when the Seaforth Highlanders went through their lines, and once the Seaforths had passed the house, respecting the flag of truce and submission, the Boers opened fire from the rear, thinking that all the Scots had gone through the gap and they could be picked off from the back.

'That was a mistake,' wrote Walter. 'The Highlanders were mad for revenge. They stormed the house and bayoneted every Boer inside.'

Jane felt sick as she read it. Walter wasn't a man to hate deeply or for long and to have written this showed how angry and moved he had been. Since then, he'd written of the horses, the heat and the flies in an African summer.

Jane wrote when she could, but knew that he must find her letters as limited as his were to her, for by the time each one received mail, the news was stale. In time, Jane learned more from the *County Press* than from his front-line, but late, messages.

She tried to trace the events, intelligently, and read accounts of the fighting at Venter's Spruit and the capture of Spion Kop. She rejoiced at each victory and mourned for the dead, all the dead who had no personal contact with her and her family, and she prayed each night that Walter would survive and come home again. The place names meant nothing to her and the children knew more about the geography of the war and the battlefields than she did. Edward had a large map on which he marked each battle.

Mr Foster had all his bulletins written on the backs of invoices which he stored on a spike hanging from a beam in the shop. To look up what happened at the retreat at Tugela, he had to climb through dozens of sheets of paper and began to wish he'd never started his collection. Far from being good for trade, he now found that it wasted serving time. When a customer came in and said, 'Have you a minute, Mr Foster?' he groaned inwardly, trying desperately to recall on which piece of curling paper he had scribbled the account of the skirmish at Rhodes Drift or the date when the Boers wrecked the bridges on the Modder.

'Do you have the Casualty List of the twelfth of last month?' someone asked. Mr Foster looked at the shopful of customers and was tempted to say he had lost it, and in any case had no time for more information that day.

'You give a wonderful service,' said Dr Barnes, who walked straight to the counter to be served before everyone. 'I'll have my special tobacco, please, Mr Foster.'

'I'll be with you as soon as I serve the Doctor,' he said, trying to sound helpful.

The doctor drew him to one side. 'We, that is certain civic figures, had a meeting last night and although it isn't settled and you mustn't take it as gospel until you have formal notice, we consider that in view of your services to the town, there is every likelihood of you being put up for the Council.' The doctor smiled. 'For your unique service and humanity to the less well-educated of the community.'

98

Mr Foster handed him the tobacco in a dream. It was the fulfilment of all his hopes, to be a councillor, to walk with the gentry to the Town Hall and to be there when Royalty came. He might even be recognised by people like the Seelys at Mottistone Manor and the titled vicar of the church at Osborne!

'Now what was it you wanted to know, my dear?' he asked when the doctor was gone. He already felt as if he stood behind the Union Jack, wearing his dark suit and gold watch chain and accepted that the inconvenience would be his proud cross to bear, so he continued to collect news and laboriously to copy it into exercise books as the invoices became crumpled and the writing faded. Caught in the trap of his own business acumen, he was doomed to waste precious selling time, telling yet again 'how the Boers picked off two hundred and ninety of our best troops as they followed Methuen's order to make the frontal attack on Magersfontein'.

However, he now derived satisfaction from his task and warmed to his own rhetoric. 'They have better rifles, Ma'am,' he'd say. 'They call them Mauser rifles and the blackguards fire and run away without giving our fellows a chance to retaliate.' He smiled at the admiring faces. 'Now if I was in command, I'd make sure that our boys had the same guns instead of the heavy guns they have on issue.'

Maudie Dove thought he was wonderful. 'Would you give one to my Ben, Mr Foster?' she said.

He waved a hand modestly, and shrugged. 'If only I could, my dear. I know what ought to be done – if I had my way, there'd be a different tale, I can tell you. That'll be tuppence and the borax will be in tomorrow, Yes, if I had my way, it would be very different.'

Maudie gathered up her groceries and left, reluctantly. Ben's name was not on the Casualty Lists after the Relief of Kimberley and she now took pride in the fact that he had been in the fighting that led to the defeat of Cronje, the famous and skilful Boer commander. She had seen the picture of Cronje in the *Daily Mail*, following his surrender before he embarked for St Helena and exile, and behind him in the crowds of British Tommies in khaki, were the rag-tag of defeated Boers. Maudie was convinced that one of the British faces was Ben, and she kept the photograph and haunted Mr Foster's shop, buying groceries she couldn't afford just to hear him tell yet again the stories she wanted to hear, of the flood of events that led to Cronje's capture.

Maudie found that more women talked to her now that she took more trouble over her cleanliness and the health of Lucy, who trailed behind her from shop to shop, the scar on her throat faint and her long legs plump with all the fresh fruit and fish that Jane gave them.

'Cronje's not like I thought,' Maudie told anyone who would listen. 'He's just a middle-aged man with a beard. Not good-looking or out of the ordinary. Just look at his suit and that wide hat! He's like any other man, and have you seen his wife? She's a mess, but I suppose any woman would look like that if her husband was beaten. My Ben was there, you know, standing quite close to them in the picture.'

The Casualty Lists were Jane's greatest concern. She dreaded hearing familiar names mentioned far more than she dreaded the news of battles. She was worried when news of the outbreak of typhoid fever came from Bloemfontein and the scurvy caused by lack of food in the camps. She longed to take them food and comforts and regarded her own well-fed children with a mixture of pride and guilt. The shop was doing well, she made a fair amount of pin-money from the sale of home-made preserves and pickles and batches of potato pies.

It would be a tonic to see the old shop looking spruce. It was almost as satisfying as having new clothes, so she gave the order for the shop to be re-painted and as the sun shone with more conviction, she knew it was time for spring cleaning.

Clare shook the carpet on the clothes line with more resentment than enthusiasm. 'Mother, why do we have to work so hard? Mrs Cooper had Dan to do all this heavy work. Why can't he do ours?'

'Dan helps us with the horses and the brickyard and I can't ask him to do any more,' said Jane. 'He's a good man and Annie Cooper puts on him far too much.'

'What about us?' said Clare.

'You live here,' said Jane shortly. 'Your father expects everyone to help and I'm not having this place turned into a pigsty because I have a lazy daughter.' She smiled. 'We all have to do our share, Clare. Now tie your head up in a duster and put a sack apron over your dress. That carpet needs a really good beating. It's full of dust.'

Janey attacked bedroom rugs with a wicker carpet beater, sending clouds of dust billowing up to hang on the sunbeams. Jack reached into the corners of the outhouse with a long-handled brush, bringing down the winter harvest of cobwebs. Edward carried more rugs into the yard and Clare groaned. 'Do we have to do *everything* today? The dust makes me sneeze.'

Lizzie wiped a strand of hair from her eyes with a soapy hand. 'I hate spring cleaning,' she said. Rainbow lights danced in the water as she swished bubbles to wash the china. She put the clean pieces to drain on the slate shelf outside the back door. China was washed twice a year and returned to the cabinet to wait for the next washing. Some was never used, but most was brought out for Christmas and used once before joining the rest until the spring cleaning.

Jane loved her cabinet of china and regretted that the only space for it was in a dark corner by the pantry door. It really took up useful room, but Jane wouldn't hear of parting with it. 'The girls will want a bit of good china when they marry,' she said, but Lizzie wished that every piece would break!

The warm spell came suddenly, and the sunlight showed up every dingy crack. The pampas grass and the limp leaves of the castor oil plants were clogged with dust from the grime of winter fires and Jane was glad that it was Saturday and the children were home to help. Buckets of strong soda water, fierce enough to remove the skin, waited for the boys to use on the walls and ceiling of the outhouse. The boiler had an extra scrub and the bars underneath had a coat of blacklead. The floor gleamed wet and fresh and for once, the smell of fish was banished through the open window.

Jane believed that anything that smelled fresh must be healthy and that clean air was purifying. Not for her the sealed-up rooms of her neighbours. Even in cold weather, she aired rooms once a day or she was conscious of the smell of animals and sweat and the reek of soot.

The water was hot in the tub and Jane rolled up her sleeves and plunged the linen valances from the beds into the soapy water. She briskly pounded them with the dolly and rubbed them vigorously up and down the washboard, shooting rivulets of dirty water back into the soap solution. When she was satisfied, she eased them out into a two-handled tub and the boys carried them to the outhouse where they boiled the linen in the scoured copper. 'Will you add the blue?' she called to Sidney, knowing that he enjoyed this.

101

He swished the bag of washing blue into the clear, cold water and waited while his mother rinsed the now snowy linen. He did his job slowly, fascinated by the swirls of dark blue that made pictures, like waves on the shore, ebbing and flowing as he added more blue. He stirred gently and the dark streaks faded, leaving a bath full of bright blue water like Cowes under a blue sky.

He stood by the heavy mangle which was kept in the yard under a tarpaulin, its grimy bucket under the outlet. Sidney looked forward to turning the handle and seeing the water flow down the wooden shute into the bucket. He traced the pattern in the wrought-iron stand but didn't touch the heavy wooden rollers. Clare had a crushed finger end, ever since her finger had been caught between the rollers. She'd been playing with Lizzie, who wanted to press her handkerchief. Clare had pushed the small square of linen towards the rollers to start it off and Lizzie had turned the handle too soon. The finger would never grow straight again with a perfect nail and since then, the handle had been tied up unless Jane was there to see what was happening.

The first valance was folded and lowered into the blue water. The effect of the yellow soap was counteracted by the blue and Jane sighed with satisfaction and exertion. She had starch waiting, made from mixing knobbly pieces of starch with borax and cold water, and adding boiling water to the smooth white paste, until it turned thick and blue-grey. She diluted it, adding cold water until it 'looked right'.

The valances needed thick starch to make them very stiff and Jane soaked them thoroughly, stacking them ready to hang on the clothes line as soon as dust from the carpet beating had subsided. Clare helped to put the china back in the cabinet and the boys swilled the path with the used and now filthy soda water, brushing it away into the drain with the stiff yard broom.

Emily sat in the shop to take her turn at the counter. She knitted as she waited for customers and enjoyed the feeling of responsibility. She enjoyed stacking the weights and wondered who had made the deep dents in the wooden counter. It must have been done with one of the round weights and she hoped she wouldn't be blamed for it, even though she knew the marks had been there since sometime after Christmas.

She took a rest from knitting and made paper pokes from newspaper to hold vegetables, then prised off the glossy brown dates from the new block behind the counter, on a shelf with Sidney's label and the long-handled fork. Two of her friends came in for potatoes and Emily took a quick peep in to the back room to make sure that it was empty, before slipping a handful of dates to each child. They wrapped the sticky fruit in handkerchiefs and stuffed them inside the leg elastic of their bloomers and went off, giggling.

Smells of washing and dust, of a suet pudding boiling and beef broth simmering on the hob came from the back room. Customers recognised it as the Spring Cleaning Smell, one to be repeated in every well-ordered house in the town. It was a smell to remain in the memory, to bring a jolt to the senses whenever a pudding was boiled, conjuring up dust on sunbeams and the warmth of childhood.

Edward dragged the last rug from the line. He spread it on clean flagstones and Sidney sprinkled it with wet tea leaves that had been kept in a huge old bathtub over the winter months, ready for the carpet cleaning. Jack gave it a final sweep, removing surface dust and the leaves in a muddy tilth that was flushed down the drain.

Upstairs, Janey swept the bare boards in readiness for the cleaned carpets and rugs and before dinner, the beds were back in their places, denuded without their modest valances and with the cases and boxes stored under the beds, exposed to view.

'I'm hungry,' said Jack, rubbing his red hands on a damp towel.

'You've all done well,' said Jane. 'We'll shut up shop and have dinner now.' She laughed with an uplift of spirits. The long morning had been hard work but fun with the children helping and being able to get on, knowing that someone would serve in the shop. When Walter was there, he made difficulties, hating the upheaval but doing little to help and wanting stupid minor things done that could wait until another day.

She ladled out the thick broth and watched the pink cheeks bending over the steaming bowls. Even dinner was better today than on other spring cleaning days, as Walter would come back late and expect everyone to wait for him, when the children were famished. She felt a pang of guilt. It was wicked to be glad that he was away, just for the morning, and she glanced up at his picture on the wall to remind herself that he was in her thoughts all the time.

'May we do the boxes?' said Clare after the last dish was put away and the valances were on the clothes line in the now clear air.

'You don't want to look at a lot of old clothes,' said Jane, but her

103

eyes sparkled as she knew that this was what the girls had looked forward to all the morning. 'Oh, well, we should turn them out to see if the moths have been busy.'

One by one, the boxes were brought down to the fireside and opened to examine all the long-lost treasures stored away from last year, and the fine clothes that were kept for special occasions. Jane heated the flat irons and put a thick towel on the end of the table and watched as each box was opened, giving her decision on what should be kept, what could be altered for a member of the family and what was outgrown and could be given away. Grubby marks were sponged with vinegar and water or ammonia and the seams and collars, crumpled after the long seclusion, were ironed.

Clare draped herself in Jane's best shawl, admiring the heavy fringing and the delicate embroidery on the cream silk. There was a peacock and a garland of flowers, with sprigs of roses in the corners. Jane examined it with care. No mildew and the colours hadn't faded. 'Why don't you wear it, Mother?' asked Clare. 'I'd wear it all the time if it was mine.'

'I do wear it,' said Jane. She sighed. 'I'll wear it when your father comes home.' She took it from Clare and folded it carefully, putting tissue paper between the folds. She had worn it twice. Once when Walter had given it to her, soon after they met, and once when Walter took her to Cowes in the trap to see the foreign ships during Cowes Week.

Emily found her favourite toy, a tiny chest of drawers with golden dragons writhing on the shiny black paper mâché. The drawers were filled with coarse sawdust to absorb the damp and to keep the contents from tarnishing. It was like the grape tubs that came from the warehouse, in which layers of grapes were protected in depths of sawdust or powdered cork. The turquoise ring and the eternity ring studded with marcasite looked incongruous on Emily's small fingers, still red from serving fish and potatoes, but she loved them, holding them up to the light to make the stones glisten.

Clare avoided rings and often hid her maimed finger in her pocket when there was company, but she pinned a butterfly brooch to her hair and Janey ran a long string of smooth amber beads through her fingers. Jane bustled in and out of the shop, ironed valances and did a dozen jobs, but was persuaded to put on jet earrings and a choker collar of paste diamonds and the 'Mother' brooch.

With the lightness of spring, the aura of expectation and the knowledge of work well done, it was easy to be more optimistic. Jane found that she could think of Walter without the dull heartache, and no longer wished to go to him, together with the ladies who flocked out on every available boat, intent on giving the soldiers nursing care and comfort. She'd been envious of the titled ladies when they left for Africa, full of a sense of adventure. It was easy for them to leave their children with nannies and their homes to be cared for by servants.

As for the other women who went overseas, Jane had a shrewd suspicion that they were no better than they ought to be! She'd heard of camp-followers. Living in a garrison town, it was impossible not to know about the girls who haunted the Barracks, knowing exactly when each pay parade took place, and draining some soldiers of their pitiful remittance.

Jane fingered a cameo brooch which had belonged to her mother. It was odd that she should be thinking of her and not of Walter. She shook out her wedding dress from the box that was always left until last. The girls gathered round, delighted as usual. Janey smoothed the hand-tucked bodice and the neckline trimmed with real lace on a stiffened band.

'What a tiny waist you had, Mother,' said Lizzie. 'Do you think I'll have a waist like that?' She held in her stomach.

'Of course,' said Jane. 'You'll all be beautiful ladies.' She held the dress in front of her and looked down at it, marvelling at the slender hour-glass figure she once had before eight pregnancies. She smoothed the folds of the skirt and straightened the lovers' knots of ribbon on the front panel. A lifetime of experience had passed since she wore it and she would never wear it again. Did Walter know that she kept it? By the time the girls brought down the boxes, he was usually away to the stables or the farm, anywhere to get away from the female scene. She knew that she would never part with it. Perhaps one day, one of the girls might want it. She saw Emily's plump hands, heavy with rings. The girls had a long way to go before they married. She sighed. They would need many more dresses, many more clothes before they need look for wedding gowns.

'Pretty as the day you wore it!' Jane let the dress slip away and Janey caught it before it reached the floor.

'Archie! You gave me a fright.'

'I saw the notice, but the door was on the jar so I came in.'

'This is for the ladies,' said Clare with her nose in the air. The boys had followed Walter's tradition and were out.

'I can see that,' said Archie. 'I met the boys on their way to Aaron and they told me you'd been slaving all the morning, but I don't believe it. Here you are, all dolled up in such finery!'

Clare picked up a black shawl and put it round her shoulders, laughing, and the other girls showed him the necklaces and beads, but Jane felt uneasy and shy with this man she had known ever since she came to the Island. His eyes showed admiration and something she sadly lacked in her life now. She removed the jet earrings and the sparkling collar, the cameo brooch and the bracelet of elephant hair, but kept the brooch given her by the children, as if it was a label that made her status clear. She was a mother, left with her children while her husband was away. That and no more to any man, even Archie whom she loved as a friend and cousin.

'Ladies offer gentlemen tea when they call,' said Jane, trying to be as lighthearted as before. 'You'll have a cup? The kettle's ready.'

Archie shook his head. 'Shouldn't be here by rights. Amy wanted something from Shide, so I popped in, to take the milk if you have any.'

'How is little Rose?'

'Tired, as usual,' he said, frowning. 'How did we make a weakly child like her, Jane, when you have seven who never seem to have anything wrong?'

'I lost one,' said Jane, quietly.

'That's not the same.' Archie watched Janey make tea, her face flushed and her mouth tight with concentration as she lifted the heavy iron kettle. 'And Rose is such a child. Your brood are grown-up and a blessing.'

'Rose is sick, so she hasn't had a chance,' said Jane. 'And there's nothing like having to do things to make a child grow up fast. I couldn't manage if they didn't do more than is fair for any child to do, Archie, but they are very good,' she admitted.

He stood at the door of the shop with the lidded can of milk. 'You look better now than when you wore that dress, Jane. Better and prettier and more of a woman a man could love.'

'Sure, I've had enough loving to last a lifetime,' she said, wrapping up the fish she was sending for Amy. 'Seven mouths to feed are enough for any couple,' she said.

'Not for me,' he muttered bitterly. 'If I had you, Jane, I'd have sons and warmth.'

She put a hand on his arm. 'No, Archie, my dear. Not you, nor Walter, nor any man can have that from me, now.' She pushed the parcel into his other hand. 'Now be gone! I have work to do, even if my favourite cousin has time to spare.' She glanced at him and he saw the plea in her eyes. 'We talk a lot of nonsense, at times.'

'I doubt it,' he said, 'but I never talk of you to Amy.' He bent to kiss her cheek and they were cousins by marriage with no hint of wanting.

Jane went back to the girls feeling sad. Poor Archie, to have no boy to carry on the farm. She sorted skirts for altering and the boxes went back under the beds for another long sleep.

'What can we do tomorrow, Mother?' said Lizzie, knowing that after the spring cleaning, they had a treat.

'We'll walk to Carisbrooke in the morning.'

'Can I tell the boys when they come in?' said Clare. 'I shall wear my new gloves and scarf and take a walking stick.'

It had been a long time since Jane had the energy to walk up to Carisbrooke Castle and the family were delighted. She felt released after the cleaning and the sun made her want to go out into the fresh air. The look in Archie's eyes was a tonic she wouldn't admit to, but which left a smile lingering long after he left.

'Will the Queen be there?' said Edward when the boys heard the news.

'Archie said the Queen is at Osborne as her standard is flying. If the weather is set like this for a day or so, she'll most likely go up to the Castle,' said Jane.

'Can we pick primroses?' said Lizzie.

'We'll go to the Castle Chapel in the morning, pick primroses and come back for a late dinner,' said Jane. She glanced at the clear sky and wanted to climb high and to gaze into distances, and next day, when the children finished all the chores early, she knew that she must keep her promise. The air was still cold and Jane put on her dark violet coat trimmed with fur. She buttoned her boots and pinned a bunch of artificial flowers to the brim of her dark green hat.

The long walk to the Castle passed quickly. They went through the town and up onto the raised Mall with its handsome houses behind tall iron railings. Some of the houses already had trim front lawns and trailing rambler roses at the base of new trellis-work. Infant privet hedges put out new shoots and the Mall was broad and level for walking, the paving clean as no wheeled traffic or horses were allowed to use it. Sidney found a stick and dragged it along the railings, making a satisfying staccato drumming sound.

Jane knew that this was not the way for a young man to behave on a Sunday morning, but she walked on and said nothing, seeing no harm in it. They walked through the shrubbery and over the path along the moat. Fields of young wheat covered with tender green partly obscured the brown earth, stretching over the hill in a voluptuous curve. Sheep grazed in the moat, birds shrilled a welcome and Jane was young again. Spring must be a new beginning in many ways. Next year, she would walk to the castle with Walter and they would laugh at the lost months.

The huge oaken gates to the Castle yard were open. The long sweep of shining cobbles led to the Chapel and Jane paused to give her family a hasty inspection. 'Straighten your tie, Sidney,' she said. She tweaked Jack's sailor hat to a more reverent angle and the girls put their gloves on again and made sure their boots were laced evenly.

This was the first time that Jane had visted the Chapel without Walter. The deep porch was dark and chilly after the sunshine and Jane blinked in the gloom. Two men stood by the entrance and she stopped. Were they visitors, too, or could they be the Queen's equerries? The Queen was coming to the service! Suddenly, Jane was confused by her boldness and ashamed to think she dared to come here. Her heart beat fast with panic, but one of the equerries saw her as she turned away.

He caught up with her. 'Please go in, Madam. Take your places if you wish to attend Divine Service.' He smiled and Jane thought he looked kind like Sam. 'Her Majesty prefers to have a congregation at the service,' he said. 'You are welcome to sit over there.'

They were shown to seats just behind the Royal pews. Jane frowned at the boys to make sure they would behave and then sat with a very straight back, her feet firmly together and her hands on her lap.

'Is she coming?' asked Sidney in a penetrating whisper. Jane nodded curtly, willing him to realise how important it was to be

108

grown-up. Other residents of Carisbrooke village drifted in and filled five rows of pews. The choir from Carisbrooke Parish Church rustled anthem sheets in the choir stalls and the organist played softly.

The simple dignity of the Chapel was enhanced by soft coloured light, filtering through fine stained-glass windows. Above the pews hug flags and pennants, coats of arms of long-dead dignatories and Sidney slewed round in his seat to read the Gothic writing on the wooden back of his pew. He traced an illuminated name with one finger. It was writing but not really writing, he thought. It was very clever. He'd try to do his name like that to make his school books look impressive. He traced the 'S' again, trying to commit the swirls to memory. Jane nudged him with a sharp elbow.

The gilded side door opened and two ladies-in-waiting hurried in with cushions which they arranged in the Queen's chair. The two equerries stood to attention, the organist played more briskly and the congregation waited silently while a short, stout figure was helped from a carrying chair in the porch. Lizzie coughed and Edward gave her a glance that was so like Walter's that Jane smiled and almost forgot how nervous she felt.

Janey tried to appear unconcerned as she made a special effort not to move and to let the Queen hear her squeaky shoe, and Clare hid her broken fingernail under the hymn book she held, but there was no visible tension as the Queen passed by, slowly, leaning on a black stick decorated with silver and with an ornate silver head. Her Imperial Majesty, Queen of England, Scotland, Ireland and Wales, Empress of India and Sovereign of all her Dominions across the seas, came slowly down the aisle to sink thankfully onto the well-worn cushions in the big chair.

The children stared. They had seen her many times, passing through Newport in the carriage but never as close as this. She was dressed in black from head to foot, with a touch of white at her throat. Her cap was of soft lace, finer than any Jane had seen worn and black crêpe made the white lace even more stark. Jet beads hung about Her Majesty like black hail and her eyes wore the blank expression of one who sees badly. Her face was very pale and her mouth turned down at the corners.

– She's old. She's very old and tired, thought Jane. She looked so weary of the world. It was sad to think that in spite of all she had, and all she ruled, she was just a tired old lady. She's lost a husband

and two children, thought Jane. No wonder she's sad. The organist played the National Anthem, and the congregation stood until it was over and the equerry signalled everyone to sit. The fat little woman sat impassively as if quite alone and had no part in the ceremony.

Jane sighed with relief. One glance at the faces lined up on either side of her showed that the family was subdued by the occasion. They mouthed the hymns, afraid to let any sound escape in case the Queen noticed that they sang out of tune, and they tried to keep their feet still on the stickily-polished floor of the pew.

Janey went scarlet with embarrassment when she forgot about her feet and her shoe squeaked loudly during a pause in the prayer, but no one seemed to notice and she wriggled the hassock closer and sat with her feet on it for the rest of the service.

The vicar climbed up to the pulpit and began his sermon. A bird, nestling on the crown of the hat worn by one of the ladies-in-waiting looked so real that Clare watched in case it flew away. Jane looked up at the arched flags and saw that they were very dusty. – Just as well she doesn't see clearly, she thought. If she's like me, she can't abide dirt.

Her Majesty sat still for the entire service, gazing fixedly at the pulpit. Her daughter, the Princess Beatrice, smiled encouragement at the vicar as he did his best to preach a sermon of hope to someone who had already heard the latest casualty figures and news of heavier losses in South Africa, and was still in mourning for many of her own beloved family.

Jane thought of the Queen's family. – She's lost one with the Blood Disease, she thought. Just as I lost Caroline. She prayed for Walter, to God, the Trinity and for good measure, to the Holy Mother, a little guiltily as she had lapsed from Catholic worship for many years. The service ended and the Queen stayed seated until the Chapel was empty. As she appeared in her carrying chair, her mantle folded in orderly folds, she had more expression and the pale eyes flickered over the small group of women and children who curtsied awkwardly if she looked their way.

The Queen smiled faintly and raised one hand. A small girl stepped forward, pushed by her mother, and held out a bunch of primroses. The tired face brightened and a little colour came to the yellow cheeks as the Queen accepted the flowers and pressed them to her cheek. She patted the girl's head and spoke a few words.

110

'I wish I'd done that,' said Clare jealously.

'We haven't picked any flowers yet,' said Edward, 'and that girl wasn't even in Chapel. We sat with the Queen.'

'Is it to be primroses or back home for dinner?' asked Jane.

'Have you brought anything to eat?' said Jack.

'Biscuits,' replied Jane. 'If that's enough to tide you over.' So they all said they wanted to pick primroses.

The path from the castle was steep and rough but dry underfoot on the way past the Priory. The hedgerows glowed with spring and the old Priory appeared gaunt and deserted against the soft yellows and greens, but through a side window, blurred by thick frosted glass, were figures passing up a stairway. Only shadows with faceless hoods that sang, as the Darwens came nearer to the main gate, picking damp primroses from the lush grass.

'I'm thirsty,' said Emily.

'You shouldn't eat so many dry biscuits,' said Jane. 'You'll have to wait until we get home now.'

She drew back from the gate, as she did instinctively when she saw a priest or a nun or passed the Catholic Church. Her family had never been devout Catholics, but she came from a mostly Catholic community and still felt the power and tug of the Church.

'I'm thirsty too,' said Sidney.

'Can't you wait till you get home?' said Jane uneasily.

Emily's lip quivered and Sidney looked defiant. Lizzie sniffed. 'It seems wrong to bother the Sisters on a Holy day,' said Jane.

'They don't mind. They like it,' said Emily hopefully.

Jane hesitated. It was well-known that the Sisters at the Priory never refused a drink to travellers, especially if there were children. The family had been a credit to her all the morning, so she hid her diffidence and knocked on the small postern gate by the lodge.

A closed grille over a wooden shutter moved slightly and a sweet voice asked Jane if she could help. It was an unexpected voice from the wall and Sidney nearly fell over in alarm. Even Jane, who knew it was only a nun sitting behind the grille in the gatehouse, was nervous, but she said, 'I have some children here, Sister. We have walked from the far side of Newport and the two smallest are very thirsty.'

Unhurried movements were heard on the other side of the shutter which now slid back to show a recess in which was a jug of fresh milk and two mugs. Jane put her hand through the bars and poured the milk, bringing the mugs out carefully.

Emily stared at the grille, a ring of milk round her mouth. 'Where is she?' she whispered. Jane shook her head warningly and took the mug to fill for the others. Once the milk was all gone, Jane put the mugs back and the shutter once more slid over, hiding them and allowing the nun to clear them away unseen.

'Thank you, Sister,' said Jane shyly. She gave Edward a push.

'Thank you, Sister,' he said, gruffly.

'Thank you, Sister,' the others chorused.

'God Bless you,' came the voice and the small sounds faded away. Jane walked down the lane and the others followed, chattering with excitement.

'Why couldn't we see her? Was it a nun or a ghost? Why couldn't we go in to drink the milk? Does she live all alone in that tiny room?'

'It's what they call a closed order of nuns,' said Jane. 'They live in the big building, the Priory, and they all have special work to do, like sitting in the gatehouse to take messages and to open the gates if a priest comes. They never come outside and nobody ever sees them. If a girl goes in there as a nun, she never comes out again.'

'What do they do all day?'

'They are saintly women who pray for the sins of the world and for very bad children,' said Jane, smiling. 'They sew clothes for the poor and give refreshment to any one who asks for it.'

Janey was worried. 'They *must* come out sometimes.'

'No, they make a promise that they will give up their homes and families and live there forever. They leave the world outside.'

'But they *must* go home for Christmas!' Lizzie's face was solemn and half-afraid.

'No,' said Jane. 'They promise God to stay there, and they don't have children, not ever. They do have a very nice Christmas, singing hymns and having services. I expect they enjoy it,' she added, without much conviction. She saw the children were too serious. 'I sometimes think it would be a good idea to go there for some peace and quiet where I wouldn't have to answer so many questions!'

'Oh, I don't want to be a nun. I think it's mean to make them stay there forever,' said Lizzie, and they were quiet until the Priory was far behind them.

112

The water wheel was turning in the mill at Shide. The millstream was in full flood and watercress glistened darkly in huge masses. Gypsies gathered the leaves into bunches on the bank of the stream and others were cutting willows from the hedge to sell in the town. Jack wanted to stay but Jane called him on severely, knowing his affinity to water and mud and him in his best clothes and boots! Tadpoles could wait but dinner could not. She was hungry. She was pleased to find she was more hungry than she had been for weeks or months. Her five button gloves were hot and tight and her best boots began to draw her feet.

'I'm glad I'm not a nun,' said Sidney as they sat down to table.

'Boys don't go in to convents,' said Clare. 'Janey and Lizzie and Emily and me would be allowed, but they wouldn't let you inside the gates, so there!'

'Men do,' said Jack. 'I read about it, Miss Knowall!' Jane explained the difference between priories and monasteries and then found herself telling them something about the Catholic Church and faith. She told them about Confession and Absolution and wondered if she had said too much. Walter wouldn't be pleased if she confused the children by telling them of the Mass, as he had a deep suspicion of the Catholic Church, and only attended the Wesleyan Chapel once or twice a year and the parish church of St Thomas for weddings and funerals.

'You have no need to think about it,' said Jane. 'You go to Chapel and Sunday School and your father wouldn't like you to fill your heads with things that have no meaning for you.'

'But we like to know,' said Jack.

'Your father knows best,' said Jane, and was shocked to realise that the words had no impact on either the children or herself.

'I'd like to have my sins forgiven,' said Jack.

'That's because you do such bad things,' said Janey. Jack's face went red and he punched his sister.

'Now eat up your dinner or I for one will not be forgiving you!' said Jane. Sidney bent over the bowl of primroses on the table and breathed in, deeply. 'Take some of them over to Granny Cheverton,' said Jane. 'She likes primroses and it's as much as she can do to walk down her garden, so she can't see them growing this year. You can tell her about the Queen,' she added, to encourage them to make a visit to the crotchety old lady.

'I'll see to the animals,' said Edward, with the same air of righteousness that Walter wore when he wanted to get out of something he hated. 'And I'll go and see the news.'

Jane closed the door behind them and put on an old pair of slippers as her good boots had made one heel sore. She picked up a novelette that Amy had given her and settled down to read and to enjoy the quiet. The unreal world of the heroine engrossed her, taking her into a place of romance, castles and wicked men and a handsome young lover. It seemed only five minutes before the children rushed back and Jane put the book aside with a sigh of regret. Then she saw Edward's face.

'What's wrong? Are you ill, Edward?'

His voice was gruff and unsteady. 'I went up to the *Press*. There's been another big battle and heavy losses. They've rushed up volunteers to the fighting.'

Jane sat down heavily. She pushed her book under a cushion and forced a smile. 'Your father is very good at looking after himself,' she said. 'We must never think of him being hurt. It's bad luck,' she said firmly.

Edward looked relieved, as if her confidence was enough to ensure Walter's safety, and in his gratitude, he helped her to prepare tea, cutting up the plum cake and buttering bread.

Jane tried to be cheerful, but inside, the pale yellow and greens of spring died and a grey misery took its place. After tea, she went to the *County Press* window and read the names, but as usual they were the names of strangers killed or wounded in faraway places that were hard and unreal written on the bulletins. The stilted prose was coloured by the fact that the Queen was now in residence at Osborne, and the account of the British forces trying to clear a corner of the Orange Free State to make communication easier for the advance to the Transvaal sounded like a game, with opposing sides gathered on two facing ridges each waiting for reinforcements. But it was a bloody game, with forty-one left dead in one skirmish and many wounded in the attempt to cut off the Boers' retreat.

Nothing was said of the regiments involved, but as she watched, another bulletin arrived with a fresh Casualty List which included the name of a man from Yarmouth, the son of a farmer who often met Walter at Newport market. Jane read on, dreading further evidence that the Artillery was involved.

'*30 April, 1900*: a body of mounted Infantry and Smith Dorrien's Brigade of the Seventh Division reached Houtney, 45 miles from Thaba N'Chu and fought Botha who occupied the

114

hills with seven big guns. General French was on his way to meet them. Known casualties are forty-five dead and wounded. Three kopjes taken by the Gordon Highlanders and the Shropshire Light Infantry, with bitter fighting continuing.'

Jane walked home slowly. The war was raging more fiercely than ever, although the politicians shouted that the worst was over. Newspapers were divided in their opinions and it was impossible for ordinary folk to decide who was right. Lord Asquith had condemned the inefficiency of the Generals. White was in disgrace and Methuen had lost more men by insisting on his Frontal Attack with fixed bayonets, a policy that was tragically wasteful. – It's all wrong, thought Jane. How can they go on fighting in the old ways? And how the Boers must laugh at us, she thought, but knew that some papers still praised the leaders and described British losses as something heroic and patriotic like the Charge of the Light Brigade.

Heroic perhaps, but what man wanted to die? And after the wounded came back, what then, she thought as a man limped out of a doorway and tried to sell Jane a copy of the poem that Rudyard Kipling had given towards the relief of the War Widows and orphans at home. Jane thanked him and said that she had a copy at home and a husband away at war and he nodded.

The words were running through her mind when she got home. She had no need to read the poem as she knew it by heart and the schools were teaching children to recite it for a concert on May Day. She had even sent a copy to Walter, knowing his feelings for Mr Kipling's poetry. The children began to chant the poem, while Jane made cocoa, to be word-perfect for school next day.

'...He's an absent-minded beggar and his weaknesses are
  great ...
And we and Paul must take him as we find him...
He is out on active service, wiping something off a slate...
But he's left a lot of little things behind him ...'

The children said the words easily, the meaning lost in the chanting repetition, but there were tears in Jane's eyes.

Chapter 9

Archie Cheverton reached down for the silvery cream churn that he had brought for the goat's milk and Jane handed up the parcel of fruit and fish. 'I hope she is better soon,' she said.

'I wish we had your secret,' said Archie.

'She'll grow out of it,' said Jane, uttering the conventional phrase that meant nothing.

'I'm healthy and Amy is fine except for certain times but Rose is like a fairy child.'

'With the days lengthening, you must bring her over here to see the children. They miss her very much and she enjoys it here.'

'I would, only Amy thinks she must stay in a warm room for her chest.'

'Well, choose a day when there's no wind,' said Jane and waved him off, looking after the trim trap with Blackie pulling it effortlessly. Archie looked back when he reached the bend and waved. – Dear Archie, Jane thought. Just to see him made her heart warm and he seemed to come more and more for the milk.

It gave her pleasure to give away the milk which came in far greater quantities than her family could use. Maudie would be round soon for a jugful for Lucy and Mr Foster took some for his daughter, as the doctor said it was good for Nellie's consumption. Rose, whose hands were translucent and her skin as pink and white as Nellie's, had been told to drink goat's milk too, but in the Cheverton household, consumption was never mentioned, as if they hoped the disease would disappear if the name was ignored.

– I wonder if Amy and Archie really know? Jane thought. They smothered her with care, keeping her in a stuffy room to avoid taking chill, but the poor little soul had been ill again and Jane longed to get her into the fresh air. After a walk in the field, breathing good air, she felt better and so did her own family, coming home with sparkling eyes and rosy cheeks – so why couldn't it be good for Rose? It was difficult enough for normal people to breathe in a stuffy atmosphere, and yet Rose lay, listless and pale, day after spring day.

The shop-bell jangled and Maudie stood with an envelope in her hand. 'Did you bring your jug, Maudie?'

'Oh, I forgot, Mrs Darwen, but I had this letter.'

'From Ben?'

'From the army.' Her eyes sparkled. 'Ben is wounded and is coming home. Isn't that good?'

'But what does it say, Maudie? Is he badly wounded?'

Maudie waved aside all questions. 'The important fact is that he's coming home to Lucy and me and I can look after any old wound!' She went to the door. 'I'll pop back with the jug, but I just had to tell you, Mrs Darwen. Have you heard from your husband?'

'Not since last week. He's joined a regiment at the Front again in some of the worst battles. He was on the Modder.' Much practice had trained Jane to keep her voice steady when customers asked after Walter. 'He's well, thank God,' she added, and hoped that Maudie wouldn't see the trains of wounded before Ben arrived, as she heard that the slightly wounded were patched up in Africa and it was only the badly maimed who were sent back to Great Britain. Jane had seen one or two groups being put into ambulances for transfer to the Garrison Infirmary.

If Walter was badly wounded, what would she do?

– It would be better that he dies than be crippled for life. Oh, God, what am I thinking? It was Maudie who had a wounded husband. Walter was fine. He was alive and well and if she could read between the lines of his scanty letters, he was enjoying himself.

The freedom and excitement suited Walter. The horses were a source of constant concern, he was outspoken about the leadership, but solid in his praise for Lord Roberts and Ian Hamilton, the General who fought so bravely at Sanna's Post. Walter hated the Boers but admired their cunning and tactics and said bluntly that it would do the Generals good to be there when the Artillery unlimbered to set up guns, knowing that as soon as the guns were free, the Boers would swoop down to isolate men and horses from the guns.

117

'If you deal with poachers, you set traps, not stand on the skyline and hope he comes your way,' wrote Walter, and Jane could picture Walter laying trip wires and fighting like the enemy and enjoying it. She didn't know whether to laugh or cry. She was becoming nervy, envying the women out there. She wanted to see for herself if the conditions were as bad as the letters from soldiers said. Newspapers were full of accounts of comforts sent to the troops in the base towns and the Cape, but letters told of dysentery, scurvy, typhoid and the terrible sufferings of the wounded before they were collected and taken to hospital.

The shop was empty for a while and she busied herself all the time she was thinking. She accepted that some tales of Boer brutality might be exaggerated, but there must be a lot of truth in the stories, and she didn't know which worried her the most, the suffering and privation or the comforts, unspecified but hinted at strongly! The women in the base towns seemed to do more than cater for a man's hunger for food and warmth. Jane stifled her dread and tried to be fair. Men away from home must live by a different set of rules. Family ties were weakened by distance and lack of physical contact and under the constant threat of death or maiming, the urgency of life would colour the wants of the moment, and the desire to indulge all bodily needs and lusts. All but Walter, she thought, hopefully. He hated dirty women.

Maudie came with the jug and Jane gave her the milk and some shrivelled russet apples and some dates so that her hands were too full to linger in the shop and she had to hurry home. Jane couldn't bear to hear another word about the war. In the back room, the primroses were fading and smelled of death. Jane locked the shop door, put her arms on the table in the back room and sobbed more bitterly than she'd done since Walter left.

She cried until she was drained of all feeling, tears and despair, and achieved a kind of peace. She became conscious of a gentle tapping at the front door and knew that she must open the shop. She doused her face with cold water and found a pot of Fuller's Earth with which she dabbed her face to take away the shine and the redness round her eyes. The tapping came again so she brushed her hair back into its knot and went to the door.

'Violets? Lovely violets? And water-cresses fresh from a running stream, Lady.'

Old Mother Lee, the Queen of the gypsies living down by the river, looked into Jane's face, her sharp brown eyes shining with a curious mixture of Romany understanding and cunning. It needed only half a glance to know that Mrs Darwen had been weeping, but Mrs Lee sensed no tragedy in the house, no death.

'You're as pretty as ever, my dear.'

Jane forced a smile. 'You say that every year, Mrs Lee.' In spite of her crying, Jane felt much better. Perhaps she had washed away her sorrow and misgivings, perhaps the sight of the old woman showed that spring was indeed come, like the first home-coming birds, but whatever it was, she was glad of company.

'I've made tea,' she said, on impulse. The old lady followed her into the back room and put her basket on the floor. She pulled out a red ribbon. 'I want no ribbons, but I do need pegs,' said Jane. 'There may be a few pieces to mend, too.' She busied herself by the range while Mrs Lee looked at the clean windows and the white-stoned hearth. There was no neglect here, even with the man away. Courage was something she understood. She took in the atmosphere, part-psychologist, part-clairvoyant and felt a bond with the Irishwoman.

'Take your tea in a white cup,' said Mrs Lee. Jane hesitated. She mistrusted her own reactions to fortune-telling but knew that Mrs Lee would tell her no lies. Hadn't she said before the twins came that they were on the way? She had said it even before Jane knew she was pregnant. She'd said, 'You've caught, my dear, and it's more than one, both girls.' Walter had scoffed, saying the old woman only came to get something for nothing, but he didn't like to be reminded of what she had said, when the twins were born.

Jane made tea and gave Mrs Lee Walter's big cup and a slice of lardy cake. Jane crumbled her own cake without eating, but finished her tea and swirled the tea-leaves, pouring out the liquid and leaving the leaves in a pattern on the sides of the cup.

Mrs Lee stared at it, turning the cup round slowly, her eyes seeming to sink into her head under half-closed lids. 'There's someone over water. It's further than the mainland,' she said. 'Someone with death all round him and no seeming end that he can see.' Jane nodded. This was to be expected. The old lady must know that Walter was away, as would be most of the husbands in houses she visited. 'He's in good health but may be hurt in the leg.' Jane drew in her breath. 'It's not much more than a bad bruise. Not bad enough to bring him home, but bad enough to take him out of danger for a while.'

She looked in the cup again, her face without expression. 'He will lack nothing. He will be given everything he needs where he is going.' She smiled. 'I see you surrounded with good friends and love. There is a love everywhere, of many different kinds. Love will protect you from one man who might want to hurt you. There are two men. One has already tried to hurt you. Be careful of him. He envies you. The other can be trusted to give you help and you can go to him safely for help.' She paused. 'You have sense to say no to another one who wants you, and you could give him nothing.' Jane blushed, remembering Archie.

Mrs Lee looked up, suddenly. 'Give the eldest boy his head. He will ask you soon. Let him be occupied in another place when the master returns. It is better for young men to have freedom. This one deserves it and will need to make his way before he marries trouble. That is a long way off, but it is here, plain as day.'

'And the others?'

'You are blessed with good children, my dear. One girl will marry and lose her husband young. It will be hard for her to manage but she is like you and is brave. One will make a bad marriage out of vanity and another will marry for a lifetime. The youngest girl will never marry but will be with you in your old age.'

'What of the other boys?'

Mrs Lee frowned. 'The wild one will travel far away. The other will never marry but you will lose him. Leave him to be happy in his way. You work hard. I can see it in your face and hands. Your destiny is to work for others, but it brings you joy. You are well-liked and will never want.'

Jane filled the big cup for Mrs Lee again. She wanted to know more but surely it was only a game! A bit of harmless nonsense, wrong to take seriously and she'd better not tell Emily she would never marry a prince!

Mrs Lee sipped her tea. 'You forgot to put the green thread in his hussif,' said Mrs Lee. 'He had to borrow but he keeps your likeness in his pocket and misses you. You will always be the most important woman in his life.'

Jane instinctively glanced at the closed door of the cupboard behind which was the hank of green thread she had found the morning after Walter left, and she knew he had her picture.

Mrs Lee stepped into the shop and came back, confident that nobody could hear. She came close to Jane. 'Have you thought what will happen when your man comes back? He will be as all men are after a long separation, more eager for you.' Jane's cheeks burned. 'Don't be upset, my dear, it's the way of life.' She looked at the troubled face of the still handsome woman. 'You know you must never bear another child, and you must protect yourself.'

'But how? We don't... we haven't since Caroline.' Jane floundered and wondered how Mrs Lee could know. It seemed natural to confide in this gypsy woman, to voice her fears for the first time to anyone. 'I could sleep with the girls,' she said, 'but he is a proud man and it would make him angry. He is a very passionate man and if he does come home and expects his rights, I can do nothing.'

Mrs Lee searched in the depths of her basket. She held up a package wrapped in linen. Inside were crude pessaries of yellow fat with specks of dark colour spread through them. 'These are safe, not like the ones they sell,' said Mrs Lee. 'With the others, you would be sore and your man would not let you use them as he would suffer, too. These are gentle and contain herbs which are safe and sure. He may not need to know that you use them.'

Jane viewed them with distrust. 'I don't think I could,' she began.

'They will never harm you,' said Mrs Lee. 'They will help you through a very difficult time.'

'And if I used them and they didn't work? Do I take this on trust when I know that I might die if they fail?'

'Each time you use one, it will protect you, but if you miss even one, and get caught, then you must take this pill at the first sign of sickness.' She took from her shawl a large grey pill. Jane started back, revolted.

'It tastes of nothing,' said the gypsy.

'But that is a mortal sin in the eyes of the Church.' Jane touched the brooch at her neck. 'The law says it, too. Walter begged the doctor to do something when I was carrying Caroline but he dared not do it.'

The sharp brown eyes looked angry. 'And if the woman obeys the law and dies, who looks to her family? Who would feed your children and bring them up as good people?' She smiled shrewdly. 'You know I never give you bad advice. Trust me, my dear. You are a good woman and have done many good things for me and my family. We never forget.'

'I can't believe that I would have to use them,' said Jane, but they were thrust into her hand. She put them deep inside her work-box and put the box in the cupboard. 'I must pay you for your trouble,' she said.

Mrs Lee finished her cake and put the pegs on the table. 'Pay me for the pegs. The other is a gift,' she said. Jane was surprised. If Mrs Lee wanted payment only for the pegs and gave the fortune-telling and pessaries free, it meant that she was in earnest and wanted to help. It would have been easy to make money from another woman's fears. Jane gave her money for the pegs and pulled out a bundle of clothes that had been waiting for the spring visit since the cleaning.

When the children came in, Jane was sitting at the table, absentmindedly winding green thread from a spool round her fingers and back on the spool again.

'Who came in today?' asked Emily.

'Maudie, with news that Ben might be back home, wounded, and old Mrs Lee, who talked a lot of nonsense.'

'Percy Cantor said that an ambulance train is coming from the boats tonight,' said Edward. 'He says that it's a big one and they're using the chapel up by the Barracks to take some of them.'

'How does Percy Cantor know?' said Jack. 'They don't know everything, those Cantors!'

'He does know,' said Edward. He glanced at his mother. 'And I'd know too, if I worked on the railway. The train from Cowes will be in about four and they want all the carts and traps we can find to help get the men to the Barracks.'

'Can I go up to Mr Foster's?' asked Clare. 'Ethel Sheath says that he has got all his books out and is answering questions.'

'Haven't you heard enough about the war?' said Jane. The reverses suffered by British troops made depressing reading. Leader columns hinted at more and more bungling and were outspoken against what had started as a popular war. The public now was outraged by the stories brought back by the wounded, and long-needed reforms were mooted in cartoons and Letters to the Editor, and the *Morning Post* was so loud in its condemnation that it was said the Queen refused to have copies in her presence.

Even advertisements, like the one for Monkey Brand Soap carried the caption, 'Clean up the War office, Lord Kitchener', and *Punch* reported scathing details of the £55,000,000 National Debt.

'What? Run the War on business principles? Good Gad, Sir, Hope it doesn't come to that!' declared *Punch*'s General Muddle.

122

Stories of disillusion grew as the wounded filled homecoming troopships. Newport being a garrison town had its share. The workhouses and charitable homes for paupers were full and conditions remained harsh, still carrying the stigma of Poverty, the Victorian sin. With no hope of work, the wounded had no alternative but to go to the Parish, as the pension was pitiful and unless there was an able-bodied member of the man's family who could work, it meant the workhouse for the couple in the first hard winter.

Jane hated to see the men in corduroy and the women in coarse print dresses working in the hospital laundry and the workhouse gardens. Each time she heard of a local family broken up and the surviving members being sent up the hill, she felt an upsurge of deep resentment. How could a hard-working and honest woman be labelled a pauper? How could they forfeit all their freedom, rights and respect? She shuddered when she saw them. – God save my children from that, she prayed.

'Maudie? I gave you the milk and I haven't time to gossip,' said Jane sharply, as the girl lingered in the doorway. 'Mr Foster is telling people about the way the war is going,' she said, knowing that this would make Maudie run up to the shop. 'Clare is there, taking it all in and getting the wrong end of the stick as usual,' she added, more warmly.

'I'm not going,' said Maudie. 'I heard that they are bringing some of the wounded back tonight and I wondered if Ben would be there.' She began to sob. 'I've been hearing such things, Mrs Darwen. I must go and see for myself, but I can't go alone.'

'I think you'd be better out of it until they tell you something, Maudie.'

'I can't wait at home. I haven't heard anything more from the Army and nobody knows if the wounded are from Ben's regiment or not. Please, Mrs Darwen, if it was your husband, you'd be the first on the platform to see him.'

'Very well, Maudie. I'll call in for you and we'll go to the station.' Jane finished sorting the fruit and was almost glad to be going with Maudie. She had avoided meeting the first small trains as she dreaded seeing a familiar face, but now she would have Maudie to support if Ben was among the convoy. It would lessen her own reactions, and having made up her mind to go, she might as well do it properly.

'Fetch the cart and Bess,' she told Jack. 'I'm going to the station with a few things for the men.' Janey helped load the cart with fresh bread and shrimps, apples and Jane's potato pies. It was the only way she knew to say Thank You to the men who suffered in this way and express her guilty relief that one of them wasn't her husband. She ripped an old sheet into long strips about three inches wide and Emily rolled them neatly into bandages. A metal jar that Walter took when on the boat with Aaron was filled with tea and another with cider. They might not want it or be able to take it, but Jane needed to give, and when she called for Maudie the girl looked enviously at the goods as if she would rather Jane gave them to her than to the deserving wounded.

'Think that this is for Ben,' said Jane.

'Oh, I do, Mrs Darwen,' said Maudie, straightening her face into a sad expression and trying to hide the fact that this was exciting, going with Mrs Darwen on the cart as if she was an important Lady Bountiful.

The first carriages were filled with walking cases, or at least they fitted into the official description of walking cases. Any man who could hobble from the train, even with a heavy crutch and one leg or one arm gone, was a walking case. One man with no hands had a Salvation Army girl with him who fed him biscuits and water before a man came to take him behind the coal heaps to urinate before being taken on a cart to the Barracks and the infirmary. Another one for the workhouse, thought Jane and her eyes pricked with pity. Better not to live than to suffer for life.

Maudie came back to the cart from trying to find out if Ben's fellow soldiers were on the train but to Jane's intense relief, the convoy was a mixed bag of officers and Other Ranks from many different regiments, the only thing they had in common being the dirt, the bloodstained clothing they still wore and in which they had fought, and the smell of stale sweat and blood that offended the noses of the helpers.

Jane longed to go to each and clean him, to change the soiled clothes and to comfort him. She thought fleetingly of the women out there, helping in so many ways and she hoped that if Walter was wounded, they would care for him, even if it ended in his infidelity.

The wounded were transferred to ambulance carts and ordinary delivery carts, and many local people lent gigs and traps to transport the walking cases, leaving the ambulances for the stretchers. Maudie was handing out pies and enjoying the experience while Jane walked along the line of men waiting for transport. A pale face looked up at her, the eyes dark with pain. They were the same eyes that Jane had seen in dying animals and old men losing their minds. She bent and smoothed the lank hair from his forehead and offered him a drink. One of his sleeves was pinned across his breast and the side of his tunic was stiff with dried blood. He gasped between sips and tried to raise his head. Jane cradled his head on her elbow and held the cup to his lips again, before the orderlies lifted him on to the ambulance. He groaned and she wiped the sweat from his face with her own pocket handkerchief and pulled the blanket higher over his shoulders.

A sickly smell that she had not met before today came from his stump. The sleeve was damp and offensive and the orderly who had helped to move him, said, 'Bad case of gas gangrene, Ma'am.'

'How do you know?'

'Once you've caught a whiff of that, you'd know it anywhere. You smelled it. I wager you'll never forget it.'

'He looks very rough. Can they do anything?' Jane asked in a low voice.

'Might as well as left him there,' he said and shrugged. 'He's beyond help.'

'But you couldn't leave him to die in a foreign land!'

The orderly spat on the ground to rid himself of the smell and the responsibility. 'He took a place on the boat that could have gone to someone likely to live,' he said.

Jane looked up the hill at the staggering line of vehicles. There were all kinds of suitable and unsuitable transport. The baskets were empty and Maudie was crying and Jane could bear no more. She left Maudie in Sea Street and took Bess and the cart back to the stable. Edward would wonder why she didn't call him, but she wanted to be alone. She put Bess in the warm stall and sat on a bale of straw, glad to dispel the aura of death by the familiar animal smells around her and the gentle sounds from Bess and the nanny goat.

It was late when she went home. She raked the fire vigorously and dropped her handkerchief into the reddest part of the fire, but it wasn't so easy to destroy the memory of the boy. He was very young. He might have been one of the youths who lied about his age to the recruiting sergeant. Death was a poor reward for patriotism and a young soul.

Jane was deeply unhappy. 'Was it very bad, Mother?' asked Sidney, who was forbidden to go anywhere near the convoys.

'It tears me to pieces, Son,' she said, but her tears wouldn't come. The poor mother who had to see her son like that, indecently dirty and with that terrible smell of death! Was it wicked to pray that he dies before his mother saw him? If it was Edward or Sidney, she would want to know everything, to see everything however maimed they were. She hated the Army and the cynical men who turned a blind eye to a lad's age to get one more soldier. She hated the incompetent Generals and the journalists who distorted the news until ordinary people had no idea of what was truth and what was lies.

If only women could sort out this mess, she thought wryly. They at least had commonsense and would make the nation's money last out better and make a better fist than some of the vain politicians. Her Irish spirit rose, first in anger and then in determination. There was so little she could do, but if every woman did a little, beginning in a small way, and helped those nearest to her, some good must come of it.

She took out the scrap of paper where she had scribbled the boy's address. He lived at a farm near Blackwater, and by now, local trains calling at Shide and Blackwater stations would have spread the news that another troop train was in. Tomorrow, the family would receive one of the buff envelopes from the army.

'Call Edward,' she said and brought out pen and ink and paper. She wrote a note to the boy's mother, not mentioning appearance but saying how sorry she was to see him so ill. 'He was being well cared-for when I saw him at the station,' she wrote. 'I spoke to him and he was comfortable.'

'Did you want me, Mother?'

'Yes, Edward. Go up to the station with this. Ask the guard to put it on the next train to Blackwater and tell the porter to take it to the farm. It isn't far. I know it well and there's something in the paper for his trouble.'

'You saw him?' Jane nodded and recalled that Edward must know the family from the weekly market. 'If he dies in the night, at least she will know that somebody cared,' said Edward.

'You saw him, too? Edward, I don't think your father would like you seeing such things! I didn't know you were on the platform.'

Edward went red. 'They let me help with the baggage and you

didn't come as far as the guard's van.'

'Well, get along with you and see that the guard knows who you mean,' she said.

Maudie came into the shop, cheerful now that she knew that Ben wasn't on the train. She stood by the counter while Jack made patterns in the floorboards with water to lay the dust. He used an old watering can without a rose, but stuffed the spout with a stick to reduce the flow of water. He made loops and whirls and even wrote his name and then Maudie's. She was fascinated and looked almost happy.

'I don't think Ben can be badly hurt, Mrs Darwen. I think they made him well at the Cape and I'll hear soon that he's back with his pals,' she said.

'It's strange that you've heard nothing since that one letter from the army,' said Jane, but she tried to feel more optimistic and shook off her depression. The evening was warm and the sky tinged with pink clouds, the swifts diving low. She put a vase of wild flowers and sprigs of mint on the table to keep the flies away, but they hung in spiralling circles, either immune to mint, or not having heard that mint kept flies away. They settled on the sweet dates in the shop until Jane waved them away and covered the block with clean butter muslin.

Flies visited the fish and walked on the windows, and the glue-papers which hung from the ceiling were covered with the blue-black bodies, but nobody took much notice of flies unless they were a real nuisance. It was natural for flies to gather where there was food, just as it was natural for mice to be found in most of the houses in the old part of the town. Flies were kept down by swatting and glue-paper and cats kept down the mice.

Women came shopping, glad to relax after the long warm day and to talk of the wounded and the war. Bad news and others' misfortunes brought trade to the shop but Jane avoided being drawn into any discussion about the men she had seen on the station. When the fish was bought and the last drop of drama wrung from the gossip, they left slowly and Jane was glad to see the back of them and be quiet for half an hour, sitting in the dusk, watching the bridge and hearing the train labour up the rise, while the bats flitted low from their hiding places in the broken brickwork of the railway bridge.

'Did you send it?' Jane asked Edward. She glanced at the clock. 'You're all very late.'

127

'I got a free ride and took it out there myself,' said Edward. 'When he knew about the letter, the guard said I could see the porter at Blackwater and wait for the train to come back from Sandown, so they'll be sure to get it now.'

'That was good of you, Edward. I shall write and tell your father what you did.' He smiled, but without the pleasure that he might have shown just after Walter went away. – It doesn't matter to him what his father thinks, she decided, and saw how tall and strong he was growing. He was a young man, not a boy any longer.

'Tomorrow, you can do what you like as soon as the morning chores are done,' said Jane. 'We have everything we need in the shop and Edward and Sidney can do the delivery.' She smiled. 'You all work hard and I know your father would want you to play sometimes.'

Once more, the faces turned to her were polite when she mentioned Walter. He was fast becoming a hazy figure and his influence was just a convention of words that gave him a place in their lives. Jane gave them all bread and cheese and milk and went up to her room to look out of the window again. From below, she heard the giggles of the girls and the muted voices of Jack and Clare and Lizzie. They were plotting something, she knew, but was too weary to wonder what it might be. It was Friday night; tomorrow morning there would be no clean pinnies to put on for school, no rush to get going, as most of the customers had children at home on Saturdays and had time to relax and shop later.

If only the war would end, life could be good, thought Jane. She drifted off to sleep with the thought that Aaron was taking his barge across the Hamble at first light to fetch strawberries. It worked out well as the Officers' Mess wanted a big order for a garden party. – I wonder if I should have doubled my order? she thought, but turned over in the broad, soft bed and stretched, luxuriously and alone.

Chapter 10

'Hurry up or he'll be gone, Lizzie,' hissed Jack as he held back the bolt and almost pushed the two girls through into the street. 'We've the goat to milk first and the hay to pull down and we mustn't let anyone see us.'

'I'm tired,' wailed Lizzie but it was only a quiet wail as she knew that Jack would leave her behind if she cried.

'Come on,' said Clare. 'Ethel said she'd be there waiting but if we didn't come, she'd go alone.' They hurried down to the stable and startled the nanny goat and Bess who looked at them as if they were mad or the sun had made a mistake. The first birds gave a sleepy call and the pre-dawn haze took on a faint glow across the river. Clare sneezed as she pulled down hay for the animals. 'Did you tell Mother in the note that we would do this?' asked Clare, suddenly guilty.

'We'll have done everything we should and I wrote it all down,' said Jack impatiently. 'And she said we could do what we liked today.'

'She didn't mean this,' said Clare, and giggled. They hurried past the warehouses and down to the quay by the sleeping houses in Sea Street, along by the iron cranes where Ethel Sheath was waiting for them, her red hair a second sunrise and her freckled face glowing with suppressed excitement. The tide was full and it was too early for Joe Matthews to operate the swing bridge, so his wooden hut was empty and the children had the quay and the dawn to themselves.

Aaron's barge was tied up below the path to the stables, high on the tide. The other boats were silent and the chimneys on the timber warehouse were cold. Jack threw one more glance along to the hut and went onto the barge. It was an open boat with coils of

129

rope in the stern and bows, a few tarpaulins and the buckets and baskets needed for fishing. Water seeped in through a small leak by the keel and the patched sail lay folded in the bottom of the boat, slowly absorbing water.

The wheelhouse was little more than a shelter of rough wood, behind which Aaron took refuge in bad weather. There was a cubby hole and a locker, a cupboard and a seat, but for the rest, the boat was open. Jack pulled at a heavy tarpaulin in the stern. It was stiff with dried salt, and so never completely dry. He breathed hard as had tried to pull it and slipped on the deck boards.

Ethel pushed him aside. 'It's no use *pulling*. I know because I've been in the boat before!' She lifted an edge and folded it back. Jack grunted but had to accept her idea and he held the edge up to let the girls crawl underneath, taking charge again and impressing on them that the whole trip was *his* idea. He made sure they were hidden before he joined them. It was hot and dark and smelled of stale fish. Clare wriggled and kicked a bucket, which fell over on deck, spilling rotten bait. The smell was almost overpowering and Clare crawled in deeper under the canvas to get closer to Ethel.

'They're coming,' said Jack. 'Don't make a sound.'

Aaron stopped and rested his wheelbarrow against a bollard and George put the brake on his barrow, by shoving a stone against the back wheel. George Crouch, the crew, handed down the strawberry baskets and Aaron stacked them against the sides of the boat. They added a couple of jars of cider and one of water, a covered basket of food and a fresh bucket of bait. George checked the fishing tackle and neither of the men seemed to notice the smell of the rotten bait.

'That li'l nipper of yourn wanted to come,' said George.

'Young Ethel? Yes, she kept on about it to me all day yesterday. She wanted all them young Darwen children to come too, but I couldn't have that. What would Walt's wife say? She'd have been in a rare old pickle if I'd as much as asked.'

The voices came indistinctly through the canvas and the children kept very still. Aaron threw more baskets on to the tarpaulin and George untied the mooring rope and pushed away from the quay with a long pole, taking the barge into midstream between the mudbanks. Aaron lifted his face to the air and grunted as an offshore breeze freshened with the dawn and the outgoing tide. He raised the sail and it flapped lazily against the mast as the barge drifted down into deep water.

Lizzie was thirsty. In the excitement of slipping out of the house before her mother was awake, she'd had nothing to eat or drink and began to wish she'd brought a bottle of water or cold tea with her. The boat quickened, water gurgling under the keel as the flat bottom slapped its way to the sea.

Gypsies by the bend in the river were too busy lighting fires to heed one barge on the river and the houseboats on Little London had closed curtained windows. The barge drifted on, and Aaron lit his pipe, tamping down the black, oily shag with a calloused finger. The smoke wafted back to Lizzie and in time penetrated the thick canvas and even hid the smell of fish. Lizzie decided that she wasn't hungry after all, and as the boat hit the cross currents of the Solent and the estuary, she felt very sick.

Lizzie stuffed her handkerchief into her mouth to avoid smelling the foul pipe. She knew just how angry Jack would be if she let herself be seen too soon. He had made the girls promise to stay quiet and hidden until they were clear of the harbour, when Aaron would be forced to take them on, or lose a day's fishing and all his strawberry picking. With the wind and tide behind him, he had better things to do than to take four bad children back home. Jack had a shrewd idea that once the worst shock was over, Aaron would see the funny side and be amused at his stowaways.

Lizzie lifted one corner of the tarpaulin and tried to gasp in some fresh air. 'What's that?' Aaron listened.

'I didn't hear nothing,' said George. 'Unless it's a rat. I'll get Bert Cooper's Jack Russell down here for a day. It's time he took a sniff round again. Best ratter in Newport, that dog.'

Aaron picked up the boat hook but Lizzie was quiet and he put it down again. He fixed bait to a line of hooks and trailed them behind, clear of the wake and watched the sail filling and the boat making good time. The sea rolled sluggishly and Jack knew that they were clear of the Island.

Aaron gasped speechlessly, as Jack clawed a way out of the stifling cover and emerged into the sunlight. Jack blinked in the light and grinned nervously, and kept his distance from Aaron. 'What are you doing here?' Aaron sat down heavily on the locker, his dismay growing as first Clare crawled out, then Ethel and finally Lizzie, who stumbled and clung to Ethel. 'How many more of you, for the Lord's sake?' he asked. Clare kicked the tarpaulin back and Lizzie sat on it, her face pale and her forehead

131

covered with beads of sweat. She looked really frightened. The water had an oily swell, light and calm but Lizzie who usually refused to put a foot on any boat, and didn't like the water, was queasy and dizzy.

Aaron frowned, bringing his eyebrows together to meet in a shaggy veil over his hooked nose and Lizzie thought he looked like a pirate. She wished with all her heart that she was at home. Aaron saw her fear and pallor and it did much to stem the tide of abuse that wanted to vent itself on the stowaways. His eyes twinkled. 'You don't look much of a sailor, my gal,' he said. Lizzie stared at him in dumb misery and he picked her up and sat her down on a coil of rope in the bows. 'You stay there,' he said. 'Look ahead and you won't get the smell of my old pipe or the fish.' Lizzie lay back in the stream of clear air and felt better. Her colour returned and for the first time in her life, began to enjoy the water.

Jack was right. They were too far out in the Channel for Aaron to take them back home again, and after a few mutterings and threats, he accepted the situation with good humour.

'I don't know what your mother will say,' he said. 'Did you think of her?'

'I left a note in the shop,' said Jack. 'There's no call for her to worry if you take us, and we did the work before we came away.' He shifted uneasily under the stern gaze. 'It's Saturday, and Edward and Sidney and Janey are there. She's all right for help.'

'Well, if you come with us, you'll have to work your passage,' said Aaron. 'I can't abide passengers.' He was ready to concentrate on the day ahead. He winked at George who listened, fascinated. 'You'll have to earn your keep and we don't feed tramps. Hope you brought plenty of grub with you?' Jack shook his head and George gave a loud laugh. 'That's too bad, ain't it, George? You'm going to be hungry.' The men laughed. 'We only brought a bite with us, enough for two,' said Aaron.

'You've a lot in that basket,' said Ethel, her face going red. 'I saw Mother pack it last night.'

'That's for when we finish the picking. Might see a few friends who are hungry.'

George chuckled. 'I expect they had a good breakfast before coming away, Aaron. Nothing like a good breakfast to set you up for the day. We had a good breakfast, didn't we, Aaron?'

'Yes, we should last out. Shouldn't need much until after the picking.' The men joked in a heavy-handed way, enjoying the situation while the children grew emptier and emptier. Aaron eyed them with tolerance. Little blighters, he'd teach them a lesson. With their father away, they needed a check.

He saw that Clare was close to tears. 'Never mind, we might give you a bite of ourn when we finish, and you can eat all the strawberries you like while you pick.'

'Are we going to pick strawberries?'

'You don't think I'd bring idle hands with me, do you? You'll be able to pick a nice few in three hours.'

Jack baited hooks and took off the catch after the girls pulled them on board. Aaron wasn't out for fish but he never sailed without a line or two over the side and even a few fish would come in handy. It was a pleasant change for him to sit by the tiller and let someone else do the work. George joined him and they took turns at the cider jar. Lizzie eyed the jar with longing.

'Want some?' said Aaron. The cider was cool in the thick stoneware. It was dark and still and potent and made Lizzie catch her breath. The sun came up hot and bright in a cloudless sky and the cider made her sleepy, so she snuggled down among the ropes and went to sleep.

The boat followed the coastline towards the opening to the Hamble River. Fishing boats coming in with lobster pots were tying up and men sat on the shingle, mending nets. Several called to Aaron as the boat drifted along under the leafy banks of the river and Aaron tied up by the Inn, under dense shade. George threw the baskets on shore and told each of the children to take some across the lane on the first strawberry field.

Already, women in print aprons and sunbonnets were picking ripe fruit for market, filling flat boxes and loading them on to farm waggons, then covering them with thick layers of straw. Aaron weighed each basket as it was filled and the farmer showed him which rows to pick and which had been cleared. Trees at the edge of the field gave a dark band of shade, and it was pleasant working between the rows of green plants.

Jack picked fast and the girls followed him, and filled several baskets quickly. George took them to the boat where he had been busy sweeping the deck with a stiff broom and water to get rid of the foul smells and rigging up a shelter of tarpaulins sprinkled with water to keep the boat cool. He stacked the baskets in the cool and the farmer kept a tally of the weight picked.

The next batch of baskets took longer to fill and the sun shifted from behind the trees. Clare's back ached and her mouth felt rough and acid. She stopped eating strawberries and looked across at the others. Jack wiped sweat from his eyes and rolled up his shirt sleeves. Lizzie looked hot and sorry for herself and Ethel's normally pale and freckled face had turned lobster pink under the carroty hair. The pile of baskets seemed as high as when they started.

'Can't we stop for a bit?' whispered Clare.

'No!' Ethel looked frightened. 'I know he didn't look angry on the boat, but just you try and stop working and he'd get wild with us!'

'Come on,' shouted Aaron. 'I didn't ask you to come. If you don't like it, you can lump it! Should've stayed at home!'

They picked strawberries until they hated the sight of them. Their hands were covered with juice, their arms bitten by midges, the sun grew hotter and the shade less and still Aaron goaded them to greater efforts.

At last, Clare faltered and then Lizzie, and Jack looked defiant. They stopped work, no longer caring what he would say or do and Ethel began to cry. Lizzie had endured all she could. At best, she had less fortitude than her twin, Clare, and at worst she gave in easily to tantrums and tears when she imagined the world was against her. She wasn't resilient and she *had* done her best and filled nearly as many baskets as Clare. It was too much.

Lizzie staggered to the hedgerow and was quietly and thoroughly sick. All her tiredness, all her vague sea sickness and a great number of pulped pink strawberries spewed out on to the grass. She wiped her mouth and felt better. Aaron saw her out of the corner of his eye and relented. He'd been very hard on them, he had to admit, but he'd meant to be. They had pluck, that was for sure. Even that one hadn't really whined. He gave the last of the baskets to George to fill and called, 'Enough! You can stop now. Have a rest and we'll catch the tide.'

The children threw themselves down on the cool grass in the shade. The last of the strawberry baskets were stacked in neat layers with enough space between to let the air cool them and George went to the Inn. He came out carrying a large fresh loaf and a flagon of beer. Aaron opened the basket and put thick layers of apple chutney and slices of fat salt pork on hunks of bread. George unearthed tin mugs from the wheelhouse and filled them with ale. The children ate and drank in silence, and he smiled at Aaron who winked and tried to look stern.

They were tired, with the weariness of overstretched muscles and long exposure to the sun. The skin on the backs of their hands was sunburned and they itched all over with bites, but somehow, all four children were happy. The food was the most delicious they'd ever tasted, or so it seemed, eaten on the grass with dragon-flies skimming the river and the bees working the hedgerow flowers.

'We'd best be off,' said Aaron, looking at the tops of the trees swaying, so the children took the rest of their food into the boat and were still eating when the barge slipped from the river and pointed to the distant Island. There was peace on the water and a deep serenity. The sea birds paused to swoop for crusts and the light was translucent. The sea darkened and there was little foam apart from the creamy wake. Water sucked at the keel, and the sail hung like a broken wing as they followed the ebbing tide, then billowed in the open sea.

Aaron sat looking at the Solent. 'She's a lovely old gal today,' he said. She was generous too, as line after line of mackerel was pulled into the boat, with the fish shoaling high in the warm water. George baited books and pulled in the catch with monotonous ease and Aaron didn't light his pipe.

Gypsy fires lit the bend of the river after the darkness between Cowes and Folley. George hummed a tune from a music hall song that came faintly from the quay at Cowes. The river was quiet and the quay at Newport was deserted, except for a woman resting on the stone wall by the barrows below the stables. There was a lantern by her side and moths dashed against the lantern windows.

'Look out! There's your mother,' said Aaron. George jumped out and made fast. The children hung back and Jack braced himself, jumping ashore and kicking stones as if he hadn't a care in the world, but glancing at Clare and Lizzie under lowered lids, waiting for the explosion.

'I brought them back safe and sound,' said Aaron.

'I didn't doubt that, Aaron, and I don't blame you at all for taking them. They should have asked me before going off like that.'

'We thought you'd say no if we asked,' said Clare.

'How could you know if you didn't ask?' replied Jane dryly. Jack

135

kicked another stone.

'Jack left a note, Mother. He said it would be all right if he left a note,' pleaded Lizzie.

'Any coward can leave a note,' said Jane. She looked at Jack for the first time, then turned her back on him. Jack tossed his head angrily but kept quiet. 'While you're here, you can load our cart,' said Jane. 'You did remember I wanted extra, Aaron?'

'Yes, gal, I remembered. They're fine berries this year.' He winked. 'Cheaper too, seeing I had help and I didn't pay for labour!' Jane didn't smile.

'I'm tired,' said Lizzie in the voice that usually brought sympathy.

'So am I!' said Jane. Lizzie went to pack the cart and they carried all the order for the Barracks to the stable ready ior the morning delivery, and the remainder of the load went on to the handcart – slightly under-ripe fruit that would be just right for sale in the shop on Monday morning.

Aaron kept two baskets and carried them while the children trundled the handcart to the shop on the bridge. Jane walked with him. He put one basket on the counter and Jane looked at it doubtfully.

'That's over and above the order,' she said.

'It's a few extra,' he said awkwardly. 'Don't be too hard on them, gal. They worked like navvies. They've been a real help: I saw to that! They ain't bad children and you've got to let them go with the tide, sometime. I didn't mind them coming, and I'll take the lot of them another time, if you'd let me.'

Jane's face softened. 'It's good of you, Aaron.'

'Give them a holiday, and give yourself a break from them.'

'You're sure they didn't get in the way?'

'They were great little pickers and they stuck it out to the bitter end! All on 'em.'

Jane looked at the tired and dirty faces. Lizzie tried to scratch a midge bite on her bottom without anyone noticing and Clare looked pale and hollow-eyed. She saw the scratches and brought a bowl of warm water to bathe the hands and arms and dabbed the bites with vinegar and put elderflower ointment on the sore patches.

'Stay for some broth, Aaron,' said Jane. She smiled and the children knew that she had forgiven them. They went to bed, too tired for food and anxious to be in bed before their mother was alone!

136

Jack gave his mother a quick hug and said 'Sorry,' and hurried upstairs. The footsteps died on the boards and Aaron blew his pipe while Jane ladled out mutton broth. They ate in companionable silence and Jane pushed over Walter's tobacco jar to Aaron.

He stayed for just one pipe, knowing that Ethel would have told them that he was home, but he knew that Jane needed someone just to sit in Walter's chair and fill it, however inadequately. He made the room masculine with the familiar tobacco smell and Aaron watched Jane over the smoke, seeing a very lonely woman.

Aaron blew a last smoke ring and yawned. He knocked the ash from his pipe. 'Best go. Young Ethel will have told them I'm back and they'll want their berries before they go to bed. It's been a good day. Pity you couldn't come, but the children were good company. You're lucky, Jane. Not a dud'un among them.'

He hoisted his basket on his hip and crossed the bridge to his own cottage. Jane closed the door and lit a candle from the guttering stump of the old one and the acrid smell of the extinguished wick hung heavily in the shop. Jane took a big ripe berry and bit into it. The juice trickled down her chin and when she put her handkerchief to her face, the juice was diluted with tears. It had been a long and anxious day, even knowing that Aaron was caring for them, and she knew they would come to no harm. – I'll have to let them go one day, she thought.

She closed the yard door and went up to the hot bedroom. She dreamed of Walter. He was back home again, but she couldn't find him. He laughed, but it wasn't warm like his laughter. It was taunting and cynical. She sensed him near but couldn't touch him and behind his laughter was the shadow of someone she couldn't see clearly, but knew to be a woman. Jane threw aside the bedclothes and tried to find a cool spot in the feather bed, but slept lightly and woke again. She wanted Walter, needed his body close to hers, his hands caressing her body and his swift, compulsive love.

Amy had Archie, and even the Coopers had each other, although both wives made no secret of the fact that they disliked the physical side of marriage and now envied Jane being without it. The act was one to be avoided as much as possible, or endured when it couldn't be put off any longer. Jane wept tears of loneliness and frustration, and dozed again, only when she had explored her own body and given herself guilty comfort of a kind.

137

She lay on the bed, hotter than ever, as the orgasm faded, and hated herself. 'Forgive me, for I sin,' she prayed to the darkness, and fell asleep.

Dawn came cooler and Jane longed for air. Quietly, she dressed and went into the yard. Nero, half-asleep, looked up from the bench in the outhouse. The air was fresh and dew hung on the grass and Jane opened the doors and windows to freshen the house before the sun came in. The strawberries in the shop smelled delicious and Jane felt a surge of energy.

By the time the children were awake, she had a hand wrapped in an old towel as she stirred the spitting jam. And by breakfast-time, she had filled all the row of seven pound jam jars and washed the huge preserving pan. The smell of jam wafted across the bridge to Aaron. He sniffed and smiled. 'Good gal. That's the best medicine. Work and more work. I'll bring you the pick of the oysters as soon as they'm ready.'

Chapter 11

Heat shimmered over the bridge, and the street by the shop was dusty with bubbles of tar in the gutters as the summer day opened. Jane wore her thinnest blouse and skirt and was glad that she had no need of corsets in this weather. She sympathised with schoolmistresses like Miss Martin who had to endure the yawns and inattention of children in the hot classrooms, and the weather seemed set for at least a few more days of heatwave.

Jack came back from the stable with more energy than he had shown for days, and Jane suspected that he had been swimming in the river again. His hair was damp and his socks looked as if he had put them back on inside-out, but she pretended not to notice, but dryly remarked that he seemed to have more life in him on Saturdays.

'We ought to have more holidays,' he said. 'You work too hard, Mother. Miss Martin should let us off school again to help you.'

'And where would I find you to help? Down in the withy beds again like last time?' He turned as if to go out again. 'And where is it this time? Percy Cantor? You stay here, my lad. Your Uncle Archie will be here soon and will want some help. Did you bring the fresh milk?'

'It's sitting in water in the outhouse,' Jack said. 'Can I go haymaking with Uncle Archie?'

'I don't know about that. Amy doesn't like to be put out by a lot of visitors.'

'You manage. You never mind how many there are,' said Jack.

'Aunt Amy hasn't my big family and she knows how many farm hands she has to feed and doesn't want unexpected people. We have the fish to cook if we have visitors.' Jane smiled. 'Run out now. I think that's Blackie I can hear.' She followed Jack into

the sunlight and laughed. 'Rose! It's good to see you, my dear.'
Jane threw up her hands in mock surprise. 'And what have you
done to poor Blackie, Miss?'

Rose climbed down from the trap and went to the horse's head.
Sidney gazed up in wonder. Rose had cut holes in an old straw hat
for the horse's ears to poke through and pinned a bunch of
poppies and cornflowers to the brim, with sprigs of mint to keep
the flies away.

Archie smiled at Jane over the heads of the children. 'Take
Blackie into the shade,' he said.

'May Rose come down to the river with us?' asked Edward. 'I'll
take care of her, and it's cool down there.'

'Jack must stay and help with the shop while I settle with Uncle
Archie,' said Jane.

'I'll stay, too,' said Janey. 'I'll finish the sweeping.'

Jane relaxed. Archie was so easy to talk to, so easy to have in the
house, but she felt safer if they were not alone, not because she
was afraid of him, but all the same, it was fitting that a married
lady should not have men to visit her in the back room. She
pushed away the thought that Sam came in, Aaron came in and so
did a few of Walter's business pals if they happened to be in
Newport for the market.

'Well, now, that's a fine lot of plums you've brought me. I've
been asked for yours from one or two who like them for jam and I
sold a few pots to the Officers' Mess. I'll make this lot tonight
when it's cooler. I can sell all the pickles and jams I can make. It
never fails to amaze me that more people don't make their own.
It's easy enough.'

'Not everyone has your talents, Jane.' She turned away from
the admiration in his eyes.

'You'll be wanting a cool drink. Will it be cold tea or lemon?'
Jane could hear her voice taking on its Irish timbre as it did when
she was nervous.

'Cold tea,' said Archie. Jack brought in the rest of the plums.
'We've a glut this year and not enough hands to pick them,' said
Archie. 'The hay is good, too, if we can stook it in the dry.'

'It must be a worry with half your men gone to the war,' said
Jane.

'Yes, and I can't stay now,' he said. 'I have to pick up some
maize for the hens and get back to the fields. With the light
evenings, we can work late but it's a problem.' But he lounged

140

back in Walter's chair in the doorway to the yard and sipped his tea as if he was set there for the day.

'What about hay?' said Jane in a business-like voice. 'How much of your crop do you think we should put aside?'

'If Walter comes back, you'll need double and more oats. He'll want Blackie as soon as he comes home, more's the pity. I wish I could buy him.'

'Shall we leave it that we have enough for Bess and you keep Blackie's fodder until we know?'

Archie nodded. 'I'd like to keep him as long as I can. He's a good worker with a nice temper and good-looking to ride.' Jane recalled seeing Archie mounted on Blackie at the Hunt and they had both looked very handsome.

'I've never seen him looking better, Archie. I feel happy knowing that you have him and care for him so well.' She sighed. 'But you know Walter. Horses are *his* affair, and I couldn't sell Blackie however long he is away.' She gazed out into the yard where Janey was putting away the broom.

'I like to help... Walter's family in any way I can. Jane.' She covered the jug of tea with a muslin edged with glass beads to keep out the flies. 'Any news?' he said, and the tension eased.

'Bad food, the state of the horses and the bad tents. Walter doesn't write about himself, but after a while, he did tell me of the terrible things they have to eat. During the sieges, they had to eat mules and horses and make puddings out of laundry starch. The men who entered Ladysmith in March, when it was finally relieved, were shocked when they saw the people there. They'd been on a ration of a bowl of some sort of porridge stuff called mealies, and a biscuit. They ate any horseflesh they could find. Walter said they ate four thousand horses during a siege of four or five months.

Jane leaned forward, her eyes bright with anguish. 'There was fever, too, Archie. That frightened me. I'm very upset when he writes of fever. It's everywhere he's been. They buried five hundred at Ladysmith. I hear all the bad news twice. It's never the same, though. The newspapers say one thing and then I get Walter's letters saying something more. He says that the parcels of comforts are not regular and some never see any.'

'Of course, it's winter there now,' said Archie. 'It seems impossible that it is cold and wet there while we simmer in this lot.'

141

'They're in camp,' said Jane, and shivered.

'Cheer up, Jane. General Buller saved them and the army does seem to be making gains all over the place now. The war can't go on forever. The rate they are going, Walter will be home soon.' He laughed. 'Old Walt must be all right if his only personal grumble is lack of baccy. He doesn't say that he is short of food, does he?'

'No, but...'

'Well, then, you mark my words. He's A.1. He's strong and has plenty of spunk and I daresay that he enjoys most of it.'

'I hope you're right, Archie.' Jane gave him a long, level look. 'I do miss him, Archie. He is my husband and I miss him.'

'And you worry too much. Why don't you take a rest? Why not come down to the farm tomorrow. You hardly ever come and you know you enjoy it when you do.'

'I don't know,' began Jane, wistfully.

'Come on Sunday and bring a bite to eat. Come by train and you can all help. There's hay to be tossed and as many plums as you can carry back. You can give the children their grub in the field and come and eat with us.'

Jane smiled gratefully. Trust Archie to be tactful. The picnic for the children would overcome any objection that Amy could have, and she would have no extra mouths to feed.

'I'll bring a basket of food and if it rains we can all eat indoors but make no extra work for Amy. Tell her I'll bring everything for us and we can help. We'd like to help,' said Jane, beginning to look forward to her outing.

Archie noticed, not for the first time, how soft was Jane's expression when she smiled. She had a dimension of femininity and more depth of character than Amy could ever possess. She now looked as eager as a schoolgirl at the prospect of a treat.

'Will you stay and eat with us?' Jane said.

Archie looked at her face, alight with warmth and affection. He shook his head. 'I haven't the time, but I'll expect you tomorrow. Now, no excuses and Rose will be delighted. She is so well just now and it will do her good to run wild with her cousins.'

Archie finished his tea and went to the door to ask Jack to bring back the horse, and Rose. It would be so easy to make a fool of himself over Walter Darwen's wife, thought Archie. He had to remind himself yet again that he was married to Amy, and Jane was married with seven children and must never have more. He set Rose in the trap with a parasol to keep her head cool and watched the lively faces of Jane's family. If only he had sons to take on the farm, and lively daughters who wouldn't spend the winter in closed rooms. He flicked Blackie with the end of the whip and gently put him to Snooks Hill.

On Sunday, Jane wore a cool muslin dress and a wide straw hat. She called the girls and told them to take hats and the boys wore thin shirts and jackets. Heat made the street outside blank and lifeless. Most of the neighbours were in church and already the dung thrown into the gutters was drying, sending up an acrid smell mingled with dust.

Edward took the big basket and Jack carried a flagon of goat's milk for Rose, while the rest carried smaller baskets and bundles across the quay to the railway station at the bottom of the town. Lines of open trucks in the sidings were full of coal, and coal-dust crunched underfoot as they walked.

Jane tapped on the shutter over the window of the booking office. The stationmaster, who was sitting in the shade, heard her and reluctantly opened the shutter.

'One and seven halves to Wootton, please, Mr Rich.' He handed over the carefully counted green cardboard tickets, having counted the smiling scrubbed faces before him. He closed the window and by the time that Jane had shepherded her family to the iron gate leading to the platform, Mr Rich was waiting to examine the tickets. He counted first the tickets and then the children again, as if he suspected that Jane had slipped in a couple more. He gave Jane the torn halves for the return journey and pocketed the rest. He glanced at the round clock hanging from a wrought-iron bar under the shelter of the platform roof, then took out a half-hunter watch and compared the time there with the clock.

'The train will be here in precisely seven and a half minutes,' he said. 'Other side. Please use the gates.'

Jane pushed open the white wicket gate at the side of the line and held it while the baskets and children went through. The gate swung to after her. It was designed to keep children and animals off the track and there was a similar gate on the other side of the line, allowing passengers on to the platform there. The white gates were Mr Rich's showpieces. He saw them as a great aid to safety on the railways and made much of them, quite ignoring the fact that by crossing the line five yards away, it was possible to do so without using either gate.

The stationmaster now became the porter and pulled a trolley

143

bearing two red mail bags along to the spot where the guard's van would stop. He walked to the exit, ticket punch in hand. Edward watched, his face aglow with interest and envy. How important Mr Rich was! How many duties he had to perform and how well he did them. Some day *he* would be like that, working on the railway, seeing the great monsters steam into the station and perhaps punching tickets, after he'd been there long enough.

Imagine being allowed to punch tickets and to wave a train on to the next station, using a green flag and a whistle – *that* was power. Edward dreamed. He would check each ticket carefully and sternly refuse a ride to anyone who tried to go on the platform without one, or whose ticket was out of date. Between trains, he could put luggage in the office for collection, tend the station garden and fill the lamps with oil. He sighed and wished that Jane would let him work with his friend at Cowes.

A plume of smoke rose from the line near the bend of the river. It hung on the still air like a great white cloud, billowing a little, dissolving slowly and leaving whisps of haze in the sunshine long after the train had passed by. The train whistle blew as the gradient was reached and the engine rasped and the brakes squealed in the dry atmosphere, as the train seemed to hover over the old bridge, with the music of the wheels changing as they crossed the iron lattice. Horses and ducks under the arches went on feeding as if nothing happened above them and the train slid to a gusty halt with the guard's van at the exact spot where the guard would open his door and reach out for the mail bags a yard away.

Edward was deeply impressed. How could Mr Rich *know* the train would stop just there? The guard threw down a sack of oats for the chandler in the High Street and carefully lifted out a crate of young fowls. He put them in the shade. Next came a mass of harness and two long-handled scythes, the blades wrapped in sacking. A few passengers got off the train and walked to the exit where Mr Rich punched the tickets, examined a season ticket with suspicion and glanced down the hill for any latecomers. Satisfied that all who wished to travel were present, he closed the gates, walked across the line and collected a package from the guard. He waited, watch in hand, for the exact moment of departure, blew his whistle and waved the green flag.

With less than twenty passengers, the train asthmatically breathed out into the open, leaving the station full of white smoke. Edward leaned out of the window to watch Mr Rich, the priviliged Head of the Station, crossing the line without using the gates.

Jane sat in the centre seat, prepared to enjoy the few minutes' journey. She read all the advertisements framed in heavy mahogany and looked at the familiar views of the Island, which were on every train, painted in gaudy colours. In the flyblown mirror over the opposite seat, she could see the reflections of the flowers on her hat. She smiled, thinking how well the pink flowers looked with the spray of wheat.

Sidney pressed his nose to the glass. Edward secured the window on the middle notch of the leather strap, but even half-open, smuts came into the carriage and Jane moved away so they wouldn't soil her dress. 'Don't lean out of the window or you'll have your head knocked off,' she said. 'Or you'll get smuts in your eyes.' She pulled at Emily's skirt. 'We're coming to a bridge. A man had his head knocked off because he was looking the other way.'

It was what she said each time they went by train and it was a part of the outing and the children would have been disappointed if she hadn't said it. It made it more exciting when they put out their heads and drew back before the train flashed under the bridge, clearing the metal uprights by yards. The children fell back into the carriage with a satisfying sense of danger.

Jane watched, indulgently. Hedges along the river fields were covered with dog roses. Clumps of cow parsley dotted the sides of the track and where the banks were steep and close to the rails, patches of burned gorse and hawthorn showed where sparks from the engine had fallen. Cows, in distant corners of the fields, went on cropping grass, brushing away the flies with long tails, their horns catching on the stunted trees and in the low bushes where they grazed. A dark girl stared at the train and a dog barked as they passed the gypsy encampment, but there wasn't time to see everything, lulled by the rhythmic clunkety-clunk of the wheels, as Wootton was the next stop.

Sedately, the Darwens climbed down from the train and went over the bridge to the road. Wootton Creek was still and cool against the soft rise of the green hill and the lane to the farm followed the path from the weir. Lizzie picked flowers, although Jack laughed at her and said they'd be wilted before they reached the farm. He threw stones in the water and watched the eddies reach the other shore.

Clare and Janey tried to keep their dresses clean so that Rose

145

would see how smart they were and Edward dreamed of trains. Sidney lagged behind, trying to pull a leaf to bits without touching the veins.

Amy was at the gate. 'Thought you'd be on that one,' she said. 'Rose is in the lower field,' she told the children. 'And your Uncle Archie is there, too. He said you must go and help him.' She smiled at Jane. 'It's such a nice day, we'll all eat in the field. You children run on and your mother and me will bring the food down later.'

Jane loosened the ribbon tying her hat and breathed deeply. A dragon-fly flashed blue fire on its dash back to the Creek. 'You are lucky, Amy,' she said. 'I love this place.'

Amy sniffed. She had been up since first light making butter and was tired and hot. 'It's all right in summer,' she said, grudgingly. 'But winter can be cruel here with the damp rising from the Creek.' She led the way to the low-ceilinged flagstoned kitchen with its wooden arch open above the stove and side ovens. Copper pans gleamed in the sun and wild flowers fanned out in a deep bowl. It looked very attractive, but Jane could imagine the warm airiness turning to cold draughts through the gaps under the doors and from the badly-fitting windows.

Beyond the living room was a room with a high, tightly shut window. There was a couch in the far corner and a fireplace, making this room snug and warm. It was the room where Rose spent most of her life when she was ill or the weather bad. In an effort to keep the girl warm, it was overheated with no ventilation and the brown marks left by heavy condensation scarred the whitewashed walls.

Jane shivered. It looked like a dungeon. 'How is Rose?' she said.

'I can't understand why she is so well. I thought the hot weather would try her badly. In there, she has no strength, even when she had rested, but this summer, she's had more energy than she's had for ages and loves to be out. I make her sit in the shade if I think she is doing too much, but she is very much better. She was pleased to know you were coming today, but I'll have to make sure she doesn't burn in the sun.'

'She may be over the worst,' said Jane. 'She's been growing fast and perhaps now she'll outgrow her delicate state.'

Amy shrugged. 'Sometimes I think she won't make old bones.' She took her tea to the wide window-seat and drank it quickly.

'I didn't come to hold you up,' said Jane. 'Just tell me what you

146

want done. I can turn my hand to most things.'

'Have you skimmed?'

'No, but I can try,' said Jane.

'All you need is a steady hand,' said Amy. 'I'll show you.'

The still-room-cum-dairy was lined with slate shelves filled with stone kegs and jars, ewers and silvery cream buckets with heavy lids and brass hinges. Each cream bucket had its own scoop, like a soup ladle, hanging from its side. The milk was ready for skimming and stood in a wide shallow bowl, a layer of thick cream already forming on the surface.

Amy took a skimming spoon and pulled it gently across the cream, until it puckered and wrinkled and collected in the bowl of the spoon. She took off all the rich yellow topping and left behind the thin watery blue-white milk.

Jane rolled up her sleeves and put on a print apron. She washed her hands under the tap and took the skimmer, making it bite too deeply into the milk at the first attempt, then caught the knack and no longer stirred the liquid, but separated the cream from the milk evenly, pouring pure cream into one of the silver buckets. She remembered her aunt in Ireland did this on her farm and the smooth, unhurried rhythm was soothing. Ladle after ladle of cream flowed into containers until only skim milk was left, which slopped into buckets for the pigs and calves, as nobody but the very poor would drink skimmed milk.

The goat's milk for Rose stood in a deep earthenware pot of water, covered with wet butter muslin. 'I can't think why the doctor likes her to have it,' said Amy. 'It looks the same as cows' milk to me, but there must be some truth in it as she has been better since she began on it.'

The women washed the milk vessels in plenty of hot soda water, pouring boiling water into each cleaned container to scald it. Amy sniffed each one as it drained, knowing that if it smelled fresh, with no lingering odour of milk, then the next batch to go in the vessel wouldn't curdle. She knew from bitter experience that new milk put in unscalded pans could curdle in a few hours. Nobody knew why this happened. It was a fact of life at which they didn't wonder, but accepted without deep thought.

Jane took up a pair of butter pats and boards and put them on the table, tracing the long furrows in the rectangular boards which shaped the butter. Amy dipped her boards in cold water, took a piece of butter from the churn and tossed it from one pat to

147

the other, beating out the surplus water and shaping it into a neat square, criss-crossed from the shaping. Jane stacked the squares as they were made, putting them on dishes and covering them with wet muslin. She carried the dishes to the cold dark pantry where the walls were so thick it knew neither winter nor summer.

Amy wetted wooden butter moulds and filled them with butter, forcing it into every crack in the pattern, to make sure that no air bubbles remained. She trimmed off the edges and swiftly turned the moulds on to wetted dishes. A sharp tap and the moulds came away cleanly, leaving the embossed pattern sharply drawn. There was a rose design on one, another of thistles and one had a cow's head, complete with mournful eyes.

'The big house has three every week,' said Amy. 'They like them for the main table.' She rinsed the churn and left it to drain, upside-down, with the wooden lid unhinged while Jane washed the cloths and wiped the table down. Amy stacked bottles of cold tea and one of goat's milk in a basket and filled another with the food that Jane had brought. She slung them on a shoulder yolk and put cider and more food in two other baskets which she gave to Jane with a yolk. Jane was amazed how easy it was to carry heavy weights like this on a shoulder yolk and hummed to herself as they walked down to the fields among the warm scents of stocks and clove pinks. Butterflies flew among the nettles by the cesspool and larks were breaking their throats with song. Jane was happy, the weather was perfect and there was no news of ambulance trains and hadn't been for two weeks. With better news from South Africa, the sharp edge of fear receded.

Emily ran to her, holding a bunch of wild scabious and clover. Jane closed her eyes as she smelled the flowers and Emily took the cloth from the top of one basket to lay on the grass. They unpacked under a tree and Jane called to the others who ran from all parts of the field, the boys with their jackets off and sleeves rolled as high as possible and the girls running barefoot through the long, dry grass.

Janey picked straw from Jack's hair. 'We've only been doing what Uncle Archie told us to do,' she said, grinning. 'He told us to toss the hay as high as we could to dry it.'

'We'll be able to stook it after dinner,' said Archie. 'It's a relief to know the hay is safe for the year. Every pound of fodder will be valuable if the war goes on. Last year we lost a lot when the damp

148

stooks built up heat and burned down, and we have no stock left.'
He smiled at the boys. 'Do you want to get rid of them, Jane? I
could do with a couple all the time.'

Archie flung himself down on the grass, his working shirt
open at the neck and his dusty corduroys tied with string at the
knees. He wiped his face with a red handkerchief and as he
smiled, his strong teeth showed creamy against the brown skin.

Jane viewed him with open approval, thinking that everyone
must know he was more handsome in his working clothes than
when he wore a tight suit and a necktie. – How lucky I am to have
such a nice-looking, kind relative by marriage. Amy clicked her
tongue. 'You look like one of your own labourers, Archie. Nobody
would think you owned this farm, and those corduroys are like the
ones they give to the inmates of the workhouse.'

The families shared the food, the children finding a novelty in
Amy's cooking and Archie eating the cockles that Jane offered,
knowing he liked cockles but that Amy would never bother to
cook them and preserve them in vinegar. Archie lay on a heap of
straw and enjoyed being spoiled, the girls helping him to
anything he wanted to eat and tickling his neck with long grasses.
He watched the two women with lazy eyes. Amy was a good wife,
always willing to help and very good with sick animals, but his
eyes turned time and again to Jane whose face was flushed and
whose hair was hanging in curling tendrils from her severe bun.
She saw him looking and an instinctive alarm registered in her
brain. She got up and brushed her skirt.

'This won't do, children. We are here to help! Put your shoes
on, girls, and come to the orchard. If you want plum jam this year,
you'd better pick plums.'

'You made plum jam last night,' said Lizzie.

'That was for the Barracks,' said Jane. She picked up her basket
and the girls followed slowly.

'They've been picked from the lower branches. The others will
be difficult to reach without a ladder. I'll bring the ladder and one
of the boys can climb up,' said Archie.

'You've hay-making to finish,' said Amy sharply. 'Jane and I
can carry the light ladder. We're not made of putty.' Archie
shrugged and walked away to the field. Amy smiled maliciously.
'Take no notice of him, Jane. I'm afraid that Archie needs keeping
in his place. My husband is fond of the ladies.'

Jane raised her eyebrows. 'Now, Amy, you *do* surprise me. I

149

would never have thought so.' She looked directly at Amy. 'He's a good husband, isn't he? Has he ever given you cause to doubt him?'

Amy's gaze flickered and she shifted her eyes. 'Never,' she admitted. 'He's been a good husband,' she said in a subdued voice.

'Then you've no cause to worry about him, have you?' Amy flushed angrily and called to Rose. 'How many times have I to tell you to put on your hat?' She raised her voice even more. 'You'll be burned and have a bad night!'

'Don't be cross, Amy,' said Jane. 'It's such a lovely day and you've been very kind, teaching me to skim. You know that you are a very lucky woman to have a good-looking man like Archie, who is faithful to you.' She smiled at Amy's confusion. 'Everyone I've met speaks well of him. Never a word of gossip and I don't think there ever will be. I'm very fond of your husband, Amy, but I've a man of my own, a good man, and I don't need to look at any other man however long Walter may be in coming home.'

Her smile had a chill in it and Amy changed the subject quickly, but insisted on making a pat of butter with the cow's head on it for Jane to take back with her.

On the way to the station, midges hung in clouds under the low branches of trees on the tow-path. Fish broke surface taking flies and Sidney argued that he heard a woodpecker.

'It's someone mending a boat,' said Jack derisively.

'It isn't. It's a woodpecker, isn't it Edward?' The boys ran ahead as carefree as if there was no war, no father away for what seemed like forever and no hard work before they left for school each morning.

Emily slipped a hot hand into Jane's. 'I do love Uncle Archie, don't you, Mother?'

Jane smiled. 'Surely. He's a warm person with a big heart.' She smiled. Archie was such an easy man to know. In some ways, she was more at home with him on a day like today than she was with Walter, who would never lie around on a pile of straw, making the children laugh if there were horses to see or a man to talk with on more serious subjects. Archie laughed easily and made her feel as if she was witty and important. There was a bond between them that made him know what she was thinking.

She shook away the thought. If Amy hadn't put ideas into her head, she would never have considered that he showed her more affection than good manners between family connections demanded.

'Uncle Archie thinks you're pretty, Mother,' said Emily.

'And so I am,' said Jane firmly. 'And so is Aunt Amy and Janey and Lizzie and Rose and you.' Of course he regarded her with approval. She was Walter's wife and she kept her family together while he was away, so Archie was pleasant to her. She was Walter's wife.

In the train, the wheels said, 'Walter-has-gone, Walter-has-gone, Walter-has-gone...' and her sadness flooded back, but it was more of an objective sadness as if she was sorry for a set of circumstances and not just for herself.

They were weary from too much sun and their clothes were limp and grubby, and Sidney was sick after eating too many plums. Jane made each one stand on a blanket by her washstand and wash all over to get rid of the itchy harvest mites. 'That'll teach you not to run in the field barefoot,' she said. 'Wash between the toes or you'll itch all night.' She helped them put vinegar and Fuller's Earth on bites and sat them down in their nightclothes to eat supper. Edward washed in the old tin bath in the outhouse to show that he was a man and didn't get washed down like children, and he hung the dusty clothes that the boys discarded on the line for airing.

Jane sorted plums while the wasps were away as she knew the shop would be pestered with them in the morning. She filled a jam jar with water and sugar to attract them and trap as many as possible, and Edward put it on the flat part of the outhouse roof away from the shop.

The dusk was warm and friendly and the smell of jam was everywhere. Jane filled the last jar and made more tea, sitting in the open doorway quietly before going to bed.

In her room, she stripped off all her clothes and washed all over, patting her skin dry and scenting her under-arms with Attar of Roses just as she had done when Walter was there to notice and caress her, putting his face to her breast and smelling the fragrance. But tonight, no tears came. No deep sadness. He was a long way off and she had learned to skim milk and make cream.

Chapter 12

'Plum jam?' Maudie sniffed, and waved aside a wasp.

'I've made enough to last us until next year and some for the Mess. We picked the plums at Wootton yesterday and Archie brought in a lot the day before.'

'Have you heard any news, Mrs Darwen?'

'Not a line for weeks, Maudie. After Ladysmith, the troops moved so fast that it must have been impossible for them to write, even if they had pencil and paper. They're a long way from the Cape and our letters are not reaching the men quickly.'

'They said one ship went down carrying all our letters and some wounded,' said Maudie.

Jane saw that she was drawn and tired. It was weeks now since she had heard that Ben was wounded, and men coming back on the convoys knew nothing about him. Some said he had been patched up and was back in the Front Line, some said he was badly hurt and some refused to say anything.

'I know it's hard not to listen to rumours, Maudie. It's best to think that he is being treated out there and will soon be well.' Maudie looked doubtful. 'When you do hear, you'll forget how worried you were. There's nothing in the papers and no fresh bulletins, so look on no news as good news and be ready, all trim and clean for when he does come back, and make Lucy a new dress from this one of Emily's.'

'If the Queen is at Osborne, we should get the news quickly,' said Maudie, brightening as she fingered the still good Madras cotton that Emily had outgrown. It was common knowledge that the Queen released the latest news to the local press as soon as possible. She loved the Island and appreciated the Islanders' attitude to her presence among them. Being used to royalty, they showed her a mixture of deference and pride. Even the poorest was not servile, but respectful, so that she could talk to many of them with far less embarrassment than to many of higher rank who tried to impress her with their own self-importance and the need to ingratiate themselves.

'They say her sight's going,' said Maudie.

'That's why she stays here for longer and longer, where she feels at home,' said Jane. 'She can't get about as well as she could. She uses that carrying chair in church and must find it trying to travel.' Now, in June, she was 'down the road' again and the outriders often drove through the town of Newport followed by the modest coach and four, bearing Her Majesty to Carisbrooke to visit her daughter, the Princess Beatrice, Lord Lieutenant of the Island.

Jane often thought of the Queen since the day she had been so close in the chapel. She imagined her lonely in that great house. Many local people had been in the state rooms, which were crammed with trophies and elaborate gifts from Indian Rajahs, the Ethiopian Emperor and African chieftans. Tapestries, collected from all over the world hung on walls and draped settles, the huge oil-paintings of Royal children dominating the walls, painted when the Prince Consort was alive and left where he liked them to be. Did men in a family dominate *everything* – even after death?

'Have you ever been inside Osborne?' asked Maudie.

'Once,' said Jane shortly.

'It must be nice to have all that,' murmured Maudie. 'The woman downstairs is being horrible about Lucy laughing. I wish I lived in a place with all those rooms.'

'I don't,' said Jane. 'It's too full and only the parts the Queen uses are homely.' She thought of the collection of marble hands and feet which the Queen kept on view, all replicas of her children in infancy. There was a model of the Duke of Wellington, too, cast in bronze but she hated to think of them all and hoped she would never see them again. Marble statues reminded her of the cemetery and the thought of those baby hands, in marble, cut off at the wrists, horrified her even while she had a very real affection for the Queen. They were both mothers of large families, had suffered the pangs of childbirth and loss. Both were without husbands. – Please God only for a while for me, prayed Jane. The loss of infants was a bond that bridged rank and age.

153

Edward called out, 'The carriage is coming from the Castle.'

Maudie brightened. 'The Queen must be ill again!' Any bad news if it wasn't her own, made life interesting.

'It's the Princess going to Osborne, right enough,' said Jane and sent Jack to see if there was a Royal bulletin in the *County Press* window. There was nothing new but in next to no time, the town buzzed with speculation as local concern grew. Later, the *Press* issued a guarded statement that the Queen was very grieved at the loss of the Duke of Coburg and that the Princess was attending the Queen at Osborne. 'Holy Mary keep the old lady safe,' said Jane. Poor soul, it was her fourth bereavement.

Edward dragged out the long black shutter and put it in the middle of the window of the shop, with a picture of the Royal family draped in black crêpe. Other shopkeepers with windows fronting the main road did the same, but apart from conventional mourning in churches, the local people were unconcerned. Love for the Queen was real but the unpopularity of the war had brought indifference to the fate of remote members of the Royal family.

Children told not to play, resented it. 'Who was the Duke?' asked Sidney. 'Has he ever lived on the Island?' To make matters worse, it was Sunday again and the children had to file into church in gloves and hats, tight collars and button boots until even the most reverent longed for the sermon to end.

Jack sat at the end of the pew and slipped out during the singing of the last hymn. With any luck, he could get down to the stables and swim before anyone saw him, in the river out of sight of the town. He went to the shop to fetch a towel and Aaron was waiting.

'Thought you'd never get out of that place,' said Aaron. Jack stared at the full baskets at Aaron's feet. The man waved a stiff mackerel in the boy's face.

'Is it a *glut*?'

The man nodded. 'Sandown Bay's full of them. Black with them. I came back with one load and I'm going again but I need help. If your father was here, he'd have come like a shot!'

Jack gave a war-whoop quite unsuitable for a Sunday morning, especially during a time of Royal mourning. He rushed into the shop, and clattered up the stairs, to change into an old thin shirt and cotton trousers. He put rope-soled shoes on his feet and grabbed a straw hat. Jane arrived and he looked at her with pleading eyes.

154

'A glut is it?' Jane smiled and waved Jack away. 'Edward, put Bess in the shafts and load up from the barge. Call at the ice factory and pack it well and tell the foreman we'll need more when the next lot comes. Then take the load to the Barracks. Janey! Clare! Take Sidney and push the hand-cart up to the Town Hall arches. Keep the fish in the shade and sell cheap. I'll stay in the shop with Emily and Lizzie. We'll have to open up. Jack!' she called. 'Tell Aaron to put the surplus on the train and I'll send Edward to collect from the station when he comes back.'

Jane cleared the window of fruit and vegetables and the neatly-staked packets of herbs and dried peas. She wiped the marble slab and put down trays of zinc covered with roughly chipped ice and flooded them with a cascade of the fish that were so fresh they stood stiffly in the hand as if carved from wood. The air smelled of salt and the sea. She changed her dress and put on a coarse sacking apron. Already, local people were converging on the shop at the news of good fresh fish being sold so cheaply. They came from across the bridge, the top of the town and even from cottages near Shide Mill. They brought buckets or deep Delft plates as they couldn't expect wrapping paper at the shop, and besides, Jane gave better measure if she just weighed roughly and tipped the fish into ready containers.

The inn-keeper's wife and Mrs Grace came, still wearing Sunday-best, but with aprons over their finery. They took six dozen for customers to eat in the tap-room, a delicacy when soused in vinegar. They ordered more from the next load for smoking and hurried back, passing the woman from the Bugle who had the same ideas.

Maudie came in with a bucket and offered to serve, knowing that she would have free fish in return, and Lucy sat and watched the activity, with Ikey on her lap. Jane was up to her elbows in fish-guts as she cleaned fish for those too squeamish to clean their own and Emily heaved buckets of fish-guts down to the water under the bridge. Maudie weighed fish and took money, putting the soiled coins in a bucket of water as there wasn't time to clean her hands. It was a simple way of ensuring that the money taken to the bank wouldn't stink of fish.

All thoughts of Sunday dinner faded, and Jane put a dish of mackerel doused in cider and adorned with bay leaves in the bottom of the oven, with scrubbed potatoes dry on the shelf. By two o'clock, there were few fish left. Jane washed her reeking hands under the yard tap and Emily sprayed water over the shop-

155

floor before sweeping up the débris with a stiff broom. Maudie put her own fish on a tray of ice while she helped Jane lay the table and the tired women fed themselves and the little girls on tender fish with a delicate flavour. They ate bananas from the shop and Maudie had stewed plums.

Jane gutted and put the remaining fish to souse, the only way of preserving them for a day or so in hot weather. They would keep now, in the cool larder. Next, she looked out the long bamboo rods on which she would impale the next batch of fish, for smoking. Smoked mackerel was a delicacy that kept well and was popular when fresh fish wasn't obtainable. Walter would enjoy them when he came home, she thought.

'Maudie, will you go up to the brickyard and ask them to make up a smoking shed? Tell them we'll be ready to start smoking early tomorrow morning. It takes that time for the oak chips to heat the house.'

Walter had made a rough brick shed in which he smoked fish and it had paid for itself, time and again. The glut would soon be over and might not come again for weeks, months or even years. In fact, this was the first time Jane had seen so many fish since Emily was born.

Emily yawned. 'I know you're tired. You worked very hard, Emily.' Jane gave her a hug, and Emily smiled happily. 'Wash your face in cold water because there is still a lot to do, but you can go and meet the others now.'

As it was Sunday this meant an extra day of trading, for mackerel – traditionally a fish eaten within twenty-four hours of landing – could be sold and hawked on the streets. No one on the Island would eat a mackerel over a day old, unless it was soused or smoked.

'Maudie, please take this dish to the surgery. The Doctor enjoys my soused fish and it's a way of saying thank you.' She watched Maudie go and wished that the idea had come from the girl who owed him so much.

Bert Cooper came in, and for once, Jane was glad to see him, as he was full of sensible ideas of building another smoking house and using the shell of an old shed with sheets of iron to back the bricks. 'You've a good eye for business,' Jane said.

'We could make a good partnership,' he said, with more boldness than he'd dared to show since the day of the Hunt.

'We're already business partners, Bert,' she said dryly. 'That works very well.'

'I hope you tell Walter that.'

'I'd never tell anything I couldn't say to your face,' she said. 'The good and the bad.'

He grinned and seemed relieved. 'I'll take a batch of the smoked fish over to the mainland,' he said. 'Get a good price for it there. How are you off for sticks?'

'We could use more,' said Jane.

'Leave that to me. I'll send one of the men for some from the nursery-men or we can use green willow.'

He paused in the doorway. 'All this fish and I'll not taste a bit. Annie never cooks mackerel as she can't abide the smell.'

'Not much smell to sousing,' said Jane, with a malicious smile. It was Bert's favourite dish and one he had often enjoyed with Walter when they sat over the books. She saw that he was tired and gave him his due. He had been working hard, helping Edward load the fish from the train and chivvying the men at the yard to get ready for the smoke. 'You can take this lot up for the men at the yard and have some yourself,' said Jane. 'And if you let them break that dish, I'll murder you.'

'I wouldn't dare,' he said with feeling, but went red with surprised pleasure. Sidney came back with the hand-cart and Jane sent him to scrub it out to be fresh for the next lot. The girls had gone back after dinner to tell late customers that there was more fresh fish at the shop. Maudie washed the marble slabs, sending a flow of fishy water through the drain at the front of the windowsill and by tea-time, all was wholesome and the last pieces of damaged fish were losing their brilliance and becoming limp and unsaleable. Jane scalded them for the dog and cats and put them to cool.

Maudie sipped her fourth cup of tea, then reluctantly took Lucy home. Jane smiled. It was peaceful at last, but there would be work to do later. She was glad that Aaron had taken Jack with him. The boy missed his father more than he knew, for in many ways he needed to do a man's work with men. He missed the trips with Walter to the farms and the days on the mainland when Walter saw contractors and met his friends. Jack craved adventure and his restless soul made him hot-tempered and impulsive. A boat-ride and hard work would do him good, she thought.

Nobody settled down to knitting or sewing. There would be fish to gut and string up when the barge came in, and Jane was hot and tired. 'I wish I had your energy,' she said as Janey began to skip outside the front door. 'It's Sunday and you shouldn't,' began Jane. What did it matter? They had worked twice as hard as any day of the week. They were good children. 'Is the tide in?' she asked Ethel, who sat on the counter, drumming her feet against the wood.

'It's on the turn. Mother said the barge will be up about nine if they wait for the tide.'

Jane felt suddenly carefree and released. Her eyes glinted and she knew that it had been a good day. 'Come on, let's walk down the river-fields to meet the barge,' she said. 'We'll find a breath of air by the water. We'll wait for Aaron at the bend opposite the gypsies and come back on the barge with him. You can carry something for your supper and Nero can come too.'

Janey made jam sandwiches and Jane packed fruit and cake while the boys carried cold tea and lemonade in bottles in their haversacks, and left the hand-cart near the mooring.

Birds drifted low after gnats, showing that it would be fine tomorrow. The river-fields were empty and sounds from across the water came sharp and brittle in the silence. Trees hung without moving a leaf and the tide pushed its way over the mudbanks to hiss on the warm gravel edges of the shore. Dry rushes stood quivering as the water eddied round the roots and a family of moorhens swam for the islet of reeds as the children waded in the shallows. Jane wondered what Annie Cooper would think and if she was too old to paddle. Did Annie or Bert remember what it was like to be young? To run over a field in bare feet and to paddle in clear water?

Jane tucked Emily's dress inside her knickers before the hem was drenched, then helped the other girls to do the same. She hung back a little and quietly removed her own shoes and stockings and smiled as the cool water ran between her toes. Nero hunted every sound in the reeds, the first dew came and a water rat chiselled his way towards them, disappearing when Nero splashed into the water. The dog came back, shaking wet fur over Sidney, and owls started hunting.

'I can see the barge,' said Ethel from the bank.

Jane climbed up through tall grasses and heard the rumble of the distant railway train and the last plume of smoke to leave Cowes hung above the trees, then stirred as the breeze came in with the tide.

Aaron's sail billowed and hung, clung to the mast and took

158

wind, but the tide did all the work. Jane saw the sail and went out on to the finger of gravel that made a natural jetty and the children shouted. Aaron looked across and saw Jane's scarf, like a flower in the dusk. He pulled over and they climbed on board. The boat was full of fish again and Jack was wet with salt and scales, but he grinned happily and stuffed himself with bread and jam, wiping his mouth with a grimy hand.

Aaron took a swig of tea. 'Parched, I was,' he said. He jerked his head towards Jack. 'Young 'un did well. Worked like a man. We sold all but this load. Thought you'd want these to smoke.'

'We'll have a grand settling tomorrow,' said Jane happily. It would be more funds for her own pin-money, the perquisite of her work over and above ordinary shop-keeping and one that Walter looked on with amused approval, as he would if he farmed and Jane claimed pig-money like Amy did, for rearing the weakly.

Aaron saw her peaceful face and was glad for her. She'd manage whatever happened, even if Walter never came back.

From the hills behind them and over Pan Down, came flickers of lightning. A distant rumble pushed back the heat and lightning once more cut the clouds. 'Someone's having it tonight,' said Aaron, comfortably. 'Might clear the air a bit, but I don't think it's our turn just yet. I'd best help you get those fish in smoke, though. It might be bad tomorrow.'

Chapter 13

Was it the thunder that brought all this? Jane looked out at the rain streaming down the gutters and turned back to the misery in the shop. Ben Dove was dead. Jane sat by the back window of the living room and pleated her apron with nervous fingers. At least the shop might be empty for a while until the rain eased. It was as if a holiday was over and now the reckoning must come.

Maudie Dove sat in the tub chair and rocked to and fro, sobbing. The letter that she had brought to Jane as soon as it came still lay on the table. Jane was lost for words, after trying for so long to convince Maudie that Ben was being cared for and would be well soon. Ironically, a letter from Ben had come at the same time as the official news of his death and threw a little light on what had happened.

After being wounded in one of the earlier battles, he had recovered so well that he was nursed in the huts behind the firing line, but as more and more wounded came to the camp after Bloemfontein, the local medical services proved inadequate and all convalescent patients were used as orderlies while the hospital waited for more doctors and nurses to arrive from the Cape. Ben wrote of bad conditions, of seriously wounded men lying on the ground in poor shelter because there was no other place to put them.

'I'm feeling very weak,' he wrote. 'What with the work and my leg aching all the time. I can't stomach the native food or the mule's liver they give us. If I was as bad as some of the poor blighters, I'd rather be dead than suffer as they do. The fever has come to the camp and never an hour goes but someone dies of it.'

Ben had joined them. In fact, he had the symptoms of typhoid fever when he sent the letter. He died a few days later and his letter arrived with the dreaded buff envelope.

This brought the war closer again. Jane was used to Walter being away, used to the bugles blowing across the river and the whistle of the troop trains. She enjoyed making her own decisions, running the shop and seeing that Bert Cooper didn't cheat over the brickyard. In her heart, she knew that Walter would return safely. Just as old Mrs Lee had forecast, he would return and her Irish feyness accepted the prediction since he had written that he'd hurt his leg when a frightened horse tried to rub him off against a tree. If that was true, then the other predictions, good and bad, would happen.

Maudie looked up through swollen eyelids. Her face was blotched and dirty with weeping and in spite of her youth, suddenly ugly. Jane saw with distaste that her blouse was grubby. It was not the grubbiness of new dirt on a hot day, but the greyness of badly-washed clothes. ... She's a dabber, Jane thought. She handed her the only remedy possible at a time like this, a large cup of tea, strong and with enough sugar in it to transform it to a dark syrup, the panacea for every grief and every crisis. Maudie sipped it between shuddering sobs and her breathing calmed down. She took solace from Jane's unspoken compassion and her strength.

Jane read the typed letter with rising indignation. The official version was so different from the picture drawn in his letters and the first-hand descriptions from the returning wounded. Officially, he died of fever following wounds, but they didn't find it necessary to tell his wife how he died in bad conditions, working as an orderly when he should have been in bed! They made it sound heroic – as if Ben had died with a patriotic smile on his face and 'God save the Queen' on his lips. 'He will be remembered as one of our country's heroes,' it said. Maudie was impressed.

'They say he was a hero!' And Jane refrained from saying what she thought. Perhaps it was better for him to die than to be wounded again and come home maimed for life. With all Maudie's good intentions, she would have been incapable of nursing a permanent invalid. A lifetime with a man embittered by war and in constant need of attention would try anyone, and Maudie had no moral stamina. It was a tragedy, but already, Maudie was drying her tears and showing a kind of cheerful acceptance. Jane bathed the girl's eyes with a damp cloth and she began to return to normal.

161

– She's an easy-going girl, thought Jane. When she isn't crying or in a bad mood, she's quite good-looking. She could marry again.

'I shall have a pension,' said Maudie.

'Not enough to care for Lucy or to buy clothes and good food. You'll have to find work,' said Jane. 'What can you do?'

'I can scrub,' said Maudie, without enthusiasm. Jane had doubts that Maudie could clean well enough to satisfy the ladies on the Mall or up at Staplers, and she wasn't a good cook. Maudie looked miserable again.

'I could ask Mrs Anderson at the laundry. I believe she needs more hands,' said Jane.

'I'd like that! I know some of the girls there and when Lucy starts school in the autumn, I could work at least half-time.'

'It's very hard work, Maudie.'

'I know, but I do want to keep Lucy, Mrs Darwen. I love her and I couldn't bear it if they took her away.'

'I'm glad to hear it,' said Jane seriously. 'But if you work, you must remember that Lucy is still small and mustn't be left alone too often. She'll be young to start school but once she does go, you'll have the School Board Inspector after you if Lucy doesn't attend regularly, or if they come and find her alone in the house at night.'

Maudie stuck out her lower lip. She knew what Jane was implying. In the summer, Maudie had been seen more than once watching the foreign barges come in, talking and laughing with the men. It was harmless enough, but in a town like Newport, tongues wagged.

'She's a husband away fighting for Queen and country while she flaunts herself in front of common bargees,' Annie Cooper had commented, self-righteously.

'And as for the child, she's left alone for hours in that terrible house,' were the thoughts of another. 'It's too near the quay and we all know what goes on there of an evening.'

'If you want people's good opinion, you have to earn their respect,' said Jane now. 'You will be judged by the company you keep and by the way you behave. I agree it's unfair – when you know that you are doing nothing very wrong but a woman on her own has to be extra careful,' said Jane bluntly.

Maudie began to cry again. 'I do try, Mrs Darwen, but they all look at me as if I'm no better than I ought to be. I'm not like that.'

'I know, Maudie,' said Jane in a softer tone. 'You are bound to

162

feel lonely without your man to care for you, but be careful who you take as a friend. You can come to me for advice at any time, and if you need something for Lucy, but sooner or later, you'll have to find your own level and stand firm on your own merits. You've left that little mite long enough now. Go and fetch her and you can have dinner here while I go and see Mrs Anderson. If you want to go out on your own, leave Lucy with a neighbour or bring her here for an hour or two, but don't leave her alone at night.'

After dinner, Jane left Maudie washing the dishes while she put on her hat and went to find Mrs Anderson. The laundry was in a back street, between the bonemeal factory and the bakery. In hot weather, the smell was bad. Smoke from the bakery chimney and the acrid smell of bonemeal blended with the stale smell of soda, bleach and soap in a cloud of steam, but today there was a breeze and some of the steam dispelled quickly.

The office was over the main cat-walk by the work room. Huge zinc baths were full of linen, and girls with heavy drab dresses, unbuttoned at the neck and with sleeves rolled high, lined up to take buckets of starch and borax, soda or bleach from the assistant, their dresses partly protected by rubber aprons and sacking.

Mrs Anderson closed the office door firmly. 'It shuts out the noise and stops the steam getting into the books,' she said. 'Steam gets everywhere. Look at the mildew on these bindings on the account books.' She offered tea which Jane refused. 'What can I do for you, Jane? Something special to be laundered? That damask tablecloth?'

'No, I hardly use that now Walter is away. I came to ask if you were taking on extra hands. Maudie Dove is now a widow and needs work.'

'I think I know her.' Mrs Anderson looked reluctant. 'A slip of a thing, isn't she? Would she be strong enough?'

She nodded to the window overlooking the work-room and a bay where women dragged heavy wet sheets from the boilers into a vast sink. They used wooden tongs but the sheets slipped and if they didn't have the knack of twisting and throwing in one movement, the hot linen had to be manhandled. One girl had bandages from wrist to elbow and several had slight scalds.

'She'd have to have her wits about her. Some of them think they can gossip and don't look what they are doing. When that happens? Accidents! And most of the time, they've only got themselves to blame.' A group of girls folded rough-dry sheets ready for the mangle. The huge rollers were padded with clean linen and were wide enough to take three sheets at a time. The slow, heavy rollers pressed the sheets so thoroughly that afterwards, they needed only a touch of a flat iron to crisp them. Jane looked away, remembering Clare's crushed finger-tip. – What a terrible place, she thought. Holy Mother, don't let one of mine come to this.

'I'll give her a week's trial. She can start on Monday and do mornings,' said Mrs Anderson.

– Monday? thought Jane. Was the term starting so soon? She'd pushed the thought aside, knowing she'd miss the help the children gave her during the holidays, but there was so escape.

That Sunday evening, the girls put out clean pinafores and Sidney rubbed soap round the neck of his stiff collar to stop it chafing. To him, it was the symbol of all the restrictions that school imposed on him and his feet dragged up the hill that first morning. Edward went with equal reluctance and Jane knew that a decision about his future must be faced. He was nearly fourteen and ready to leave school. He had a fair amount of commonsense and practical ability but hated lessons. School was now a waste of time. He hated reading unless it was about the railway and inventors and people who dreamed up the noisy, smelly monsters.

– I shall miss him, thought Jane. He had Walter's strength and dependability, but Jack was eager to take over some of the deliveries as it gave him an added kudos among his friends at school. If he took over that, Edward could be spared, as the others liked tending the animals, looking on it as pleasure and not work. Jane thought of him all the morning, and when Edward came home again, looking bored and miserable, she said, 'Let Jack take the cart, Edward. I want to talk to you.'

Jack grabbed the list of addresses and went before his mother changed her mind. This would show that idiot Percy Cantor who could do responsible work! He would hurry with the deliveries and give some of his friends a ride back to the stable.

'I've been thinking about when you leave school,' said Jane. Edward bit his lip and looked down. 'Cheer up! I thought you hated school.'

'I do, but I don't want to work in the shop all my life,' he said, with a touch of defiance. He glanced up apprehensively, and found his mother smiling.

164

'Anyone can see that,' she said drily. 'You make no secret of it. I've been thinking... With the others coming on and being useful, and your father returning home one day, it might be possible for you to do something you want to do.'

'You mean – *work on the railway?*' Edward was incredulous. 'Really, really, work on the railway?'

'Now don't jump to conclusions. I don't know what your father will say when he comes back and finds you've left school, but you can try it until he says different. I think it would be best all round.' Edward hugged her. 'But remember, if your father comes back and says you must leave, you do as he says, with a good grace! If you don't, it will be very awkward for me. Do you promise?'

'I promise,' said Edward. 'Thank you, Mother. I'll do anything to help when I'm home.' He smiled. 'I'll take the others for mushrooms tomorrow before school,' he said.

'That's a good boy. I can sell as many as you pick.' It was sad to think of autumn again, but as she looked out jars for the bramble jelly soon to be made and when the mushrooms came in, waxy-white and cool, she knew that summer was gone and with it a happy time that a few months ago she would have thought impossible without Walter.

With the children at school and the shop empty for a while, Jane sat mending. The shop-bell rang and she went out expecting customers. She smiled and held out her hand in greeting. 'It's good to see you again,' she said.

André Duval stood in the doorway, grinning. He hesitated as if unsure that she remembered him, but her warm smile dispelled his doubts. 'Once more I come,' he said. 'I bring the first of the load for you, Madame, as always.'

'It must be five years that you have been bringing onions for Walter,' she said.

'Six, Madame, and a better bargain each time!'

Jane laughed. André came each year with a barge of Breton onions, good hard onions, full of flesh with a touch of purple between the layers, and crisp brown skins. The Frenchman shifted the rope from his shoulder and lowered a dozen strings onto the counter. The two men had always enjoyed arguing over the quality and the price, each knowing that a good sale would be made. It was a yearly ritual between good friends, begun when André had first come with his father, before the older man made over the barge to his son. André now lived on the barge until the crop was sold and for the rest of the year he was a farmer,

165

growing the onions as his father and grandfather had done.

André talked of the war, in good but heavily-accented English. He was concerned that Walter was still away. 'We were sure that it would finish when Pretoria was taken,' he said.

Jane sighed. 'The newspapers led us to believe that it would be soon. They said the last of the Boers would be captured and would take a vow of allegiance to the Queen, but there have been many battles since then and more men and horses killed.'

'It is bad for you. It is bad for Walter.' André pulled a bottle of wine from an inner pocket and put it on the counter. Jane hesitated. It was a part of the yearly ritual. Walter enjoyed a glass of French wine and so did she. It made her feel like one of the gentry, to sit and sip a fine wine and daintily nibble a biscuit, but how could she entertain Walter's male friends when he was away?

One glance at André's ingenuous face decided her. Where was the harm? She picked up the bottle. Would her husband want her to turn away an old friend just because some old busybody might think it wrong to entertain a man in the back room in the middle of the morning? She felt amused and defiant, but timid enough to look up the road before beckoning him to the back room.

André held the bottle to the light so that she could admire it. The ruby glow cast on the wall make the dun paint bright. 'Pretty as a jewel,' said Jane. She dusted off two glasses and after the first sip, closed her eyes for a moment.

'It is good, yes?' André chuckled. It wasn't at all like the coarse red wine the men smuggled on the timber barges. Walter brought some home that tasted like vinegar. André was delighted with Jane's obvious enjoyment. He helped himself to more and ate the cold rabbit pie that Jane set on the table. He told her news of his family in Roscoff – his daughter's marriage, the death of an uncle and the First Communion of a niece. It was as if he brought news of her own family.

'Walter will come soon and see me before the barges are empty. He will drink with me and all will be well, I know it!' He saw Jane's sadness and produced another bottle. 'For you when I am gone. If Walter is not here before I return to Roscoff, I will leave more for him and you will drink my health, yes? *Yes?*' He laughed and great gusts of sound echoed through the room. He took more wine but Jane put a restraining hand over her glass as she already felt lightheaded.

'You must come back to supper so that the children can see you,' she said.

'You are very kind. Très gentille,' he said, as he went towards the shop. 'I like to come again.'

It was certain from the acid look of triumph that Annie Cooper had been in the shop for some time.

Jane raised her eyebrows. 'Why, Annie! Why didn't you knock on the counter like you always do? You usually let me know, if I don't come running at once.'

'I was over at the butcher's and I saw you had a visitor, so I didn't like to disturb you. I bought my meat and came over here to wait until you'd finished entertaining.' Annie gave a self-satisfied smirk. 'I could tell that you were busy. You are good at feeding the men, aren't you? Even my Bert gets fed on soused mackerel up at the brickyard when my back's turned.'

André saw the sour smile and gave Jane an agonised glance. 'Zut alors!' he muttered and left the shop.

'And what can I do for you now that you are here, Annie?'

'He's a foreigner, isn't he? Sounded *very* foreign to me.' Jane smiled grimly. The old cat. She'd make a meal out of this. Jane wondered who had told her that Jane had fed the men at the brickyard when they were up to their eyes in work in the summer?

'Mr Duval is an old friend of Walter's. A very good friend and a businessman.'

'Of Walter's or yours? I didn't think Walter liked *foreigners* off the barges.'

Jane clenched her hands under the counter. 'Walter's friend, of course Annie. Why – what did you think? While Walter is away, I have to do business on his account. I have to deal with old friends, new customers and even with people I know and heartily dislike and would not have over my doorstep if it wasn't for business! There's no choice in business, Annie. Bert knows all about that.'

'Well, I suppose you know best, but I'd be careful if I was you. People talk, you know. I don't know what some would say if they knew you had men in the back room, not even in the shop, but through there, *drinking*. I can smell it now. Foreigners, too.' She picked a penny from her purse. 'I'll have a penn'orth of potherbs,' she said.

Jane stooped to find a carrot, an onion, a piece of turnip and some thyme and parsley. She thrust it across the counter and

167

Annie gathered it up hastily, her eyes like malevolent coals of excitement.

'Any order I can leave in at Mr Foster's?' said Annie, just to make sure that Jane knew where her next visit took her. There'd be quite a crowd in there, to listen and comment. This was the time when Mr Foster read the bulletin. It was the perfect time to take that Jane Darwen down a peg or two, and when she saw the sniggering faces come into her shop, she'd be less proud and sure of herself.

Jane turned away, the morning sour and dirty. She washed the glasses and corked the bottle firmly. – I might need another drop of that tonight, she thought. She cleaned the shop windows and the marble in a fury of activity and when Aaron came in and caught her reaching for the furthest corner, she felt better and almost ready to laugh at Annie's sour face and insinuations.

Aaron heaved a basket onto the counter. He tipped the fish over the marble slab; plaice with bright orange spots and silver hake slid down into a shining pyramid. He hauled a large skate onto the shelf and Jane took the cockles and put them on the counter with lemons and parsley. Aaron wiped his hands on his hessian apron. 'Will I be giving you tea?' said Jane.

Aaron noticed how Irish she sounded, which meant there was something on her mind. 'Are you too busy?'

'No, Aaron. I could do with a cup myself.' She smiled, wanly. Two men in the back room in one morning! What a pity Annie hadn't waited. She'd hate to miss anything.

Aaron sat down carefully on a whitewood chair, conscious that he left a trail of fish smells wherever he went. Jane poured out strong tea and he helped himself to sugar, stirring it for so long that Jane became restless.

'What's the matter, Aaron?' she said at last.

'I was going to ask you that. You don't look yourself, gal.' He looked wily. 'Missing Walter bad?'

'No, it's not that.' She gave a guilty start.

Aaron sucked at his tea noisily, and regarded her from under shaggy brows. 'I seen Annie Cooper up at the shop,' he said.

Jane sighed. 'She didn't lose much time spreading lies about me.'

'No, she's quick off the mark when it comes to gossip and lies,' he agreed. 'She does like to cause a bit of mischief, does Annie.' He gave a crafty grin.

168

'It's nothing to laugh about, Aaron. Tell me what she said? I might as well hear the worst then I shall know where I am.'

He laughed as if he knew a very good joke. 'Annie's a tartar and no mistake. Nobody like her for vinegar.'

'Aaron! What have you done?' Jane put down her cup. 'Aaron! I know you. You've a look about you, Aaron Sheath that means no good.' She was very pale.

Aaron laughed until the tears ran down his face and as his shoulders shook, the smell of fish came in waves. His red hair bristled on his head, in his beard and even in the short tufts in his ears. His reddened face with the bulbous nose and shaggy brows made him ugly, but the fierce expression that frightened babies had given place to a wicked sparkle. 'I settled she!' he said. He took another noisy swig and wiped his beard with the back of his hand.

'Aaron!' Jane was really worried now. 'What have you done?'

'Never could abide her, hikey old faggot! Can't ever forget her father made a bit of money. Gives herself too many airs.'

'What happened?'

'I saw her come out of here after your Johnny Onion man went and I wanted some flour, so I followed her. She were in there, all right. Just opened her mouth to tell them a tale about you Jane, but you know Annie. Never gets it out until she's spun it out into a yard-long tale, so they didn't hear anything. Just warming up, so to speak, and getting the interest going. She just got as far as saying you had to do a lot of business with men that Walter knew now he was away, then Mrs Duncan asked to be served and Annie waited until she was quiet.'

'She isn't the only one to spin things out!' said Jane.

'There were near a dozen of 'em in that shop, all hoping for some dirt. Women like them make me puke.' He slapped his knees with both hands. 'I gave a sort of cough, like, to make sure everyone knew it was me, then I went up and kissed her! I said with Bert away again, I'd be up to see her as usual. "Let me know," I said, "when he goes to Portsmouth next and I'll be up there with a nice bit of jellied eel."'

He roared with laughter, thinking of Annie's stricken face when his rough arms enfolded her and the stench of fish caught her nose. 'Aaron,' said Jane weakly.

'She was all of a heap, me gal.' He gave Jane a penetrating look. 'She took it hard,' he said, suddenly serious. 'She knew what I

169

wanted and she won't be spreading tales about you for a while.'
He began to grin again. 'I think she believed me, at least – half of
her did. Frightened to death she'll be, every time she sees me!'

'Aaron, you old devil! You are a disgrace.' Jane cut him another
slice of cake.

'Couldn't have that old faggot sewing bad seed. I know one
thing – she'll never live *this* down.'

Jane shook her head at him. 'You're a dear man. A dear man,
but do be careful. She's petty and backbiting and I wouldn't have
her harm you for the world.'

Aaron levered himself to his feet. 'Don't you fret on my
account, gal. Her can't hurt me. I owe nothing to nobody and
anyway, I gives her Dan jobs to do. It's them beholden to me, not
t'other way round and Bert likes a night fishing sometimes. He'd
be real mad if I said no the next time.'

'Dan isn't like them,' said Jane.

'Don't worry. I wouldn't take it out on him. He's the best in
that stable by a long chalk. Pity he has to stay there. He did say
once he'd move away if he could get work.'

The shop-bell rang and Jane laughed. 'You'd best be going
Aaron, before they think you're in here giving me a cuddle now
they know what a one you are for the ladies!'

From the amused hints given by customers, the tale had spread
and been embroidered. Not only had Aaron Sheath kissed Annie
Cooper in the grocery store but someone even tried to say that
they had been childhood sweethearts before Bert arrived on the
scene! Most women were glad to laugh about it, but Jane refused
to be drawn or to give her opinion. She listened and served, and
smiled indulgently, full of a warm haze of gratitude for Aaron. By
the time the children came home, she was almost sorry for Annie.

The back door was open and the air passed freely through the
shop but Clare sniffed.

'Mr Sheath was in here,' she said.

Jane threw up her hands. 'Holy Mary, can't I do anything
without you knowing the minute you come through that door?'
André came with sweets for the children and sat down to stew
and savoury dumplings and another glass of wine. The children
wondered why their mother had secret and very amusing
thoughts but were too busy learning French words to think too
deeply.

'You see the Queen, often?' said André when Sidney described
her horses and carriage.

170

'Not as often just now,' said Jane, 'but they say she will be at Osborne for Christmas. I miss seeing her go by and when she is here, the bulletins at the *Press* window are far more detailed than when she is away.'

'The horses go very fast, Uncle André, and there are sparks from the hooves.'

'But the Queen isn't well,' said Jane. 'The last time I saw her, she seemed to have shrunk. I suppose being all in black makes her look extra pale.' Jane sighed. 'Who will take her place? Carisbrooke will never be the same again when the royal rooms are used only by the Princess; and no choir in the chapel.'

'No ladies with birds on their hats,' said Clare.

'And no need to sit still for so long in Chapel,' said Jack, with a grin.

'She's over eighty and frail,' said Jane and André listened to it all so that he could tell his wife all about the English Queen that the Darwens knew well enough to sit with in Church.

Jane wondered why she was so fond of the Royal Family. The presence of the Court at Osborne made life more interesting and snippets of gossip about the people who visited the Queen there were welcome, but the remote members of the family meant nothing, as Jane had seen too much of poverty to have time for the idle rich. There were too many hungry children for her to accept the cynical disregard which many wealthy people had for the poor. Poverty wasn't brought on by laziness when it came to families ruined by the war. Daily, men returned wounded, with disabilities that cost them all hope of earning a living. The war pension was not enough to support a family and to keep them off the Parish.

'One old lady?' André shrugged.

'There are plenty younger who could be better spared,' said Jane sharply. 'She has lost her husband and rules her dominions alone, while other women are the chattels of their husbands. She has her government but she makes many decisions alone.'

'She has help! She has much help, not like you, Jane. You rule also your little kingdom while Walter is away. And you do well.' André said goodbye and Jane sat thinking long after the children were in bed.

When Walter came home, he would take control again and she must expect it to happen. When Walter came home. It was something she said less and less – and sometimes when the thought came unawares, she stifled a guilty dread. The family

171

worked hard, were happy and healthy and she had no constant fear that one day he would come home in an undisciplined and amorous mood after too much to drink and risk making her pregnant.

Sexual security gave her a kind of content, although she missed him and cared for him, but there was no nagging unhappiness any longer and the waves of loneliness flowed over her at less frequent intervals. It was like being a widow with no grief. Even the idea of the women in Pretoria giving the soldiers comfort and release from sexual lust no longer appalled her. If she was honest, it would provide a solution if it could be done without her knowing who and where it was.

– You are a wicked woman to have such thoughts, she told herself. No right-minded wife could think like that. It was wicked and immoral and if Walter suspected that she thought like that he would be angry – for of course, he would never go with another woman.

But it was so good to relax completely, stretched out alone in the big double bed.

Chapter 14

Christmas came and went, clouded with an air of mournful expectancy. It was said that the Queen was in poor health but nobody knew what was happening. Every month, of late, the old lady had heard of relatives dying, either because of the war or because, like herself, they were ageing. Good friends and high-ranking officials went, the Queen's sight and concentration failed and more and more audiences were cancelled for one reason or another. She saw very few people and the rumours grew.

Lord Roberts, now the hero of the Boer War, with a string of successes to his credit and the genuine regard of his troops carrying him on the crest of public acclaim, was the only visitor the Queen received with any pleasure outside her family. He was given audience on 14 January and the news agencies reported this meeting with the assumption that the Queen must be feeling better. The Islanders watched the bulletins and odd snippets of news came from the kitchen staff and the maidservants who worked at Osborne, but no official news was forthcoming, until 19 January, when the Queen's physicians issued a hint that the Queen was unwell.

By the twenty-first, there was another definite change and many members of the Royal Family and others from the Royal houses of Europe came to see her. Cowes and Southampton saw many luxurious foreign craft and an amused ripple of disbelief greeted the rumour that Kaiser Wilhelm had insisted on seeing her.

'I don't believe it,' said Aaron, in the shop.

'It's true. He came yesterday,' said Dan Cooper. 'I saw one of the gardeners and he told me he'd seen him. Never seen moustaches like it, he said, and looked as if he had a rod up his backside.'

Aaron sniffed. 'Poor old lady. Him coming will do her a lot of good, I don't think! She never could abide him near her.'

But Her Majesty was beyond caring who sat by her bed and who assumed precedence in the conventional mourning. She died, peacefully, on 22 January and a whole Empire mourned the passing of a century and a Queen. It was the end of an era.

Jane dusted off the black mourning shutters. They were chipped, so Edward gave them a fresh coat of paint. 'Pullers', the drapery shop by the Mall, quickly ran out of black crêpe and black-edged handkerchiefs as the local gentry hastened to show respect. The wider the black border, the more expensive they were, and therefore the greater the respect shown. The printing works in Chapel Street worked all night to churn out black-edged visiting cards and memorial cards with pictures of angels, lilies in abundance and marble urns. Photographs and prints of the Queen and every close member of the Royal Family appeared in every window, surrounded by Christmas roses and wreaths of evergreen.

Purple was the only fashionable colour after black, and only the most daring of new Sunday clothes were ordered in grey or semi-mourning.

Jane saw money being wasted everywhere and decided that even if she wanted to show respect, there was no call for waste. She searched the boxes under the beds and found an old velvet gown of black which smelled of mothballs, dust and stored apples. She hung the dress out to air and looked out black ribbons and gloves for the girls. The boys had black armbands and black neckties as it was far too expensive to dress growing children in black, just as she had no intention of buying full mourning for herself. Only the children of the very well-to-do dressed in black from head to foot.

Jane trimmed a hat with black tulle and purple flowers and bought new black gloves. She wore a miniature of the Queen on a velvet band round her neck and the black dress came up well after steaming.

Clare sulked, lost in envy of the girls who wore full mourning. She wanted to dress in the hideously dull crêpe and compromised by enveloping herself from head to foot in the voluminous black shawl with trailing fringes, that usually only saw daylight once a year.

The small picture of the Queen that Jane wore seemed

174

insignificant when compared to the rash of embroidered Union Jacks and other ornaments which appeared on muffs, coats and dresses. Jewellers did a roaring trade in cameo brooches and charm bracelets hung with sovereigns. Jane was tempted to buy another cameo of the Queen and wore it every day.

Flags flew at half-mast and the guards at the Barracks wore full ceremonial dress on the day of the funeral. Jet beads and earrings jingled, black velvet chokers and bows embroidered with yet more jet adorned the matrons of the nation and the children wore bracelets of black horsehair.

Perhaps it was an empty show, a sop to convention, but it was the custom and there was satisfaction in making some sort of show during the horror of the war. It was also, for the ordinary folk of the Island, a sincere outward sign of a very deep affection for the Queen.

The funeral took place with solemnity and pomp; a vista of black horses, some of which were dyed for the occasion, draped flags, black ostrich plumes, ribbons and muffled hooves.

Sam Walmsley twisted his hat in his hands and looked at the picture of the Queen on the counter of the shop. 'It'll never be the same again,' he said. 'But I'm glad she came home to the Island to die. It's right to think of her at Osborne, even if they did think fit to take her away to the mainland to bury her.'

The town went about its business, quietly, trying to keep up an outward show of mourning, but gradually the children were checked less and less often as they ran or shouted, and laughter instead of solemn reminiscence came from the snug bars.

With the coming of spring, the nation was tired of black. The brighter sun showed up bad dyes which turned cheap mourning rusty or tinged with green. Efforts at home cleaning only accentuated the stains made by underarm sweat and the harsh remedies left patches of bleached and weakened cloth.

Jane took out a white blouse and a grey skirt. She left them hanging by the bed and looked at them day after day, then removed the black tulle from her best hat and added white flowers instead. She put it on. Dare she wear it to chapel? She had seen Dr Barnes' wife in pale mauve with a purple hat and it was rumoured that the gentry was out of black. The black tulle lay crumpled and soiled on the white counterpane and the white flowers were crisp and clean. Jane pinned the hat to her bun and smiled at her reflection.

Clare had long abandoned her black shawl and now spent her free time gazing at the new spring fabrics in the only two shops in Newport that sold fashions. Light fabrics of pale grey, mauve and white were arranged with handkerchiefs, and bright trimmings of ostrich feathers from South African farms. Granny Cheverton bought a new black satin apron exactly like her old one, and even the Coopers had fresh curtains at their front windows.

Jane breathed deeply as she discarded her old clothes and hoped that she wouldn't have to wear black for a long time. Her health was good, the sun shone and trade was better than ever. When she needed extra work done, Edward saw that it was done well. He was eager to please her now he was about to start work at Cowes, but on the first Monday morning, when he set off, Jane had a lump in her throat. The first of her children to go, even if it was only five miles away and he'd be back for supper! She pressed a packet of food into his hand and put fruit in his pocket. She watched him go across the bridge, her hand touching the cameo at her throat. Edward looked back before turning the corner, as she let him go with quiet and understanding.

'What will Walter say?' said Amy.

'I don't know,' said Jane. 'I've written to him and told him, but I can't keep Edward kicking his heels forever.' She sounded more confident than she felt. 'He'll be used to the idea before he comes home.' She smiled. 'Archie thought it wise to let him go.'

'Archie would.' Amy gave Jane a sharp look. 'But anything that you do is right where Archie is concerned.'

'He's very helpful with suggestions, Amy. But so are you,' she added hastily. 'I put the goat's milk to sour and drain as you said, and it's very good.' She sent Amy away with a pat of her first attempt at goat-cheese and went back to read the *Morning Post*.

The latest Casualty List added many names to the men killed, whose homes were on the Island. The Boers were still a force to be reckoned with and their knowledge of local conditions still gave them many advantages. Their tactics made them difficult to find among the kopjes and along the river banks. They were defeated, but refused to recognise the fact and even with many leading Generals coming home, and talk of the first volunteers being released from duty, it was only the wounded who followed the Generals back to Great Britain and Ireland and more horses and supplies were being shipped out daily.

News from Walter was scanty. The last letter seemed to be

from a stranger. She opened it again, the print becoming a blur and a tear dropped on the page making a blister which soaked away, dimming the ink.

'Bad news?'

'Oh Sam, I didn't see you.'

He picked up the paper and saw the Casualty List. 'Not Walter?'

'No, Sam. You just came in when I was feeling a bit sorry for myself. Edward started at Cowes today, and the news tells me nothing. I wish I knew when Walter would be coming home. They say it will be soon, now.'

'Tears – and with Walter coming home? It's been a long time, Jane. Too long, perhaps.' He looked at the woman sitting by the table, trying to see her as Walter would and his heart sank. She had blossomed and her whole bearing told of her confidence as a businesswoman capable of handling traders, farmers and customers. Even Bert Cooper had to admit that she had a full say in the running of the brickyard. She took the partnership seriously and never gave an inch where money was concerned. Sam grinned. 'Bert might find Walter easier to handle than you, Jane.'

She laughed. 'He's a slippery one.'

'You're his match, gal.' Sam knew that people looked to Jane for advice and everyone who was worth their salt had a deep regard for her. As to business, she could get more with a smile than Walter could get in half an hour's argument. 'It'll be strange when he comes back,' said Sam. 'Strange for you and not easy,' he said.

She looked at him gratefully, touched and surprised at his sensitivity. 'It's not that I don't want him home,' she said. 'It's just that, well, I can't really say what I mean, Sam.'

'I know. It won't be easy to hand back the reins, even to Walter.' He dragged the banana boxes into the shop and put a bunch of Canary bananas on the counter. 'A few for you, Jane.' She bit into the peeled yellow fruit. 'Maybe the last we'll have for a while. Shipping is still too busy with the Cape to bother about these.'

'Then it's time the war ended,' she said, and entered the tally in the ledger. Sam saw her unhurried efficiency and his heart ached. When Walter came home, he would expect to take over as if he'd never been further than Portsmouth for the day. Everyone would have to move over, make room, as if he had never been to the other side of the world, and he would never suspect how difficult his homecoming would be for his wife... Sam went off hoping that his friend would stay away for a little while longer.

Jane was washing jam off Emily's blouse when Sidney rushed in with an envelope in his hand. Jane dried her hands and took out the paper with the Field postmark on the corner. The children gathered round, the fire crackled, Jane's heart beat painfully and Nero scratched and thumped his hind-leg on the floor.

'Your father is coming home in five weeks' time,' she said. She hardly recognised her own voice. Janey and Clare went on eating and Jack frowned. Everyone in the room was uneasy. Walter had been away for so long that his influence was blurred. Jane allowed more fun, more latitude, although she expected good behaviour and cooperation. She was invariably fair and had the knack of knowing when they were doing their best even when the results fell short of perfect. Walter wasn't like that.

Emily rushed to her and hugged her. 'It's wonderful,' she said, and the tension broke.

'Does it mean we'll have Blackie back again?' said Sidney. 'You don't think Father will let Uncle Archie keep him for ever, do you?'

'Did he say anything about me?' asked Edward anxiously.

'He was against it until I told him how much the others help now and how you had settled there so well. When he comes back, I think he'll let you stay,' said Jane.

'That's a relief.' Edward almost ran from the shop, catching up his haversack as he ran. The train whistle from the Shide line told him he had three minutes to get to the station and catch the train to Cowes. Jane smiled. He was so happy. The work satisfied him and he found the smell, the noise and the majesty of the huge steam engines the fulfilment of his dreams. He was important in his own right, entrusted to deal with baggage, to handle fragile packages and mail-bags and to care for livestock on the way to the boat or to the farms. He swept the platforms and helped passengers, often receiving tips for willing service and it was a relief to Jane that she had settled him there before Walter could refuse permission.

She read the letter again, conscious that she must make sure the children welcome him without the air of 'what difference will you make to my life?' that now was plain to see. This letter was warmer and contained more news. He was excited at the thought of coming home and his humour showed through the stilted words. Unconsciously, she began to tidy the room as if he might walk in at any moment. She folded linen, putting it in the airing cupboard and took out her mending, making a pile of the most urgent needs. After dinner, when the shop was empty, she started on the pile and searched for a blue button.

She riffled through the contents of the sewing-box and found a small bundle. For a moment, she couldn't remember what it was, then she slowly unwrapped the herbal preparations given her by Mrs Lee. She sat with the package in her hand, made a movement as if to throw it on the fire, then wrapped it up again. In her bedroom, she put the package in her drawer under her handkerchiefs in a box containing a few trinkets, a lock of Caroline's hair and a rosary.

She went back to the mending and when the children came home, she was gentle and attentive, with an air of resignation. Even the flies, gathering as summer heat made the fruit go overripe in a week and the fish go stale overnight, failed to annoy her as much as usual. During the next few weeks, Sam noticed her serenity and loved her for her courage in coming to terms.

It was a busy time. The troops were coming home, even though as late as mid-April, sixty thousand troopers took to the field in the hunt for prisoners to finish the resistance in isolated Laagers and villages. Pressure from ordinary citizens and those sick of the cost of the war in money and lives made the press campaign for a speedy finish to the fighting. It was estimated that a hundred and forty seven million pounds had been spent, and the war was still costing the nation another million and a half each week.

Excitement mounted and lists of honours to leading soldiers grew longer. Over a thousand were gazetted for meritorious service and Alfred Milner, in *The Blue Book*, gave his account of the war and his personal view of the present military situation. He was given three months' leave and much publicity attached to his idea that the Boers would accept the loss of their independence. Mrs Botha, the wife of General Botha, resumed peace negotiations with the British and now only scattered Boer commandos wandered, ragged and starving, from ruined farm to empty compounds, in a land laid to waste. With the coming of the winter rains, the Peace Party begged the remaining dissidents to work for a representational government that might be superior to a Republic in the Transvaal dominated by the Hollanders.

Leading politicians were honoured, but for the returning

wounded, there was little hope. Medals for some of the campaigns and a great deal of stirring phrases in the newspapers about the devotion and loyalty of 'Tommy' and a cheer for the troopships bringing the men home to Portsmouth was all they could expect and the shadow of the workhouse and the pitiful pension brought fear and disillusionment to hundreds of families.

'Did you see the names of firms hammered at the Stock Exchange?' asked Bert Cooper. 'Glad I got mine out before they went.' Jane went on scrubbing the counter. Bert picked up the ledger that Jane had checked and handed to him in the shop so that there was no need for him to enter the back room.

'I'm sorry for the ones with little enough in the first place who have gone bankrupt,' she said. 'I'll stick to selling food and not be bothered with the fancy things you talk about, Bert.'

'Nothing is right,' he said. 'Some of my men asked for more money and had the nerve to say that they wanted to join a Trade Union. I told them they were luckier than the workers in America where they have the contract system that makes the workers no more than slaves.'

'The ones coming back have a right to better times,' said Jane. 'I don't know how it will come about but surely in England they will do nothing wicked as they did in Germany, throwing an iron bar at the Kaiser!' She wrung out the cloth and Bert could see that it was no use hoping for a cup of tea from her. 'In any case,' she said, 'I have work to do to make sure all is well for Walter when he comes back.'

'About time he got home,' said Bert bitterly. 'I might even get invited in for a glass of beer or a cup of tea.'

'Annie will get your tea,' said Jane. 'She wouldn't like it if I entertained her husband here.' She smiled and Bert wondered what she had told Walter about him and if their first meeting would be difficult, but Jane had never said anything to him about the day he lost his horse and he couldn't ask her now.

But soon, in Newport, all apprehension was forgotten as they made ready for the returning heroes. Flags flew all over the Island on public buildings and private houses, and Newport High Street was a mass of bunting. The railway station was decked out with more flags and the town band lined up under an awning at the side of the station approach. As much of the coal-dust as possible had been swept up and hidden behind a huge placard bearing an out-of-date army advertisement to call men to arms – not the

180

most tactful greeting and hardly better than the coal-dust – but everyone was in a good humour and the platforms had been sluiced with water to remove the topcoat of grime.

The paintwork in the booking office had been renewed so hastily that the wooden partition stuck badly and the green paint on the seats was tacky. The Mayor inspected his watch for the fifth time and shifted his weight from one tight shoe to the other. Mr George Foster, resplendent in a magnificent silk hat stood proudly among the councillors with the Mayor under the arches of the Town Hall. It was cooler there but the air was still and tar at the side of the station approach bubbled in the heat. Emily stooped to pop the blisters until Janey pulled her away and wiped her fingers on a handkerchief. Jane looked on, taking no notice. She had other things on her mind, but nobody could guess what she was thinking, standing in her Sunday-best with her well-turned out, healthy family.

The first batch of troops would return to a civic reception in spite of a few dissident voices that hinted it was a waste of money and an increase in the rates. The Mayor, who had been chosen more for his good works than for his scholastic ability had appealed to a local schoolmaster to write his speech. He was terrified he would be struck dumb or forget his words, but nothing was going to rob him of his moment of glory. He wished there were fewer words to read and distrusted his ability to make the rhetoric sound eloquent, but he supposed the schoolmaster knew what he was about. The mayor was a successful draper and milliner and had never spoken like this in front of so many people.

Schoolchildren lined the route from the station to the Town Hall, waving streamers and flags. They had rehearsed the National Anthem, and a patriotic song composed by the same busy schoolmaster, set to an unfamilar tune just a note or two uncomfortably high. It was the type of tune that made anyone new to it go up when, in fact, the music went down and the children had little interest in learning it.

The Head Boy of Barton School stood rubbing the dusty toe caps of his shoes on the backs of his socks and tried to remember the words of *The Absent-minded Beggar*. He had been told to recite it with expression and appropriate gestures by the schoolmaster, who now walked to and fro, flushed with self-conscious superiority, clucking at children who stood out of line, or dropped their flags and creased their music-sheets. He carried a tuning fork and hoped that the military band could pick out the tune or better still, leave it alone.

The new barmaid at the Bugle wore a red hat, white blouse and a blue skirt. Aaron sniffed. 'You know what they say? Red hat and no drawers.'

All the local girls were out, ready to catch the eye of the unattached soldiers and Jane noticed with some misgiving that Maudie Dove was standing with the other girls from the laundry, laughing and giggling. Lucy was not with her and the girl looked bright-eyed and reckless. Jane was sad. Poor Lucy, with a mother who looked like a trollop with her low-necked blouse and her hair fluffed out round suspiciously rouge-pink cheeks. And Ben not dead a year.

The train whistle penetrated the eager chatter. Children climbed on walls to catch a glimpse of the white smoke from the funnel as the train came slowly into the last bend before the station. The engine seemed as if it would stop before it reached the platform but came on in a dignified last movement.

Jane clutched her purse so tightly that the clasp snapped. The children were pale in the heat and her own throat was dry. A pulse began to beat deep in her head and she took deep breaths and tried to relax. – *I must not faint.* Men filed from the train and lined up on the platform, ready for the short march to the Town Hall. Even from a distance, Jane saw that all the uniforms were spruce and the brass was highly-polished. Headed by two officers, sons of the Manors in the West Wight, well-valeted, they waited until the band struck up a march then marched stiffly, eyes front, as if on a barracks' square.

'No horses! Where are the horses?' demanded Sidney.

'They can't take horses on the train,' said Janey. 'It doesn't matter that they aren't here. Our father is coming back, that's the important thing.' Janey searched the faces under the various uniform caps. There were red, buff and green uniforms. Some men were from foot regiments and some from the Horse, but all had the common factor of the Island as their home. She could see no face she knew.

Emily began to cry. 'He's not here. He's not coming.'

'Wait,' said Jane. 'There's a lot more on the train.' It was with a sense of anti-climax that she saw him. Walter's hat was set at a slight angle, giving him an independent air. He was lean and

182

tanned and his moustache was well-trimmed. His spurs shone in the sunlight and he carried his shoulders back and his arms swung with disciplined ease close to his sides. The children waved and one or two of the women called to their husbands by name, but the soldiers were still on parade and could look neither to left or right.

The crowd followed to the square and the Darwens arrived in time to hear the children from Nodehill School, who hadn't rehearsed with Barton, piping uncertainly as the schoolmaster led them into the unfamiliar song. Children not in the parade climbed on horse troughs, and sat on the bars in the market place so that they could see over the heads of the crowd. The Mayor droned his speech and remembered most of the words, and the schoolmaster relaxed as each of his literary gems tumbled out.

The vicar climbed onto the platform and paused for a moment with his back to the crowd, just long enough to show off the full splendour of the splash of bright silk on his academic gown, before turning to ask a blessing. He preached a sermon on love of home and country, self-sacrifice and rest after toil, a homecoming after labour, which produced coarse giggles from the laundry girls.

The officer in charge shouted, the bugles called dismiss and an uncertain and suddenly disorganised assembly of men looked among the crowd for someone to claim them.

Emily pushed forward and pulled at Walter's tunic. He swept her shoulder-high and kissed her. The others lost their inhibitions and went to him, clammering for attention, the girls pulling at his hands and the boys standing near, grinning.

Walter looked over their heads and Jane met his gaze. She smiled, slowly. He had the same bold look that was there from the old days before their marriage, and it was as if he saw her for the first time, a good-looking woman among a crowd who immediately took his attention. His eyes took in every detail of her dress, her face, her shining dark hair, and with growing satisfaction, her figure. He pushed the children aside and embraced her.

'How's it been, gal?'

'We've managed,' said Jane.

There was no time to talk, no time to do anything but stop half a dozen times on the way home while friends and acquaintances shook Walter by the hand, slapping him on the back and saying,

'Walt Darwen! Well, I'll be hanged! We've missed you, Walt. Coming up the Wheatsheaf later? Bet you've a tale or two to tell!' Jane smiled serenely, but she watched his face, looking for something she badly needed to see, but couldn't find. She couldn't put a name to it and hardly knew what she was looking for, but what she didn't care to see, she saw plainly.

Walter's mouth was harder, his eyes smiled less than his lips and even his handshakes had a new controlled ruthlessness. He dragged himself away from the men and took Jane by the arm, his smile now warm and more like the man who went away. 'What's for tea?' he said.

The afternoon was a confusion of eating, drinking and laughing. Sam and Aaron dropped in and stayed to eat boiled ham and potatoes and apple pie. Jane was glad of the extra apple pie in the baker's oven, as every crumb was eaten. She made endless pots of tea and Walter was in his element. He answered questions about the campaigns and the fighting briefly, but talked more freely about the Boer prisoners, the native Africans and the horses.

'There was a poor broken-winded horse we found, left by the Boers when we overran one of their Laagers. He was so bad, we kept him for a lark and let him run with the mules. We called him Jeddah, after the Derby winner and when anyone came trying to scrounge a horse, we offered him.'

The children hung on every word. 'Is it true that the black children wear no clothes?' asked Lizzie in a whisper.

Walter laughed. 'Some of them do most of the time, but they were glad enough of a few rags to keep out the rain that comes in a deluge when it does come. They're poor little blighters. Not much cop at our kind of fighting but we were glad of them to look after the horses and to find us mealies when we had little else, and they buried our dead.' Lizzie's lips trembled, and Jane gave a warning glance. Walter laughed. 'Once we had a nice fat little boy who followed us wherever we went. I nearly brought him back to help in the shop!'

'And what would I be doing with an extra mouth to feed of any colour?' said Jane drily. She stacked the plates and the boys slipped away to do the work in the stables. Janey went with them to milk the goat and Clare tidied the shop. Emily took the dishes to the scullery to wash them and Walter smoked and talked until the air was blue with tobacco smoke, seeming unconcerned with time.

184

The boys returned and put the shutters over the shop windows and Jane brewed fresh tea. Walter sat in his old chair as if he hadn't a care in the world, enjoying being home again and the frequent visitors. George Foster looked in to ask if Walter would go over some of his bulletins and give him more detailed information of some of the battles. Bert Cooper came and accepted the cup of tea that Jane was forced to offer him. He smiled wryly, but with a certain caution, not knowing what was under her smooth smile.

'So, you're a free man again,' said Bert.

'Not officially,' Walter told him. 'I've to report to Albany every day until they call me to receive the campaign medals, tie up the loose ends and be demobilised.' He was almost apologetic. 'Give me a week or so to get settled in and I'll be ready to take over.' He saw Jack sitting and listening to the talk and suddenly thought there must be work to be done. 'What about the stable, lad? I'll come and give you a hand. It's getting late.'

Jack didn't move but looked puzzled. Walter stood up and stretched. 'It's all done, Father. They're all bedded down,' said Jack.

Sam had been about to fill his pipe again but he put it away. 'It's another day tomorrow, Walt. You'll be up early no doubt.' Sam went through to the shop and Jane unbolted the door for him. He pressed her hand. 'Don't let him see how well you've done. Not yet, Jane. Don't be too efficient.' She nodded. She had noticed the fleeting expression of annoyance on Walter's face when he realised that life had gone on without him and everything was running well.

The children were in bed and the smoke haze thinned, leaving a faint acrid smell. Jane opened the back door wider while she filled the kettles and the tank at the side of the range. She took her time over the last-minute duties, hoping that he might fall asleep in the chair and let her get to bed and be asleep before he came up.

Walter poured ale into his old tankard and sat back, dreamily looking round the room. Jane saw that he was becoming maudlin and knew that he had drunk more ale than tea even when she pressed fresh cups on him as often as she could. Nero lay with his head on Walter's slipper. 'Good old dog,' said Walter. 'You remember me. It's as if I'd never been away.'

'What will I do? Holy Mother what now?' whispered Jane in the dark scullery. She was aware that he watched every move she made in the night routine and he gazed at her now as she came

185

back into the living room.

'How have you been?' he said. 'In yourself, I mean.'

She shrugged. 'Well enough. Tired at times but there's been plenty to do as you know, but otherwise, well.'

He took her hand. 'You look better than I've seen you for years. You look pretty, Jane.' He smiled. 'Do you think, as I do, that perhaps Dr Barnes is an old fool?'

Jane turned to stone and wondered how he could avoid feeling her chill. So he'd come right out with it. He was wasting no time! 'I don't know. You heard what he said, Walter. I've been in good health without that worry.'

'But that was long ago. After such a gap, you might well be barren. Many women find they can't bear children after a while without a man.'

Jane pursed her lips. 'I don't believe that old wives' tale.' She saw his colder eyes. 'I'm still seeing,' she said. 'I'm still normal in that way.'

'Are you today?' She shook her head, her eyes wide with misery. 'Well, there must be ways. There must be ways other than those things I bought over in Portsmouth. I wouldn't use them again for the world. Made me sore enough to think I had the clap.'

'We can't. The Doctor can't give us anything. It's against the law. Against God's law, they say.'

He moved impatiently. 'There are women who never have more than they want, or not often. How do they manage?' he began to pace the room. 'What do you know of the law? What right have you to quote God's law? You aren't a Papist any more.' He turned to her, his eyes hot with anger and sadness. 'Where was God when they killed at the Modder and Bloemfontein? Where was He in the hunger and death in Mafeking and Ladysmith? Where was He while they mutilated and raped? Yes, they raped women, beat and humiliated them. Where was God then?'

'Don't,' pleaded Jane.

'I'll tell you where He was when all that was going on! He was with the women following us from camp to camp. He was looking after their dirty tails. They didn't get caught! Not with child. They had plenty of disease, I suppose, but they never got caught. Was disease their punishment or didn't He care about that, either?'

Jane shut her ears with her hands to blot out the bitter,

blasphemous voice, the voice of a child who has suffered and is refused comfort.

Everything about him said, 'It isn't fair!' He was a man with a sense of injury and a new selfishness born of deprivation. In this mood, he wanted to take from life, not to be soothed. The echo of the violence he had left was there between them. It was a man's problem and Jane was powerless to comfort him and restore his lost faith. Faith? How strange that at the moment when she needed to ignore the teachings of her lost faith, it was to that faith she prayed. – Holy Mary, Holy Mary, she said over and over again in her mind. Help me! Dimly-remembered dogma, her commonsense and her own selflessness fought and she could see no salvation.

The rest of the house was quiet except for the snores of the dog, Jane saw with painful clarity that the peace and continuity of the future with Walter depended on her, and she braced herself to smooth the hard line of his mouth with one finger.

'Perhaps that's what he is,' she said. 'Perhaps he was wrong and the Doctor is an old fool.'

Walter filled the coal-buckets while Jane went upstairs. She lifted the linen wrappings from the package under her clean handkerchiefs and took out one of the fingers of cocoa butter and herbs. She inserted it and it was odd and unfamiliar. She was tense with agony of mind and fear. – I must relax, she thought, and remembered the wine that André had left. She crept down while Walter chopped an unnecessary amount of wood in the outhouse and drank a tumblerful straight off, pouring another which she drank while she waited in bed for her husband.

The strong wine dulled her guilt and her sense of reality and when Walter came to her, she was all soft arms, whispered comfort and wifely love.

At four o'clock, Jane turned over in bed and touched her sleeping husband. Wide-awake, she saw him in the dawn and her tears soaked the pillow. Her head ached after too much wine drunk quickly and late, her thighs were sticky with cocoa butter and semen and she felt dirty and lonely, deep in an abyss of sorrow greater than she'd ever known.

Chapter 15

'I can milk her all on my own,' said Janey.

Walter smiled. 'I'll stay and watch.' He was relaxed after making love the night before and everything he saw filled him with pleasure. He was home, his wife was even more desirable than he remembered and she'd kept the shop and run the business well in his absence. The animals were in fine fettle and even the little goat that Janey was milking was pretty.

Janey sat on the stool, sending squirts of warm milk into the bucket. She liked milking, but not when someone was watching. She glanced up at her father, hoping he would go and she could push her face into the warm flank and feel the nanny nuzzling her ear, but he only smiled as if he thought she was looking for praise, so Janey sat upright and got on with the milking as quickly as possible.

Walter bent a straw and closed his mind to matters that troubled him. It was a relief to know that Jane would come to him again and to know that he wouldn't have to look elsewhere for sexual relations. – I'm clean, he told himself. The doctor out there had given him a clean bill of health and any he had taken had been a better type like the woman in Pretoria after he was wounded.

It wasn't fair that women like that one should enjoy themselves and never get pregnant, or if they did, they seemed to know what to do. They went out to the Cape to look after the troops and once there, they deserved all they got. There was no room for guilt. They supplied a need, had their fun and must know that nothing permanent could come of it. She would soon find someone to fill the bed he'd left. He smiled dreamily. She'd been very good and had taught him a thing or two. He sat up and saw that Janey was leaving, the milk pail in one hand and the eggs in another bucket. He followed slowly. There were things he'd miss, but he couldn't think of forcing whore's tricks on Jane.

Janey went out of sight, hurrying back to the shop. It was good to have Father home but he did get in the way of her freedom, as if she needed telling what to do. He was in a very good temper this morning, and it was odd that her mother didn't seem as happy ... When Janey found her in the outhouse filling the copper with dirty linen, she was crying.

Walter looked up at the windows in Sea Street and wondered if Bert still had his fancy-piece in Portsmouth. Some said a dose of pox made a woman barren and there had been no signs in the woman in Pretoria. He wondered uneasily if she had been as clean as she said. No! He was being stupid. He'd have known the signs. He was well and hearty and had nothing wrong with him but a bit of soreness that went off. That was a long time ago and the doctor had found nothing. He turned at the corner and went back to the stable, harnessing Bess ready to take the cart to the Barracks when he reported. He'd be more at home on Blackie and must get him back soon. He clicked his teeth at the old mare and she lumbered out of the stable.

Gradually, Walter did more and the boys welcomed some time to play, but Jack still did more of the deliveries and Sidney was allowed to go with him and sometimes Aaron took the boys fishing.

'That young 'un did a man's work when we had the glut of mackerel,' said Aaron. 'He needs a long rope, that one. A bit like you, I reckon,' he said, as Walter frowned. 'Let him wear himself out. Do him good and do you good to get back slowly.' Aaron made no mention to him of any of the incidents that had happened concerning the Coopers while Walter was away and nor had Sam, for which Jane was grateful, so Bert relaxed and Annie tried to be pleasant when they knew they were safe from his displeasure.

It also meant that once more, Walter and Bert spent hours together in the brickyard, with nothing to do but play cards in the office while they said they were going over the books.

'Where's father?' Emily asked. She sighed. 'Up the brickyard, I suppose. I wanted a ride with him on the cart.' She was the only one who seemed wholly delighted to have him back and resented him being away from the shop, but Jane secretly wondered what Bert was doing with the books now that she didn't keep an eye on things. After two weeks, Walter would soon be free of military service, Blackie would be home from Wootton and Jane need never see Bert Cooper again at the brickyard. That would be a relief even though it meant having less to do in running the business. There was no time to dwell on those problems. She must start again and let Fate take its way with her.

The depression that had built up over the past two days made her bend over the dolly tub and rub the clothes furiously on the washboard. There was work enough to do and if she was no longer alone, she might even get down to see Amy once in a while.

She dried her hands and drained the suds. There was dinner to cook and ironing to finish. Listlessly, with a blinding headache, and a heavy feeling in her pelvis, she went to her room. She knew that she must be pregnant. What did it matter? Her linen drawers stuck to her. The heat of the boiler must have made her perspire more than unusual. Jane hated to smell of sweat, so she found fresh drawers and felt the soiled ones. They were quite damp. Feverishly, she tore them off and found, to her surprise and rising joy that her underwear was stained with the beginnings of a period. She changed and put on a cotton diaper. She wasn't pregnant!

She soaked her wet things in a bucket in the corner of the scullery. 'I'm not caught! Mother Mary, I'm not caught!' she said. Ikey the cat licked the piece of fishskin she'd found by the drain and hardly looked up.

'Ikey! I'm all right,' said Jane, laughing hysterically. They'd made love four times and she wasn't pregnant.

In the bedroom, she opened the box in which the remaining pessaries lay. She had used one each time and there were several left. She should have trusted old Mrs Lee. Dear clever, kind witch that she was, she should have trusted her! Jane was overwhelmed by a sense of deep gratitude and sang as she mangled the clothes. Just a few left, and a week's grace while she was losing blood. – I must get some more, quickly, she thought. I must never be without them again. A week's grace and others to use after that, then she must visit the gypsy encampment. Jane wondered how she could do this without arousing comment. All the time she made bread and butter pudding and prepared fish, she was thinking.

Walter liked a quiet drink with Bert on Saturdays, so if she suggested that Bert brought the ledgers to the shop, she could leave them in peace and take the children for a picnic in the river-fields.

On Saturday, she looked at the sky and knew it would be a lovely day, so she packed a basket with food. 'They've all been such good children while you've been away and had little time to play,' she said.

'Take them,' said Walter, heartily. 'I've things to talk over with Bert and I'll see to the shop.' It suited him well as he had tales to tell Bert that would never do to be heard by the family, and Bert was good for a laugh when they were alone.

Jane walked through the fragrant fields, the trees heavy with late summer. The gypsies would be back after the rounds of the summer fairs and would be making pegs and baskets. She had seen the men in the town, recognisable by the bright neckerchiefs and shocks of untidy black hair, leading strings of donkeys past the shop on the way to the Agricultural Show at Nine Acres field, but she had seen none of the women. Soon, they would make their last round before winter, selling pegs and telling fortunes when the last of the summer seaside visitors had gone.

The food was spread out under the shade of a tree by the old tower at the bend of the river and when they finished eating, Jack brought out rags soaked in paraffin to burn at the foot of the tower, hoping to smoke out the bats that lived in the ruin. Jane knew that this would absorb them for hours and the whole family would want to watch.

'I think you're cruel,' said Sidney. 'How would you like to be smoked out of bed?'

'Don't be silly. Bats can't feel,' said Jack.

'I bet they can! It's cruel and I'm not staying to watch,' said Sidney. He followed his mother along the towpath by the houseboats. At first, Jane nearly sent him back, but she knew that he would be upset to see the bats fly and to be honest, she was feeling shy and glad of his company, as they got very close to the encampment. Rough piebald ponies were in the stockade, bred by the gypsies, hardy and hardworking. Sidney climbed the gate, calling softly, using Romany words he'd picked up at horse fairs and the ponies came to him. Jane went on, round the corner to the waggons where barking dogs cringed under the tailboards. Two dark-eyed children with bare feet and expressionless faces stared as she went towards the central caravan.

191

The open door of the painted waggon reflected the sunlight in its highly-polished coloured glass. Glimpses of brass and decorated pots and pans could be seen on mahogany shelves and Mrs Lee sat on the bed at the back. She smiled a welcome. 'I expected you,' she said. 'I saw it this morning.' Jane licked dry lips. 'Don't be afraid,' said Mrs Lee. 'There's nothing *here* to harm you.'

Her eyes were dark as sloes and as blank as she opened a wooden box bound with hoops of brass and took out a bulky package. 'Mrs Lee,' Jane began.

'You came for these, didn't you? I have them all ready.' The old voice sounded tired.

'You have no idea what they mean,' said Jane. 'I can't tell you...' Mrs Lee held up a hand and her eyes now pierced Jane's thoughts, giving out compassion. 'You helped me so much,' said Jane.

'I help when I can, but the time will come when I can help no more. The young ones haven't the power and they learn too slowly to take in all I know. They think I shall live forever. I haven't time to teach all I know and much will be lost.' Her face was sad.

'How can I thank you?' said Jane.

'I know how it is. None better. Men are the same the world over. Take care.' She put a hand on Jane's wrist, her fingers digging into the skin. 'You have the other safely?'

'The big grey pill?'

'Keep it safe for if I can't help you. There may come a time when you will need it.'

'But you will be here all the winter!'

'The waggons will be, but I may pass on.'

Jane pulled out her purse, thrusting the package deep inside her reticule. The woman looked at the money, hesitated and then waved it aside. Jane couldn't understand her. No gypsy that she'd met in the shop ever refused money, especially when freely-offered, but she knew that she must not offend. On impulse, she unpinned the cameo with the Queen's head in relief and pinned it to the gypsy's shawl. A sweet smile creased the brown face and old Mrs Lee touched the brooch, gently. 'Sweet Sara and Mary go with you,' she said.

Sidney was still sitting on the fence but now was surrounded by gypsy boys. He was sketching one of the ponies, using a worn

192

pencil stub and a scrap of paper. He had shared his apples with the boys and they were teaching him new words. He appeared to be completely at home with the strange wild-looking youths. He gave the sketch to the smallest and jumped down from the gate.

'I like them,' he said. 'Do you, Mother? I like the colours they wear, their waggons and their dark hair. Your hair is like that, Mother.'

'They are good people,' she said.

'Bert Cooper says they are bad,' said Sidney. 'I don't believe him. They care for their horses and love them, which is more than he does.'

'They are kind,' said Jane. She smiled. – You don't know how kind, she thought with wonder. She saved my life. I can live in peace for at least another three months. 'I think that you and I are a little bit like them,' said Jane.

'May I wear an earring?' asked Sidney.

'Indeed you can't!' retorted Jane. 'I wonder if Jack has burned down the tower yet?'

Jack was covered with smuts and they had seen only one bat but the children were happy and sang all the way home, and Jane could look forward to anything that life offered.

Walter looked up, smiling. He winked and nodded over to Annie Cooper who sat straight in a hard chair. Bert's expression was annoyed. 'Did you want me, Annie?' said Jane.

'I thought you'd be here,' said Annie.

'There's no need now my husband is back. I have handed all the business over to him now and I have no need to entertain, on business.'

Annie blushed and was about to retort but Bert stopped her. 'We'll be on our way, Jane. Can't expect you to make tea for us both.'

'Please don't go.' Jane beamed at them and Bert looked apprehensive. 'Now that Walter is back, it makes it so much easier to have people in for a chat.' Walter looked pleased, and Jane poured water into the big brown teapot from the kettle that was as usual, singing and ready for use. She brought out a lardy cake, secure in the knowledge that Annie could never make them as light and was mean with the fruit and the sugar crusting.

'I can see that you got on together while I was away,' said Walter.

'We had our ups and downs,' said Jane, 'but it worked out, and I

193

had a lot of help from friends.'

Annie took another slice of cake. – There'll be no supper for Bert if she can get away with it, thought Jane. Silly woman, she drove him out to the Wheatsheaf and the potato pies and smiles of Mrs Grace. She smiled at Bert with a feeling of pity. The Coopers had nothing she wanted and now she had her man at home and a full married life. In her new mellow mood, she even thought with nostalgia of the spice of business tension when she queried something shady that Bert had in mind for one of the brickyard contracts. She would miss a lot, but it would be worth while if Walter was happy.

Walter leaned back and began one of his African stories while Jane cleared away the dishes. Bert looked bored and Annie was restless. Jane smiled. Walter had so many stories to tell that lost their impact if the audience knew nothing of the country in which he had fought and the men who featured in the tales. He and Mr Foster were great friends now, and a sigh of relief went round the Wheatsheaf snug when they were in a corner deep in conversation, surrounded by Mr Foster's noteboooks. – It will even out, she thought complacently. Everything would even out once the first emotional tensions lessened. In the back of her mind, one disloyal thought haunted her.

She looked across at her husband, relaxed and laughing at something he remembered. He was better-looking and very healthy, but harder. When he made love, it was with a new haste, almost a fury and he hinted that she might enjoy making love in other ways. She had only a dim idea of what he wanted, but refused to hear of this and he seemed content. How had he learned of such things? Who had told him these things or who had shown him and been a partner in the love that belonged only to his wife?

'Blackie will be back tomorrow,' said Walter. 'He'll come back in double harness with the big cart of Archie's and he can bring the winter feed.' He eyed Annie with a wry smile. 'He'll need a bite to eat, Jane.'

'I know it,' she said shortly. 'I'll leave it for you but I have to see Miss Prentice about winter coats for Emily and Lizzie and Clare.' She dreaded seeing Archie when Walter was there. Archie couldn't keep his eyes off her and Walter would notice.

'You seem glad to be relieved of the need to see Walter's friends,' said Annie.

'I'm glad to see anyone but it's good to have more time to see to my girls. They're growing up fast and like new clothes and they work very hard,' said Jane.

'I suppose Miss Prentice will make hand-me-downs of old clothes,' said Annie, and sniffed.

'Of course. You know all about that, Annie, and I do have seven children to clothe as well as Walter and myself.' Everyone knew about the coat that Dr Barnes had given Annie for charity. It had come from a patient who seemed to think the doctor was a sorting house for such things and Annie had eagerly offered to dispose of it for him. Three months later, it appeared in church, on Mrs Cooper, altered by Miss Prentice and barely disguised by a fur collar.

'Yes, take more time for yourself, Jane,' said Walter expansively. 'It's time for blackberries. You always did go picking at one time.'

The autumn days were dry and fine, summer had forgotten to leave and life was less demanding. There were late blackberries and crabapples and the girls dragged long streamers of old man's beard from the hedgerows to trim their hats. Walter laughed, saying they were like the ostrich plumes of Africa, and the weeks passed pleasantly.

On Sundays, Jane visited the cemetery with bunches of bright berries and leaves and late flowers, and each time, she went to the gate by the river and gazed across at the thin lift of smoke from the gypsy fires. She made sure that Sidney took fruit for the gypsy children and sometimes fish for Mrs Lee, and as many clothes that she could give away with a clear conscience. When the gypsy boys brought the pegs round, they were given tea and stale buns and more fruit for the old lady.

When the last of the shining chestnuts had been gathered from Parkhurst Forest, the kernels sweet and crisp and easy to sell in the shop, there was a mushroom smell in the woods and time was passing quickly. Jane knew that she must go down to the camp again to see Mrs Lee. On Sunday, Walter would be at Wootton and the children in Chapel, so she could walk down to the camp.

Jane put on a warm serge skirt and jacket and packed a basket of cake and fruit. Walter left in the trap and Jane listened until the hoofbeats faded up Snooks Hill before she put on her hat. Sidney ran after her and caught her up on the quay. 'Why aren't you in Chapel with the others?' she said.

195

'I said I'd meet someone in the fields,' he said, and looked embarrassed.

Jane tried to sound cross. 'If I tell you to go to chapel, then you go there, my lad. Your father would be angry if he knew.'

'I'm sorry, Mother.' He grinned. 'Father never goes to chapel and you don't really like it, do you?'

'That's neither here nor there,' she said severely. 'You must be brought-up well and chapel is a part of it.'

'Come on, Mother. It's too late to go in now and I want to show you something.' He dragged at her hand.

'What do you mean? I'm not going near the tower. The bats are back and I don't like them.'

'It's not the tower. It's the camp.' He pulled at her hand and she followed, slowly. 'Come on, we'll get a good view from the bend.'

They followed the river where the reeds lay brown and dark against the low-tide mud and Jane could smell the acrid wood smoke and even see the billows of black and grey between the trees. It was a big fire but there was wood in plenty along the banks and the air was colder today.

'Come on, Mother, let's get closer. I know we shouldn't watch as we're not Romany. They say the gorgio must never see this.'

'What do you mean? What mustn't we see?'

'Didn't you know? Old Mother Lee died and they're burning her waggon.' He looked up at his mother's disbelief. 'They have to do it. It's their law.'

Jane put out a hand to steady herself. Sidney's voice came through a mist of fear and pain. Pain? She looked stupidly at her hand where it had clutched the first available branch and the long bramble thorns embedded in her palm. Drops of blood welled from the bluish wounds and she had a sudden vision of the crude pictures of the Sacred Heart with flame and thorns that she had seen on her mother's bought Indulgencies. She shuddered violently.

'Holy Mary, Mother of God, be merciful,' she whispered.

Sidney dabbed her hand with his handkerchief. 'Are gypsies Catholic, Mother?' She stared at him. 'Only, you did pray for the old woman in that way. You know, the prayer you told us went with the Rosary.'

'She said, "Sweet Sara and Mary go with you",' said Jane.

'So she was a kind of Catholic.' Sidney sat on the bank and Jane sat with him, unable to walk. They watched the fire from the line of trees that hid them from the camp. The shell of the waggon, lit by the consuming flames, stood empty. The glass splintered, the colours erupting, the painted wood curled and the oil in the lamp exploded.

The roof fell in a shower of gold sparks and the flames died. Summer died and with it, all Jane's peace of mind, her hopes and her happiness.

'Come on, Mother. We ought to get back before Father comes home.' Sidney sounded anxious now. 'They'd better not see us here watching.' He hung onto her arm and Jane could never recall walking home that day, but somehow, she was there, waiting with her apron on when Walter came in with the hot tray from the bakery. He had worked up an appetite going to Wootton and the smell of roasting meat was irresistible. The huge joint of glossy beef was surrounded by baked vegetables. He started to carve while Jane stirred gravy and piled boiled potatoes into the blue Delft tureen. Nobody noticed her silence and she was glad to hide under the general chatter. She ate little, mentally sitting outside the family, watching but having no part in it. How soon would that be true? How soon would it be before she left them, to die? Or could she make Walter understand?

Her husband was eating, his face flushed from the heat of the room and the amount of food he was consuming. Since his return, all his appetites were grosser, as if he had to get more and more of the good things in life to make up for the two years of deprivation. Jane was getting heartily tired of hearing at every meal, 'better than mule's liver! Better than mealies, better than flour with weevils in it!' Even the children, at first eager for tales of the war, were bored by his preoccupation with food and drink. He talked of little else at meal-times and drank a good deal.

Walter wasn't the man who had gone away. He wasn't the man who had been almost tender after that first night back. Jane hated the coarse laughter she interrupted when she came in and found Walter with his friends. Sam and Aaron no longer spent whole evenings with him, but other men came, who had fought in the war and shared the experiences. Some were good men who talked well and held Jane's interest with vivid descriptions of life in South Africa. When they came to see Walter, she would hear how the Boer farms were run, how the Veldt looked in the different seasons. She heard of the beautiful animals and birds and the types of houses they had in Pretoria and the Cape.

197

On these evenings, she could visualise the herds of wild buck by strange river banks, the Boer women, tough and wiry, fighting with their menfolk, forming their waggons into circles of defence and taking rifles to fight the British. They were her enemies but she admired and envied them. She loved those evenings, and looked forward to them, but when the other sort came, the ones who looked at her as just another woman, not the wife of their host and a person of importance in her own home, men who drank and brought out the worst in her husband, often ending the evening in the Bugle, she went to see Granny Cheverton or took the children to chapel concerts.

From snippets of conversation, she gathered that these men had been with camp-followers and the local whores and she now was certain that Walter had done the same.

Jane spooned out hot custard over the stewed apple and cleared away the meat. Tonight he would want her, ending a day of self-indulgence with a love what was no longer tender. Sometimes, the act of love now filled her with revulsion as he insisted on more abandoned 'refinements' and she now faced the fact that this meant a lot to him and he would not give up his pleasure easily.

The day dragged on, and the long-awaited rain came in cold glassy sheets, making the road an evil-smelling stream. Jane closed the front door and made up the fire. Walter stared out at the rain and decided that it was too wet to go to the Bugle. He sent Jack to the stable and settled at the harmonium, a full glass of ale at his side. Jane saw that the back of his neck was thickening with all the good food and lack of real exercise. He drank and was more and more sentimental as the evening wore on.

– Five more! thought Jane. Five more times when I can be safe and then? Long after Walter was asleep, Jane lay stiff with misery and frustration. He had taken her with no tenderness, but with rough urgency, showing no consideration, and her breast was badly bruised. She wanted to leave his bed and never let him touch her again.

The last leaf fell and the river under the bridge lapped the parapet as the water rose with the autumn storms. Jane searched her work-box and then the handkerchief box for the third time, but only the big grey pill remained. She had pretended to be asleep and so kept Walter away with one excuse after another for two weeks. If she could keep him away until her period came, she

198

was safe for another week as even he would not touch her then, in spite of his new habits.

Walter wound the clock and put Ikey into the outhouse. At the stair door, he took Jane's hand and squeezed it. His eyes were red-rimmed and bloodshot. 'Not tonight, Walter,' she pleaded. 'I'm so tired. I had a heavy wash today.' His grip tightened, and he half-dragged her to their room upstairs. He put a candle on the chest of drawers and looked at her. 'I'm very tired,' she repeated.

'What's wrong with you, gal? Are you sick?'

'It's not that, Walter. I'm frightened.'

'Frightened? After all these years? You enjoy it. What's to frighten you? We've proved that I was right and the Doctor was wrong, stupid old fool.' He laughed. 'You're barren. The last lot left you barren. It must have or you'd have caught long ago. I can have you whenever I want you. I do want you now.' His face hardened. 'You're my wife and my property before the law and I'll do with you what I damn well want to do, in spite of all your lady-like objections.'

'Listen. Walter. Since you came home, I've used some herbs that Mrs Lee gave me. I didn't tell you because I thought you'd be angry, and I could always get more to use without you knowing. She's dead, Walter. I can't get any more. Dr Barnes could be right. I've used the last of what she gave me and I don't know what to do.' She sank onto the side of the bed and sobbed.

'You agreed with me that the Doctor was a fool! You've been with me for months!'

'I was using the herbs.'

'And do you want me to believe that a few herbs would stop it? It's the same as I say, you can't get caught any more. It's Nature. You've had enough and your body won't grow any more babies.'

'I'm not that old. I see regularly.'

Walter shrugged. 'That's as maybe but you won't *take* now, Jane. Come on, what's a man to do? Get into bed and you'll see I'm right.' He slipped out of his clothes and began to unbutton Jane's dress. He pulled it roughly from her shoulders and smothered her neck and breasts with moist kisses. He pushed down her skirt and drawers, leaving her naked.

'No, Walter,' she moaned. 'Do you want to kill me?'

'Be still. Can't you see how I want you? Come on, gal. I must have you.'

Jane broke away, trying to cover herself with her ripped skirt,

199

hating her nakedness. Walter grabbed her arms from behind and came up close behind her. 'No!' she cried.

'It's one way or the other,' he gasped. 'Some of the men would take mules but I drew the line there. It's front or back and I don't care a damn which!'

Jane collapsed on the bed. 'That's a mortal sin. I couldn't.' She shivered with cold and revulsion and he rolled on top of her, making no attempt now to kiss her or to touch her with gentleness. Jane's hand was stiff from the thorns and she could see the burning waggon. – It's a judgment on me, she thought. I've sinned against Nature. She lay like a log until he had finished with her, then groped for her shift and turned away to stare into a well of darkness.

Walter turned in bed as if he, too, found sleep impossible. Drink and Jane's passive resistance had made an enjoyable climax evade him. He was tense and his loins ached with congestion. He was aware of her still form and a cold air of rejection. As his head cleared, he wanted to touch her and say he was sorry, but he dared not touch her now. – Tomorrow she'll have forgotten, he hoped and resented having to be sorry.

– If this was Africa, a woman would give me release if it didn't come naturally, he thought, and felt injured at Jane's lack of understanding.

Chapter 16

Christmas came and went in a foggy drizzle. Everyone had perpetually muddy boots and the dog had distemper. Sidney was in an agony of concern as the poor animal dragged its weak haunches to the backyard and coughed, spasmodically, in the damp air. The boy dosed Nero with distemper mixture that Sam brought for him and the dog was getting better, but Sidney couldn't forget that it was his father's fault.

Since his return, Walter had insisted that Nero was *his* dog and seemed to resent Nero's devotion to the boy when he gave him the daily dish of strong tea. He said that in future Sidney needn't bother as he was back and would see to his dog, so Sidney did as he was told, not knowing that nine times out of ten, Walter forgot the tea and sometimes even to feed him.

The fact that the dog in the brickyard had distemper and had bitten Nero badly, did nothing to convince Sidney that Walter wasn't wholly to blame. Jane tried to say that the giving of tea as a preventative of distemper was an old wives' tale and that the dog would have caught it anyway, but Sidney wouldn't listen.

Walter wondered uneasily if he should listen to the old remedies. He began to wonder if there could be truth in other tales, the ones that Jane believed, like the gypsy and her herbs. He glanced at his wife when he thought she wasn't looking and knew that she had changed. She hadn't been the same since that night he had taken her against her will. Now, she came when he wanted her. She silently allowed him to take her to bed when he demanded his rights but never showed any sign of love or encouragement. He was torn between shame and anger. It was like sleeping with a tailor's dummy.

Jane was quiet most of the time. Walter caught her once with the old Rosary in her hands. He tried to forget how tired she looked. Women were fanciful creatures and the weather they were having after the hot summer was enough to make anybody moody. Jane was one for the sun. She was cheerful when it shone. He shook off his own depression. She would soon be showing and that made her moody. Yes, it would be all right once that was over. If she was losing, there wasn't much point in staying in tonight. An evening in the Wheatsheaf would do him good and he could get away from the silence and Sidney's accusing eyes that seemed to follow him everywhere.

Jane heard him slam the door and she took out the gophering iron. There was linen to iron and the pinafores to crisp. Lizzie wanted to try her hand at it, so Jane gave her a piece of paper on which to practice. Lizzie liked housework and embroidery and Jane was glad of her help. 'You and Emily are quite little housekeepers,' she said.

Clare and Janey were washing their hair and Emily braided it for them. They were giggling and teasing and winding bright ribbons in the braids and pretending to be music hall actresses. The boys were in the outhouse, laying the fire under the boiler ready for the morning, and the animals had been fed.

– If I should die, they could manage without me, thought Jane. I wonder if they would miss me, and for how long? She smiled at the laughter. They've had so much work to do, far too young, that they can manage. Perhaps it's as well. It might be that this was intended and they will have all that experience to carry them on in the future when I'm gone. The Lord moves in a mysterious way, she decided.

Lizzie gave a little cry of pain. She put out her hand to Jane, tears pouring down her face. The gopher had made a red weal on her hand and Jane crooned over her as if she was a baby, soothing the burn with butter and covering it with a clean rag. Lizzie sat on a stool, calmed and self-important. – Perhaps they do need me after all, thought Jane, but this gave her no cause for pleasure but rather added to her despair.

Walter rose early as it was his day to deliver to the Barracks. He sluiced his head to clear away the fumes from the night's drinking and heard a noise in the outside privy, like a cat or a person being sick. – Someone stepped on Ikey, he thought. He climbed into his trousers and went down to breakfast, glad to see Jane pouring tea.

'I can just do with that, and so can Nero,' he said with the false

202

heartiness he found necessary these days. He put down the dish for the dog and added more sugar to his own big cup. Nero wagged his tail fairly strongly, but Jane ignored him after setting his breakfast on the table. – At least the dog bears me no grudge, he thought crossly. Anyone would think I'd half-murdered her, the way she goes on, sitting there like a plaster saint!

He ate hurriedly and left without a word. Jane cleared away and put more water on to boil. She tidied and swept through the shop, sending the dirt from the potato sacks into the gutter where it lay in a muddy heap. Rainwater slowly surrounded it and Jane watched it being washed away, like sandcastles that children built, washed away on the tide.

Annie Cooper stepped over the mud and walked into the shop, shaking the rain from her cloak and giving Jane a sharp look. Jane beat down the nausea that seemed to last longer each morning and she put a hand to her throat.

'You don't look well, Jane,' said Annie

Jane shivered. 'The cold gets into me.'

'Cold?' Annie raised her eyebrows. 'I was thinking how close and muggy it is. I feel too warm in this cloak, but it's hard to know what to wear in this unseasonable weather.'

'What can I get you, Annie?' If only the woman would go! Her eyes were everywhere. She missed nothing and remembered everything.

'You look real peaky,' said Annie, noticing the pallor on Jane's normally glowing skin, and the pinched look round the nose. Suddenly, she knew. Jane glanced up and saw that Annie knew. 'I'll take a cabbage for now and some herbs,' said Annie. 'I have to go to Mr Foster's. I'll come back for fish later.' She thrust the cabbage into her basket and hurried out, her bottom wriggling with importance.

Jane went into the back room to look in the mirror. It was there for all to see. Like all married women in the town, she needed no doctor to diagnose a pregnant women. If Annie knew, then the whole town would soon be coming in to buy and see for themselves if what Annie said was true.

'I'll feel better after the sickness is over,' she said to Nero. Since Caroline's death, she had recovered and been strong again. She pushed away the memory of that tiny, dead face and hoped that she could carry another child. By dinner-time, her colour had returned and she was stronger and hungry, craving for something

203

sharp to suck. When the children came in, she was sucking a raw lemon.

Walter went to the brickyard on the way home from the Barracks. He talked to the men and went to see Bert in the office. 'Annie says that Jane is poorly,' said Bert. His eyes were malicious. 'Annie went in the shop and Jane looked rough. Not a thing to say for herself. Real peaky. Annie was quite worried but Jane never wants sympathy.'

'First I heard of it. She was fine when I left. She was up early to get my grub. Annie's spinning you a yarn.'

Bert smiled. 'Was she all right early this morning?'

Walter forced a grin, but he remembered the sound he had heard. 'She's all right. You know women. Up one minute, down the next and this weather's enough to drive anyone to drink. You don't look so good yourself, Bert!' He took the cart back and hurried home.

Jane sat with a half-lemon on a saucer in front of her and Walter looked at it as if it might strike him. Whenever Jane had been pregnant, he had brought home the finest Italian lemons on the market, however expensive they were.

He buried his head in his hands. 'Oh God, what have I done,' he whispered. Jane didn't seem to hear but prepared tea for later, cutting bread and butter and arranging cold meat on plates. She took meticulous care that the milk should not slop on to the tablecloth and arranged knives and forks precisely. She sat with her hands folded in her lap and Walter watched her, unable to speak or to show his feelings.

Suddenly, her expression of meek acceptance was too much. It was foreign to her warm vitality. He put his arms round her, his tears running into her hair. 'We'll go to Dr Barnes! That's it. He'll help.'

Jane smoothed his head as if he was one of the children in distress. 'No,' she said gently. 'He can do nothing. He can't do it as it is against the law. I've been to him.'

Walter shook her. 'Jane! There must be a way. If he can't, then you must... aren't there women?'

The first flicker of annoyance came to her face. 'And would you let a dirty back-street woman mess me about, Walter Darwen?'

'Some women manage it on their own. *Gin!* That's it. It might do it.' He ran to the Jug and Bottle and bought the biggest bottle of gin they had. Feverishly, he poured some into a cup, spilling it on the clean cloth. Jane regarded him with detachment. 'Come on, Jane. Drink it!'

She moved away. 'I've the children coming in for their tea. Do you think I want them to see their mother swilling gin out of a cup, in the daytime?'

Walter was abject. 'Please, Jane, you must.'

'I'll take some tonight, in bed where I can do no harm. I'll not be able to drink it without something sharp. I'll press some lemons to help it down. Thank you, Walter.'

He was upset and he still cared. He was desperately guilty and didn't want to lose her after all. Jane gave the family their tea and climbed the stairs with the bottle of gin, a jug of lemon juice and a tumbler and drank herself into a stupor. Walter lay on the extreme edge of the bed listening to her drunken snores and he prayed.

In the morning, Jane felt like death. Her tongue was furred and her head ached. She went down to the privy and was very sick but after this she felt better than she had done for weeks. But she remained pregnant, performing her duties as usual but inside a vacuum. The children didn't notice how quiet she had become or how Walter took over the heavy lifting and served in the shop as often as possible. He did his clumsy best to show that he cared but it was impossible to get through the thick barrier that separated them, cutting out communication but allowing life to go on, as if nothing was wrong. Slowly the brittle barrier showed cracks and Jane was not as well.

Dr Barnes examined the scars of the old varicose ulcers and clucked his displeasure. Jane bandaged her legs to stop them swelling again but knew that the thumping in her head meant that all was not well. – If I could fade away with dignity, she thought, it would be easy... but the prolonged sickness and headaches were tangible and very uncomfortable and as she realised how serious her condition would become, she resented the discomfort, and her natural resilience burst through her apathy. At last, she permitted herself the luxury of hate and anger.

She hated herself for being in this condition and hated Walter for forcing it on her. She was deeply and bitterly angry that women should have to endure pain and humiliation and even death because the law, made by men who didn't know what it was like to suffer in this way, offered no way out. Walter had been right. Where was God? Where was justice? Men considered their animals more than their women. Walter had forced this on her as his *right*. She was a chattel and it didn't matter that she had managed all his affairs while he was far away.

She saw him talking to Dr Barnes and both the men were shaking their heads as if they regretted something that couldn't be altered, and Jane knew that Walter now accepted the fact that they must let the law stand and not interfere with nature. There was no way out that would be respectable, no way that society would allow.

Jane removed the wedding ring that cut into her swollen finger. – I must do something. I must lose the baby or die. Perhaps both of us will die, but at least the others will be spared the sight of me in the last stages of the condition.

Walter was in the outhouse and the children were at school and Edward wouldn't be back from Cowes for hours. Jane dragged her swollen legs up the stairs and rummaged in the handkerchief box. If she was to die, then it was better now before she grew too bulky and the baby was too much a human being. She glanced in the mirror and saw that she was still handsome, if a little fatter and slightly more bloated. The children would never need to be frightened as they would be if she became gross and had fits. They would remember Caroline and think the same had happened now.

She dabbed her aching temples with eau de cologne and took out the grey pill.

Jane sipped some tea and her throat constricted when she looked at the size of the pill. She hated swallowing pills of any kind and this was enormous. It was as big as one of the horse pills that Walter used on Bess. She had no idea what to expect or what its effect would be. She hesitated, then heard Walter shut the outhouse door and swill the yard with the broom and water. She put the pill in her mouth and it was cold and heavy. It tasted of nothing. She swallowed and the pill lay heavy on her tongue so she drank and gagged, swallowed again and drank more tea until the pill slid painfully down her gullet.

Walter came up and opened the door, Jane was sitting on the bed holding her throat. 'Feeling sick again?' he said. 'Can I get you something?'

'No, Walter, I think the sickness will be over soon.'

'Come down and have fresh tea. I can't think why you carried it

206

up here.' Walter took the cup and she followed him. The pill lay heavy and she was full of flatulence. Jane drank cup after cup of tea to make the pill go down further but she couldn't eat. By evening, she got rid of the wind and felt better. It was almost disappointing, but what did she expect? She went to bed with a chamber pot near the bed, thinking that the pill was only a harsh aperient and she might not have time to go down to the yard. If it was based on castor oil, it might work soon. Women used castor oil to bring on babies or to have an abortion, she knew, but she had never actually met anyone who said it worked. All it did was to produce belly-ache and the runs.

At three in the morning, Walter heard Jane call out in her sleep. He lit a candle and saw that her face was grey and covered with sweat, but she shivered as if she was very cold. He patted her hand. 'Wake up, gal, you're having a bad dream.'

She moaned and turned away, tossing her head from side to side as if to shake off the pain. She looked not at him, but through him, her eyes dull in the candlelight. He'd seen this look in the eyes of dying men and horses on the battlefields and in the abandoned houses of the Veldt. He was terrified. Walter put a hand under her to draw her to his warmth and his hand met a sticky patch of oozing blood.

He jumped out of bed and hammered on the door of the boys' room. 'Run for Dr Barnes! Make haste! It's your mother!' He opened the door and pulled the bedclothes from the nearest bed. 'You, Edward, go for the Doctor, and you Jack, get more candles! Sidney, light the lamp in the shop and bring it up.'

Walter went back and flung open the shutters but the night was dark and even with the curtains back and the windows bare, there was no light from outside. 'Candles!' He took them from Jack and lit them, filling the spare candlesticks and telling Jack to bring plates to hold more, stuck on in their own grease as there was no gas upstairs. He glanced at the face on the pillow and wanted to weep but there was no time.

Dr Barnes came running, with his overcoat over his nightshirt, and by the time he came upstairs, the room was well-lit and Walter was lighting a fire in the small grate. The room was cold and the doctor nodded his approval. 'Put some bricks in the oven, boy,' he said to Sidney. 'We need all the warmth we can give her.' He put down his bag and pulled back the bedclothes.

Jane clenched her teeth as talons of pain clawed through her subconscious mind. She was floating above her body, looking down at the pale body on the bed and she only knew that it was her body on the bed that felt pain. It was confusing, being two people. She could hear screaming and knew that it was the Jane on the bed, a woman who couldn't tell anyone about the pain. She was sinking down through the bed in a whirlpool of darkness that throbbed like a heartbeat. Her head was lighter than it had been for days but she could think only of the pain.

Hands were pulling, pushing at her, pressing on her distended abdomen. The stickiness that had seemed so uncomfortable was gone and she saw a woman's face. Mrs...? Mrs...? She was too tired to recall the name but she had seen her somewhere and she had something to do with the Doctor.

Caroline was there. Two Carolines with many child faces behind her, all waxy yellow with closed eyes. She tried to turn away so that she couldn't see them but strong hands were on her arms forcing her to lie on the bed with that other Jane. The cold rim of a cup chattered on her teeth and she fought again, but gave up weakly and swallowed. Was it more pills? Not grey pills? She screamed again. It was all a mistake, and she had to let them know.

'That's better,' said Dr Barnes, tucking back the cuff that Jane had ripped from his nightshirt. 'She'll sleep now and the bleeding has stopped.' He took the basin that was full of blood and a small bag of transparent membrane. He slit the bag with a scalpel and held it for Walter to see.

Walter looked away. 'Look at it,' the doctor said sternly. 'You must see it. Are you afraid to look at what is yours?' Walter saw the tiny foetus, the perfect human being that might have been his son. It had tiny, perfect hands, but the skin was rubbed-looking as if it had a rash.

'What did she do?' The doctor's voice broke through the horror.

'Do?' said Walter, stupidly.

'Yes, man, DO! She must have done something. She didn't use an instrument of any kind, that's for sure. No sign of a knitting-needle puncture, but she must have done something. Did she have a draught of any kind? Pills?'

Walter continued to stare at him without comprehending. 'What do you mean? She had nothing. You told us both that you could do nothing to help her.'

'That's right. There was nothing I could do within the law. There are times like this when I wish I could, but the law and the Church would be down on me like a ton of bricks. I wanted to help your wife and many others like her.' He shrugged. 'There are women who do these things. Did your wife go to any such as that?'

Walter shook his head. 'A while ago, I suggested that she might find one, but she was very angry. Jane is far too proud to have such a woman anywhere near her. She told me she refused to have a dirty back-street slut to touch her.'

The doctor made a note. He wasn't anxious to know what had happened, but he had to go through the motions of investigation, so he did his duty.

'She drank a bottle of gin,' said Walter. The Doctor grunted. There was no law against a woman geting drunk in her own home, even if the side-effect was abortion, so he wrote, 'Spontaneous abortion aggravated by alcohol in excess'. As no probe had been used, there would be less risk of infection inside the womb and the rest lay with God and Mrs Darwen's own powers of recovery.

'Give her more laudanum when she wakes, Mrs Gregory. Stop her threshing about and starve her. If she asks for food, give her some thin gruel but nothing to overheat the blood. The blood loss may have done good and now the baby has gone we might pull her through, but we'll have to watch her. Her mind may have escaped damage as she had only one fit. If she has another, make sure she bites on a folded towel. She bit her tongue with the first one and she'll have a sore mouth as it is.'

Walter watched his wife as the woman tidied the room and washed the pale face. She looked as she had done when Caroline died and now she was hardly breathing, as the heavy dose of drugs calmed her. He wished that he was dead. Janey led him downstairs and gave him a hot drink while Mrs Gregory made herself comfortable by the bedroom fire and Clare prepared a truckle bed for Walter in the boys' room. Emily was still asleep and Lizzie kept away as she hated to see her mother ill, and Janey was so like Jane that Walter couldn't look at her.

He called to Nero, who must have thought he was mad, and tramped the river-fields until dawn, wishing that he had stayed

209

away in South Africa and spared his family this pain. He couldn't walk for ever and when he went home, he lit the boiler for the washing that Janey was doing and then made up the orders for the day that had to be delivered even if the sky fell.

Chapter 17

Emily put the first primroses in a china bowl and carried them safely upstairs. She went into her mother's room and placed the bowl on the chest of drawers, only breathing deeply once the bowl was level and she knew that none of the water had spilled.

Jane was staring into space, propped up in bed and vaguely aware of the sun shining on the window. – It must be spring, she thought with surprise, but where had she been? There had been terrible dreams of pain and faces, warm hands and kind voices. She remembered the pain but it had gone and she was content to sleep, to drink and to look at nothing.

Sidney looked at her with diffidence. He had drawn many pictures for her but she didn't take any notice. He finished the new drawing for the shop, showing oranges and lemons and took it to her. He saw that she glanced at the flowers. 'Primroses, Mother,' he said.

'Primroses? Oh, the Queen loves primroses. She used to gather them every year at Osborne. Did you know that?' She smiled. 'But of course, the Queen is dead. Did you know that she died? I heard it somewhere.'

Emily looked blank, wondering why her mother spoke as if to strangers. Sidney took his mother's hand. 'Yes, Mother, we knew. The Queen died last year before you were ill.'

Jane wrinkled her forehead. She could recall Walter coming home from the station and Emily popping tar bubbles on the hot road. She thought of Maudie with paint and powder on her face and wondered if Clare had remembered to milk the nanny goat. 'How is Rose?' she said. 'The sun's shining and she should be out of that steamy little room.'

'Rose is very well, Mother.'

'You said I was ill,' said Jane. He nodded. 'Let me smell the flowers,' she said, and Emily brought the small bunch to pin on her bed-cape.

'They'd stay better with a brooch,' said Emily.

'My cameo with the Queen on it. That would do very well, but I've no neckband to pin it on.' Jane put a hand to her throat. 'Have you seen my cameo?'

'Don't you remember, Mother?' Sidney drew closer and sat on the bed. 'You gave it to old Mrs Lee when we went down to the camp. You told me that she admired it and you gave it to her for a keepsake.' He smiled, urging her to recall that day. 'You know, we went there and I sat on a fence and talked to the gypsy boys. We ate some apples and I learned some more Romany words but you wouldn't let me have an earring like them.'

'I should think not, indeed!'

'Jack tried to smoke out the bats,' said Emily eagerly.

Jane tore at the webs clouding her memory. Mrs Lee? Her colour came in bright patches, her eyes too bright. Emily slipped away to tell Walter that Mother was restless again, but Sidney stayed, stroking her hand and talking about the picnic, the blackberry hedges, the piebald ponies, running with wild manes flowing. His hands were small and comforting and she gripped them tightly.

'Tell me about Mrs Lee,' she said. Something about the old lady had to do with her being in bed, and with Walter.

'Mrs Lee died and they had to burn everything she had, Mother. We saw the burning waggon and you were sorry and said a prayer,' said Sidney.

Walter appeared in the doorway as she tried to find the link between him and Mrs Lee, and the last shreds of the veil drifted away. Jane wept for her lost babies, her sins, her illness and her present weakness. She cried as if nothing would ever stem the flood and all her guilt and desolation washed away until she was empty and exhausted and she slept.

Walter dared not touch her when he saw that she recalled why she was ill. He went away and left her with the two children and the best deep sleep she had enjoyed for months.

Three hours later, Jane woke and smelled fish frying. From the darkening room, she knew it was supper-time. Janey came in to see if she was awake. 'I'm hungry,' said Jane. 'I've been lazy long enough. I must get my strength back.'

212

The news seemed to spread that she was better and as soon as Jane was able to be helped down the stairs, she found that all her old friends wanted to see her. Jane liked to see them but there were things to be done that only she could supervise as yet and she spent a lot of time on the couch telling the others what to do, and visitors knew that they were welcome but for only short visits. Annie came to see Jane and to feel superior, but went away amazed at the serene spirit she found in the neat back room. Dan Cooper came to help Walter paint the outhouse and stayed to sort fruit or anything that needed doing, and it was time again for the annual spring cleaning.

Jack grumbled happily that he had to beat all the mats and said that it seemed only yesterday that he had brushed down the winter cobwebs and why did he have to work so hard? But Jane knew that he loved to see her colour rise and it did him good to be told off once more. Jane supervised but did nothing to tax her strength, as a girl from Barton now came in to do the rough work and it seemed a good idea to keep her on for a few more weeks. Jane walked a little more each day and her legs no longer felt like jelly. Afternoons on the couch were pleasant, sewing and making new shifts for the girls, often falling asleep in the middle of a line of stitches, and finding one long French seam enough for a day.

Walter was full of ideas for the shop as his spirits rose. He bought a new display cabinet which he filled with dried herbs in packets, split peas and lentils and bottles of sauce. He hung a new mirror behind the counter to replace the flyblown one with its advertisments worn away. Jane wondered if he had bought the new one for business reasons or from a sense of nostalgia, as there was an engraving of a voluptuous woman holding a basket of cape oranges against a background of Table Mountain.

In spite of her weakness, Jane was thinking hard. There would have to be changes for the sake of her own health, the wellbeing of the children and to remove temptation from Walter. Edward was settled at work and Jack was still happy to help his father, but Sidney needed a refuge for his painting and to have somewhere to call his own where he could think.

The rugs were in the yard and the rooms bare of everything removeable for the cleaning, so Jane climbed slowly and painfully to the attic, a tiny room used only for storage. It had a window and a skylight and a good big cupboard. She pulled rubbish from the room and called the girl to take it all downstairs and then to sweep the room and wash the furniture. It smelled fresh with the window open and seemed bigger without the rubbish.

'Sidney?' she called. He ran up the stairs. 'Would you like this room for your own?' she said.

'All alone?' His eyes were bright.

'Just you, but you would have to distemper the walls and ceiling.'

'Not share with anyone, ever?'

'No, you're a big lad and you need somewhere to keep your paints and stuff without them being spoiled.' He hugged her. 'You can choose what colour you like,' she said. He grabbed his cap and rushed up to the High Street to ask for a shade guide and brought it back to show his mother. The main colours were drab, a variation on a sludge theme but under them were some pastel colours.

'Really choose?' he said, and pointed to the mauve.

Jane looked uncertain. 'Well, you'll have to live with it,' she said, and wondered what curtains she could use to tone it down if he painted it all mauve. 'It will be a change,' she conceded.

Jane was anxious to get the house straight before Walter knew what she had planned. He had been very good of late and nothing was too much trouble for him to do for her; he showed a devotion that surprised them both. She knew that he had been very shocked and frightened by her illness and she was shrewd enough to make the most of his mood of contrition to effect all the changes she deemed necessary. He half-believed that Jane must have brought on the miscarriage herself, but hadn't the courage to ask her. Today, Walter had gone to Ashey with Bert Cooper and he had taken it for granted that Jane didn't need him. He fussed over her less now and she was relieved.

Jane called the girls, and together, they made the boxroom a bedroom for Lizzie and turned all the trunks and boxes into the shed that Walter had bought recently when Jane said she needed more storage. Lizzie was delighted with her new room, and Jane watched them hang fresh curtains of white with pink roses on them. – He'd never force me again, she thought. Would he? On some days, she was convinced that Walter had closed his mind forever on all thoughts of intercourse with her, but on other days, when he swung up on to the driving seat of the trap, dressed smartly to go to Ashey Races, with his hat at a jaunty angle and a flower in his buttonhole, she knew that he was the same lusty,

214

virile man she had married, and just as selfish.

Wasn't it enough that she had twice nearly died? There had to be an end to it. The next time that Walter was away, over in Portsmouth with Bert, they moved Sidney's belongings into the still damp and very mauve attic. There was an old table under the skylight, a shelf for books and a warm hook rug on the floor. Even Jack was envious. 'But you know you like to share with Edward,' Jane consoled him. 'You couldn't talk at night if one of you has this room, and you'd sleep the clock round if Edward didn't pull you out of bed in the morning.'

Finally, Jane moved her clothes into the room she would now share with Janey. It was a big room with good cupboards that would take all her clothes.

'Why are you moving in with Janey?' asked Sidney.

'There's no need to talk about it,' said Jane sharply. 'This is a family matter. I don't sleep well and I don't want to disturb your father, but there's no call for any of you to spread that all over Newport.'

'Uncle Archie was up at the Town Hall,' said Jack. 'He asked after you, Mother, and said he'd come for you one day and take you up to the Castle in the trap.'

'Your father will be doing that soon,' said Jane. Dear Archie, who would be there at any time if she wanted him. Dear Archie who had shown only too clearly how much he loved her when she was ill and who must never be allowed to expect anything from her.

Annie Cooper peered beyond the bead curtain that let a current of air pass from the shop to the sitting room now the door could be pushed back against the wall. She saw that the house was spring-cleaned and said nothing. Jane's serious eyes told her that there was no chance of learning what had really happened when the baby was lost and anyway, she had her own worries, with Bert going over to Portsmouth more and more, on business that kept him there for hours and sent him back with a self-satisfied smile.

Walter came home to change his clothes before going down to the town. The roads were filthy and the wheels had thrown up a fine spray of dirt all day. He smelled lavender polish and Sunlight soap and thought it about time the shop and house were back to normal. Spring cleaning went on for weeks, or so it seemed, but with Jane so much slower, it wasn't surprising. 'Humbugging nonsense,' he muttered as he went upstairs.

He sensed that something was different. The bed in the big front room was freshly made-up with newly-starched valances, and clean curtains which moved slightly in the air from the open window. There was something missing. His hair brushes and pomade were on the chest of drawers but there was a bare patch where Jane's brushes should be. He supposed she'd taken them for washing.

He opened the top drawer. The orderly chaos of gloves and ribbon boxes was gone. The stocking drawer was empty too and fresh paper lined the drawers as if waiting for a new tenant. Jane's wrapper no longer hung behind the door.

Walter glanced into the other big room and saw Jane's brushes on the washstand where Lizzie usually kept her set of toiletries, and saw the old thick wrapper behind the door. He touched its shapeless folds and remembered Jane wearing it during the long nights of teething babies, of measles and mumps and chest colds, and he wept.

Jane didn't trust him. He was torn by an emotion that was worse than sorrow. As if he would do anything to hurt her now! But he had. He had nearly killed her and he saw the wisdom of her actions even if his heart and pride were wounded. She was casting him out forever.

At teatime, he thought she looked happier than at any time since her illness and although she gave him a quick and apprehensive glance, he made no comments about the new arrangement. Jane hummed softly as she sliced bread. It was done and she didn't care what he thought about it. – I'm finished with all that, she thought with calm pleasure, but as she watched him and he said nothing and tried to be helpful, she found a warm maternal affection forming for him and hoped that he would be spared for many years to look after his family and her.

To be content and safe was wonderful. Holy Mary, she prayed silently as her family ate and argued and filled the room with laughter, thank You for Your intercession and God rest the soul of Mrs Lee, who didn't sin but helped me according to her lights.

The new bed was hard but Jane smiled as she turned over in it. Janey went to sleep as soon as she sank on to her bed and it was like having a room to herself, with safety. She stretched in bed, not anxious for sleep. She thought of all the pin-money she had put away with Sam's help after the sale of pickles and jam and

216

smoked mackerel. It gave her a certain independence. The girls will need things and a bit of money to keep, she thought. I can buy little things without asking Walter each time and when I'm stronger, I'll walk up to Carisbrooke.